NIALL LEONARD

SHREDDER

Definitions

SHREDDER
A DEFINITIONS BOOK 978 1 782 95146 9

First published in Great Britain by Definitions,
an imprint of Random House Children's Publishers UK
A Random House Group Company

1 3 5 7 9 10 8 6 4 2

Copyright © Niall Leonard, 2014
Cover artwork copyright © Blacksheep UK, 2014

The Random House Group Limited supports the Forest Stewardship Council®
(FSC®), the leading international forest-certification organisation. Our books
carrying the FSC label are printed on FSC®-certified paper. FSC is the only forest-
certification scheme supported by the leading environmental organisations,
including Greenpeace. Our paper procurement policy can be found at
www.randomhouse.co.uk/environment.

Set in 10.5/15.5pt Palatino by Falcon Oast Graphic Art Ltd.

Definitions are published by Random House Children's Publishers UK
61–63 Uxbridge Road, London W5 5SA

www.randomhouse.co.uk

Addresses for companies within The Random House Group Limited
can be found at: www.randomhouse.co.uk/offices.htm

THE RANDOM HOUSE GROUP Limited Reg. No. 954009

A CIP catalogue record for this book is available from the British Library.

Printed and bound in the CPI Group (UK) Ltd, Croydon, CR0 4YY

Trafalgar Square was smaller than I'd remembered, but it
s[...] taking Pirbal and Dean a long time to cross
[...] [t]ime had slowed down, like it used to in
[...]g, when adrenalin would heighten all my
[...] [coul]d make out every face in the crowd around
[...] see the hi-viz jackets of the coppers by the
[...] [beh]ind us, somehow; I could smell lemon in the
[...] woman sitting at the next table, and hear
[...] [h]er bangles as she rooted in her handbag.

[...] to my right, skipping down the steps from the
[...] [G]allery, I could see pale, broad-nosed Martin,
[...] [slee]ved shirt and sunglasses, carrying a folded
[...] and strolling nonchalantly south, his path
[...] [to] pass behind the Turk and Dean just before
[...] [reach]ed our table.

[...] turn my head towards him, but kept my eyes
[...] the Turk, and noted the twitch of his lips as he
[...] [se]ated there beside the Guvnor. He was smiling,
[...] [totall]y unaware of Martin, now twenty paces away,
[...] his free hand into the folded newspaper. I
[...] [th]e paper concealed a pistol, and saw now what
[...] [would] happen: the Turk and Dean would each take
[...] [in th]e back of the head before they'd even reached
[...] and the Guvnor would walk away, unscathed
[...] [u]ninvolved.

[N]ow Martin was eight paces away.

Seven . . .

'This thriller travels at a gripping pace'
Publishers Weekly

To Hoot and Lori
with profuse thanks for their hard work
and boundless enthusiasm

'Finn, why do you think you are still alive, and in one piece? I have a job for you.'

'I'm not for hire,' I said.

'Of course not,' said the Turk. Reaching into his pocket he took out a smartphone, unlocked it and started flicking at the screen. 'You don't need money, you have nothing to lose, there is no one you care about.' He held out the phone so I could see the screen.

The footage was smooth; whoever took it had been so close there was no need to zoom in. Close enough to see the stud glinting in Zoe's nose as she laughed at some crack her friend had made. The two women were sitting in some huge cafeteria – a dining room at her college maybe. Now she was emerging from an old house, pushing a bike, wrestling with a bag of books. Every turn of her head and quirk of her mouth burned into my heart, and my aching guts tightened in fear. I couldn't look up at the Turk – I knew I'd see triumph in his eyes.

'What do you want?' I said.

'There is someone I would like to meet. A friend of

yours. I need to put a proposition to him.'

Something told me this proposition was going to involve a lot of lead and explosives.

'I want you to introduce me to the Guvnor,' said the Turk . . .

ONE

After about three days I stopped pissing blood. By then I could open my left eye all the way, and the welts and bruises on my torso and legs were shifting in colour from imperial purple to sickly yellow-green. I'd barely been able to get out of bed, but I hadn't been able to sleep either, partly due to the pain, but mostly because summer had arrived at last – the sort of summer we weren't supposed to have any more, with the sun blazing down day after day from a cloudless sky, and the air hot and still and sticky, even at night. But as soon as I found I was able to stand up, dress myself and walk, I locked the house and limped towards the tube station.

I could see people in the street glance towards me and look away, some even shifting their path to give me a wider berth. They seemed to think getting worked over with chains and crowbars was an infectious condition, and if they bumped into me they'd wake up the next morning with a black eye and a split lip. At the station I stumbled onto the next tube train, lowered myself gingerly into a seat and stared at my dark reflection flickering in and out of existence on the carriage windows: just short of two metres tall, mousy-blond hair, built like a boxer, right now with the face of a punchbag. As the train rattled its way east and dived under the city the relatively fresh air of the suburbs gave way to the hot humidity of the Underground, its tunnels and platforms stinking like a sauna full of pigs. As more passengers crowded in their tension and fatigue and irritation were as tangible as the sweat running down our backs.

Even on the broad granite-paved concourse of King's Cross Station, sheltered from the sun by tall walls of red brick, the air was close and stale. Heading for the ticket office I passed armed coppers strolling slowly through the crowd, fingers twitching on the trigger guards of their submachine-guns, caps pulled down over their eyes so you couldn't tell when they were watching you, or profiling you. There'd been a terrorist attack on London a few days back, I remembered now, somewhere in the city centre – I'd heard about it on the radio while I'd been washing bloodstains out of my clothes. A suicide bomber had detonated a rucksack full of explosives in a department store packed with shoppers for a summer sale. Seven people dead, a score injured, some seriously; but if the Londoners around me were anxious or apprehensive that the same thing might happen to them, it didn't show. I guessed we all felt the same – that the slim chance of sudden, messy death and dismemberment was just some more shit we city-dwellers had to deal with, like the heat and the traffic and the sweaty, heaving crowds of other Londoners.

The train for York stood sleek and gleaming at the platform, its engines thrumming on standby. The interior was so fiercely air-conditioned I shivered with cold as I settled down in a seat towards the centre of a carriage, with a table where I had room to stretch out my long aching legs. It was an off-peak service, so few people had bothered to book them-selves seats, and as departure time approached several other passengers staggered up, hefting bags slightly too big for the aisle, hoping to join me at the table. I didn't exactly glare at them, but my body language and my battered face must have shouted that I wouldn't welcome company. They hefted their bags and staggered on. Fine by me; I needed time and space to think about what had happened, and what I had been told to do, and what I was going to do instead. I'd been thinking about it for days and even now I wasn't sure if this was a good idea. But almost imperceptibly the train jolted into motion and slid from the dark station platform out into the hard blazing sun, heading north, and it was too late to turn back.

My name is Finn Maguire; as a teenage amateur boxer I'd been nicknamed *Crusher*, because I'd been good at it. It was my dad who had signed me up for boxing lessons, to try and straighten me out after a stint in juvenile detention. The ploy had worked, mostly – I'd abandoned my early career as a petty criminal and gone straight, and the skills I'd learned in the ring had come in handy, especially after my dad had been killed.

That was ages ago now, way back in the spring. At seventeen years of age I was alone in the world, though not exactly penniless; I owned a poky house in West London, a few hundred thousand Euros in the bank and a castle in Spain I hadn't seen since I was a kid. I'd inherited all that after my dad died, and none of it made up for losing him. When I'd set out to discover who'd murdered him, the trail had led to a gangster called Joseph McGovern – 'the

Guvnor' – undisputed king of the London under-world, if you believed the tabloids. I'd been there when a bent copper working for McGovern had turned on him and got shot, and I'd only survived to not tell anyone the tale because the Guvnor had taken a shine to me. That was an honour I would gladly have avoided.

McGovern had had to leave the UK while the fuss died down, and in his absence contenders had been scrapping over his empty throne; the eventual winner turned out to be not much older than me – a foreigner known simply as 'the Turk'. Somehow he'd heard that I was McGovern's pet, and had turned up on my doorstep four nights ago with half a dozen heavies in tow. It was they who'd worked me over by way of payback for interfering in their boss's business. They would have kept going until I was nothing but minced offal, but it turned out the Turk needed me to introduce him to the Guvnor. He'd made it clear that if I refused it wouldn't just be me who would suffer.

Beyond the train's tinted windows the northern countryside was tearing past in a green blur. A podgy, bored young woman in a polyester housecoat pushed a rattling trolley loaded with junk food up the aisle. She didn't flinch at my battered face when I flagged her down and ordered some food, because she never even glanced at me. She plonked a shiny plastic apple and a slopping beaker of scalding coffee onto my table, slowly counted out my change, and moved on, thanking me in a singsong voice that sounded like a voicemail droid. I sipped carefully at the coffee, waiting for my swollen lip to sting. It didn't. I always healed quickly; it was one of the few things I had going for me.

I wasn't scared of the Turk, any more than I'd been scared of the Guvnor. I felt fear, yes, but not for myself. I'd learned in the boxing ring that you can channel fear, so it focuses you and drives you, and it was driving me now, north to the city of York. I had no close family, and few friends any more: the only person I cared about was a girl called Zoe Prendergast. Somehow the Turk had learned about her, and how I felt about her – and that was weird, because I hadn't known that myself. Not until the Turk had shown me that video of her going about her student life, unaware she was being observed, oblivious to the fact that she was a cheap chip in a poker game being played by two psychos hundreds of miles away. As soon as I'd seen the footage I'd known that if it was the last thing I did on this earth I'd see to it that Zoe was safe.

SHREDDER

I had two choices: I could do what I was told, and track down the Guvnor somehow, and not tell Zoe of the danger; or I could take her out of the equation – warn her about what was happening, urge her to run, to find safety somewhere. Maybe the Turk knew beforehand which I would choose – he'd already been playing me for weeks, tugging me back and forth on a string like a cheap plastic yo-yo – but I'd given up trying to second-guess him. All I could do was what I thought was right. And I was pretty sure that meant telling Zoe everything. I couldn't phone her – I wouldn't have known where to start, and I wasn't sure she'd even believe me. If I was going to tell her, it had to be to her face.

If I was going to tell her.

Suddenly I felt the train slowing; we were already approaching York station, and I could see up ahead the golden walls of the old city, gleaming like a Disneyland castle and dotted with tourists. I wondered if they knew that not so long ago those walls had been decorated with heads on spikes and bodies rotting in cages being picked to pieces by crows. As I stepped down from the train onto the long curving platform of York station a wall of hot air hit me – fresher than London's second-hand smog, but just as oppressive. According to the street maps on the Net it was a ten-minute walk from here to Zoe's place; ten minutes to change my mind. I could give myself more time, I knew, if I joined the sun-burned tourists waddling up and down, taking badly composed photos of each other on their compact cameras. But I turned right out of the station and headed south towards Zoe's house.

Soon I felt as nervous as a thirteen-year-old on his first date. Would Zoe even be glad to see me? Her Facebook page still said she was 'not in a relation-ship', but last time I'd looked one particular guy seemed to appear in every recent picture she'd posted, rubbing elbows with her. Maybe offline he was rubbing more than her elbows, but if he was, Zoe didn't care to advertise it. To hell with it, I thought, I'm not bringing her flowers, I'm here to warn her that her life is in danger.

Except . . . *I* was the reason it was in danger, and by disobeying instructions I'd made that danger much, much worse. Suddenly I understood that I wasn't here just to help Zoe – I was here because I wasn't prepared to take orders from a sick, vicious little shit like the Turk.

It wasn't too late; I could still turn back, let Zoe go on living her blissful student life, drinking and shagging and sleeping through lectures, unaware of the Turk's knife at her throat. Even now, when I was right outside her place – the tall, crooked, crumbling student house I'd seen in Zoe's postings – with my hand resting on the latch of her garden gate, looking up the path to her dented front door, even now I could turn back. The next train back to London left in twenty minutes. If I set off now I wouldn't even need to hurry.

I dropped my hand from the gate, stepped away and turned round. And walked right into her.

Into them, I mean.

She was with him, the guy from her Facebook photos. He was nearly as tall as me, and wiry, with startling ice-blue eyes, reddish-blond hair and cheek-bones that could cut steak. You could tell he and Zoe were together – *together* together – just by their proximity, the way he hovered within grabbing-and-snogging distance. Also by the bright pink flush on Zoe's face when she saw me standing at her gate. She looked guilty, I realized, as if I was some Victorian husband who'd found his errant wife in a brothel. Her big green eyes were staring, her full lips had parted in surprise, and for once she seemed lost for words. A tiny part of me felt gratified by her reaction; the rest of me felt as excruciatingly embarrassed as she must have been, because it suddenly felt as if we were in a cheesy TV soap. It was Zoe's friend – boyfriend, whatever – who cracked the awkward silence, with an easy laugh. He had beautifully white and even teeth, I noted, trying hard not to hate him for it.

'Hi,' he said, as if he already knew who I was. Did he? I wondered.

'Finn . . . what the hell are *you* doing here?' I could see Zoe struggling to comprehend my presence here in a different city; I was a character from another life, a dark, bitter and sordid one she had tried to leave behind. And I hadn't even told her the bad news yet. 'And what the hell happened to your face?' she said.

'The usual,' I said. I looked at her companion.

'Patrick, this is Finn . . . a friend of mine from London.' She didn't look at him, I noticed, or at me when she made the introductions. Perfect Patrick flashed his perfect teeth again and extended a hand. I shook it; his grip was cool and firm, strong without being macho. He worked out, I could tell, and the easy way he moved suggested he'd trained in fighting – something trendy, I guessed, like kickboxing or capoeira. I could see him measuring me up the same way, and hoped my livid scars counted in my favour.

'Finn, hey,' said Patrick. 'You coming in?' A Londoner, and expensively educated, by his accent. He stepped forward and opened the gate.

'I need to talk to Zoe,' I said. 'It's kind of private.'

I could see Zoe trying to read my battered face, and I tried to keep my expression neutral, because this was none of Patrick's business. But Zoe had already guessed that I wasn't there to take her to tea, and what Patrick couldn't pick up from me he was picking up from her.

'You can use our room,' he said. 'I'll chill in the kitchen, fix us some coffee.'

Our room. He'd hardly spoken ten words, but he'd already established ownership. Slick. Zoe noticed it too, and a frown flickered across her heart-shaped face.

'No, we'll take the kitchen,' she said. 'I'll see you in a minute.'

Patrick shrugged as if it made no odds to him, gave me a friendly nod and flashed his dazzling smile. 'No problem,' he said. 'Laters, yeah?'

The kitchen was badly painted in bright colours and filled with shabby mismatched furniture. It smelled of mice and old teabags.

'What was wrong with those halls of residence?' I said.

'Everything. And you can't stay there during the summer break. Patrick suggested I move in . . . Into this house, I mean.' She was blushing again. It occurred to me briefly that I should let her off the hook, make some comforting comment about what a nice bloke Patrick seemed to be and how glad I was to see her doing well. I didn't, though.

'Is he in your IT class?'

'My *class*?' Zoe snorted as she plonked the kettle down on its base and clicked the switch.

'Year group. Study group, whatever.' Now I was the one getting embarrassed. I didn't know how university worked, and as the world's worst dyslexic I was never likely to find out.

'No. He's a second year, studying international law and languages. Speaks three or four.'

'Right. Good with his tongue, then?'

She looked at me, pained and amused at the same time. I remembered how we'd used to fence like this, needling each other when we talked, and how she usually gave as good as she got, and I realized how much I'd missed it. Missed her.

'So what did happen to your face, Finn? Was it something to do with that phone?'

She'd hacked someone's smartphone for me recently; someone I'd needed to find. It was weird, me coming to her for help – when we'd first met she'd been a stoned school dropout, whose greatest achievement had been to star in a hardcore porn movie. Since then she'd cleaned up her act and won some amazing scholarship to study IT at York – the youngest ever candidate with the highest ever marks, I'd heard, though not from her. I was the only part of her old life she hadn't tried to wipe from the records, and I hoped that meant something.

She slid a cracked mug of hot coffee across the greasy table, and I sat down and told her what had happened since I'd seen her last, and how I'd tangled with the Turk. And I told her what the Turk wanted me to do, and why I had to do it.

'Did he say what he was going to do? To me, I mean?'

'He didn't have to.' I spared her my knowledge of the Turk's methods. She didn't need to know how that loan shark got disembowelled, or how Winnie and Delroy, the old couple who'd cared for me, got run down like dogs in the street. 'The real problem,' I said, 'is that I don't know where to find McGovern. Last I heard he was in Eastern Europe somewhere, hanging out with the Russian mafia.'

'How long did the Turk give you?' asked Zoe.

'A week. That was last Sunday.'

'Jesus Christ, Finn, what the hell have you been doing?'

'Bleeding,' I said.

'God . . .' She tugged at her spiky black hair. 'Why did you have to tell me all this?' She looked up again, glaring now, her green eyes full of anger.

I wasn't just a shadow from the past – I was a shadow on an X-ray. I wondered again why I had come up here. Was it really to warn her – or deep down did I resent her new life? Did I envy perfect Patrick upstairs, primping in front of a mirror right now, I imagined, tousling his own lovely blond locks? Was I trying to drag Zoe away from him, down into this stinking pit I seemed to be trapped in, so she could keep me company?

'I thought you should know,' I said. 'I thought you deserved to know. So you could decide for yourself what to do.'

'What? What am I going to do? What can I do?'

'Go to the cops,' I said. 'Tell them you've been threatened, ask for protection.'

'Oh, for Christ's sake, Finn . . .' She didn't need to finish. She trusted cops even less than I did. Her father had been a cop – the bent one who had got shot working for the Guvnor. After his death the Met had closed ranks the way they always did and sold the public a fairy story about the brave undercover detective who'd died in the line of duty.

Even though Zoe was his daughter, they wouldn't believe her story about needing protection unless I backed her up. And I couldn't do that. It would mean confessing everything I'd done, and in the last month I'd done plenty, from perverting the course of justice to murder. And even if the prosecutors offered me immunity for testifying against the Guvnor and the Turk, I'd never make it to the courtroom – the Guvnor had too much influence. I might get as far as a remand cell, but when the screws opened the door in the morning they'd find nothing but a heap of broken teeth.

'Run,' I said to Zoe. 'Leave.'

'Where the hell would I run to? And why the hell *should* I? I have a life here, Finn – your problems have nothing to do with me.'

'I know,' I said. 'I'm sorry.' That was true, but I was indignant too – did she think life was fair? Did she think shit only happened to people who deserved it? Those people in London the other day, caught by that suicide bomber, blinded and maimed and burned alive in a storm of fire and flying glass – they hadn't deserved what had happened to them, but it had still happened.

But I didn't say that, because Zoe being singled out wasn't simple bad luck. It was because of me, because of the way I felt about her. I'd never been in love – I didn't even know what it felt like – but I knew that just being close to Zoe my heart flew, and the thought of her getting hurt felt like being burned alive. I was pretty sure that meant I loved her. And now I understood that loving anyone is stupid and weak and dangerous because it makes you vulnerable.

I might suffer for that weakness, but Zoe might die.

'Amobi,' I said.

'What about him?'

I wasn't sure why that name had popped into my head. Amobi was the one cop I'd ever respected, the only one who'd ever treated me as anything other than a pain in the arse who needed a good tasering. Amobi had worked with Zoe's dad, but as far as I knew he'd been clean.

'I don't even know if he's still a cop, but maybe if we contacted him . . .'

'Of course he's still a cop,' Zoe almost snapped. 'He's with the NCA now.'

'NCA?' I said.

'The National Crime Agency. Basically SOCA, with a new name.'

That figured. I'd assumed Amobi had quit the force – any copper with brains and black skin was at a double disadvantage – but instead he'd transferred to the Serious Organized Crime Agency. Glutton for punishment, obviously.

'Then he's the one we should talk to,' I said.

'You talk to him,' said Zoe. She stood up and tossed what was left of her coffee down the sink, or in its general direction anyhow – some of it hit the window and dribbled down in brown streaks.

'Zoe—'

'Finn, I'm in the middle of a really shitty assignment and I can't think about this right now. And where the hell would we go? Where would we stay? I sold my dad's house, and the place you're living in isn't even yours, and it's not exactly safe . . .'

She seemed to realize how shrill and angry she sounded, and stopped, and took a deep breath.

'Look,' she said. 'Thanks for coming up. It was good to see you. But I really wish you hadn't. I don't want to go into hiding for the rest of my life over something I didn't do and know nothing about. If you'd never told me, if you'd just found McGovern, I would have been fine, so . . . why don't you just go home and do that?'

Of course I should never have come up here. I'd

made everything worse, not better – and I'd fooled myself that I was being noble and righteous. A trouble shared is a trouble doubled, my dad used to sigh, and I'd never known what he'd meant, till now, when I had tainted Zoe's perfect life. I'd screwed up my own a little more too: from now on I'd never be able to think of Zoe without seeing Patrick's glinting smile and golden tresses, and hearing Zoe's moan as he slipped her bra straps off her shoulders.

I hadn't been the only one living in blissful ignorance.

'Fine.' I stood up. 'I'll . . .' *See you around*, I wanted to finish, all casual and cool, but the words were so feeble they died in my throat. Restraining my polite impulse to rinse my cup out in the sink, I plonked it on the table and headed for the door. 'Bye,' I said. Maybe it looked like I was flouncing out, but I couldn't say any more – I'd already said too much.

Our parting had been pretty final, I realized, as I crossed the road outside and strode back towards the station. But maybe that was for the best. What had I to offer Zoe except bad associations? She was right to try to ignore me, to forget about me. If she carried on with her life and pretended I'd never been here, the Turk would have no need to act against her – he couldn't, in fact, without jeopardizing the only hold he had over me. No, Zoe would be safe if she stayed put and I did what I was told. All I had achieved with this visit was to give Zoe nightmares, and to shit all over the only real friendship I had.

I was five minutes from the station, and the next train left in eight minutes, so two hours from now I would be back in London. I would try, somehow, to find the Guvnor, or at least get a message to him. Then the Turk would forget about me and Zoe, and let us go back to our ordinary lives . . . wouldn't he?

I suddenly remembered Geronimo, the young cat my parents had adopted when I was little. She'd bring mice into the kitchen from the garden, and let them go, and catch them again, and let them go, and do that all morning, until she got bored. Then she'd rip their heads off for the fun of watching the blood spurt and their bodies twitch.

The next train back to London was the last one before peak hours, and it was crowded with cheapskate travellers like me on discount tickets. All the table seats were taken and I had to wedge myself into one of the rigid cramped single seats facing backwards, cursing at the pain from my kneecaps where the Turk's playmates had stamped on them. Though the window seat was empty I took the aisle, hoping size and surliness would put anyone off the idea of clambering over me to get to the empty one. It would give me a little space to stretch out later. And the ploy worked, right up until the last minute.

Through the thick tinted train window I saw the platform supervisor blow her whistle and wave her ping-pong bat at the driver, and the train jolted gently into motion, and at that moment I felt someone waiting at my elbow. I smelled her scent before I turned round, so I knew it was Zoe before I looked up; but when I did, I saw her eyes were filled with tears of anger.

'Move,' she said.

'Take a seat. Can I get you anything? Coffee, glass of water?'

'Thanks, I'm good, I said. Zoe just shook her head. The young Chinese bloke in the lightweight suit nodded and shut the door as he left the conference room.

Zoe had barely said a word to me on the train down, even when I'd dug out Amobi's number on my mobile phone and called him to ask for help. To my surprise he'd agreed to see us thirty minutes after the train got in, at an address in Victoria not far from New Scotland Yard.

I knew Scotland Yard itself was not what most

tourists expected – they looked for some Victorian palace and found a bland and ugly office block built in the 1960s – but I thought the new National Crime Agency headquarters might be exciting, with blast-proof walls maybe and full-body scanners at the door. But the address Amobi had given me turned out to be yet another bland office building with a fat, bored security man in the lobby who wafted a metal wand in our general direction. The working day was nearly over, and we passed a lot of empty desks as the young Chinese copper led us through into this conference room, with its long polished beech table, wipe-clean presentation board and sealed windows overlooking a poky south-facing courtyard densely planted with shiny green bushes. Even now it probably felt like the Congo down there, but here in the conference room it was pleasantly cool, thanks to air conditioning that throbbed away quietly out of sight.

Zoe was staring out the window at nothing much, radiating resentment and indignation. I realized she hadn't brought so much as a toothbrush with her, or a change of clothes, and felt again a sharp stab of guilt. I must have frightened her into panicking; but there was no point in apologizing yet again. I'd given her the information, and she'd made her own choice.

As if it had been much of a choice.

Amobi entered briskly, alone. 'Finn, hello.' He'd always been a snappy dresser, I remembered, but now there were some creases here and there on his smart suit that made him look less like a model from a menswear catalogue and more like flesh and blood. There were creases on his face too, faint lines of age; his skin was still so black it shone, and his head was still shaved bald, but I thought I caught a glint of grey from the stubble on his skull. He's barely thirty, I thought. How much stress is he under? Then I remembered I was here to stress him out some more.

Amobi's handshake was cool and light, as if he didn't want to really connect. He glanced over at Zoe and flashed her a huge grin; a genuine one, I saw.

'Zoe, hey – long time no see.' He actually went over and hugged her, and she actually hugged him back. He'd helped her a lot after her father had been killed, I recalled. She'd wanted to know what had really happened to her dad, and he'd sent her to me, because he knew I knew. He was shrewd and sharp and subtle; that's why I'd called him.

'Please, take a seat,' he said. He folded himself into a chair and leaned back, like a sympathetic copper with all the time in the world.

'Tell me these aren't your offices,' I said. 'You're not fighting organized crime from this dump?'

Amobi smiled. 'This is just an admin building for the Met,' he said. 'They lend us space when we need it. So what's the story with you two?'

Zoe shot me a look: tell him what you told me. So I did.

Amobi's face throughout was thoughtful and impassive. He took no notes, but that didn't bother me, because I knew he was listening. All the same I began to get a weird feeling that not much of my story came as a surprise to him, and that he even knew about the stuff I was leaving out – the shit I had pulled myself, mostly in self-defence, but not always.

'So this man you call the Turk,' Amobi summed up. 'He threatened Zoe, to force you to get in touch with McGovern?'

'Yeah,' I said.

Amobi nodded. He glanced over at Zoe, who still hadn't sat down, but was leaning against the far wall with her arms folded. It wouldn't have taken a mind-reader to see that she was furious and didn't want to be there, but didn't know what else to do. And suddenly I felt angry too, at Amobi's bland facade, at how much he was hiding from us.

'You know this guy, don't you?' I said. 'The Turk.'

Amobi blinked. 'If it's the same guy, yes, we know him,' he said. 'Describe him for me.'

25

'One metre eighty, slight build, very fit, seventy-five kilos, mid-twenties, dark Mediterranean complexion, brown eyes, black hair kept short, and he'd feed you your own liver,' I said.

'Any distinguishing features, birthmarks?'

'Not that I saw.' Amobi had taken out a notebook and pen and was scribbling rapidly.

I stared. 'You don't have all this already?' I said.

'We have conflicting descriptions,' Amobi said, not meeting my eye.

'So what's his real name?'

'He goes under half a dozen names. We call him the Turk too.'

'Christ,' I said. 'You don't know who he is, what he looks like – you've got nothing.'

'I wouldn't say that,' frowned Amobi.

'Why not? Because you don't want to admit it?' I said.

'We're on to him, Finn,' insisted Amobi. 'We're going to track him down and bang him up. We've handled thousands of wise guys like him, believe me.'

Not like this guy, you haven't, I thought. But I kept my mouth shut. Amobi knew this business better than me – he had to. Maybe the Turk *was* just another hoodlum. Maybe all his cool swagger, all his perfect calculation, was just bluff and front. Maybe.

Amobi turned back to Zoe. 'We'll get you into witness protection,' he said. 'That won't be a problem.'

'It will be a problem,' said Zoe, 'because I have coursework to do.'

'You can work at a safe house,' Amobi reassured her. 'In fact it'll be easier – no distractions.'

'Really? Will I have access to the Internet?'

Amobi sucked his teeth. 'Sorry. Internet access can be traced, which would compromise the safety of—'

'Oh, for God's sake,' said Zoe. 'How long would this go on for? I haven't witnessed anything – and it wouldn't be like I was waiting for a trial, would it? I'd be stuck in some shithole with a bunch of plods miles from anywhere, maybe for years. I'd lose my place at college, lose touch with all my friends—'

'It wouldn't be for years,' said Amobi. 'We should be able to resolve this in a few weeks.' His look slid over to me.

'You're kidding,' I said.

'Finn . . .' I knew I was in trouble when he used my name. He leaned forward, earnest and appealing. 'I'm flattered you came to me. I know how much you distrust the police force, and I know you have good reason. But we're not superheroes, you know? We can't save the world by ourselves. We need the help of the public. We need you.'

'Then we're all screwed,' I said.

'If the Turk wants you to introduce him to the Guvnor, do it,' he said. 'Arrange the meeting, tell us where and when it's going down, let us do the rest. We'll look after Zoe.'

'And who's going to look after me?'

'You've managed pretty well so far,' he grinned.

I said nothing, because this was exactly what I'd asked for. Zoe would be safe with him, and the sooner McGovern and the Turk met up the sooner this would all be over. With any luck they'd kill each other. I wondered if that was Amobi's plan – to sit back and watch, then move in with mops and bleach and bin bags. But this way Zoe would get her life back; and even if that life didn't include me, I owed her that much.

'How's he going to contact you?' asked Amobi.

'The Turk? He's not. I have to call him, at midnight, three days from now.'

'He gave you a number? Why doesn't he just call you?'

'I wondered that myself,' I said.

'What number did he give you?'

I told him. 'If you call it, he'll know I've spoken to you,' I said.

'We're a little more subtle than that,' smiled Amobi.

'Great, said Zoe, her voice tight with sarcasm. 'Except McGovern's in Moscow or somewhere, and Finn doesn't speak any Russian, so finding him might be a problem.'

Amobi raised his hands, flashing his pale palms. 'It just so happens that McGovern has recently returned to this country. We don't know exactly where he is, but we can point Finn in his general direction.' He smiled at me. 'And the Turk's right, isn't he? McGovern does like you, a little.'

'He won't like me for long if he thinks I'm running messages for his rivals,' I said.

'Then just tell him the truth,' said Amobi. 'That the Turk threatened you.'

'Assuming I can find him,' I said.

'You'll find him, Finn,' said Amobi. 'You're a very resourceful young man.'

That was all I needed, a pat on the head. I felt like a spaniel being offered a biscuit before being sent into a minefield.

'I'll give you a new number to reach us,' said Amobi. 'A voicemail drop. Just ring and leave a message, or send a text.' As if on cue, his own phone pinged. His message alert was an incongruously tinkling little fairy bell. Amobi slipped his smart-phone out of his pocket, glanced at the screen and frowned.

'Bad news?' I said.

He looked up, his poker face sliding back into place before he calculated that what he knew we'd soon find out. 'Another suicide bomber,' he said. 'Bristol this time.'

'Jesus,' I said. 'Is it bad?'

'We caught him before he had a chance to detonate,' said Amobi.

'How?' asked Zoe.

Amobi smiled. 'It's what we're paid for,' he said. 'But I have to report in.' He stood up, pushing back his chair.

'So you lot cover terrorism too?' I said.

'We cover everything,' said Amobi. 'And there's not enough of us to go round.' He reached for the door handle, then paused and turned back. 'Zoe, I'm going to get you into a safe house tonight, so you two need to say your goodbyes. I'll be back shortly.' He slipped out, and the door clicked shut behind him. In the silence that settled over the room I felt a tube train far below making the building rock.

'I'm sorry about this,' I said to Zoe.

'For Christ's sake, stop apologizing – it's really

getting on my tits,' said Zoe. Softening, she added, 'Anyway, it looks like we're doing the right thing.'

Now we had a plan, now that she was safe, her anger was dissolving, but she didn't know what she ought to feel instead. She unfolded her arms and perched them on her hips, then seemed to realize that made her look like a bossy ten-year-old. She raised her hands to her face and ran them through her spiky hair. Then she turned from the window, took three strides towards me, grabbed my face and pulled it down to hers. Her tongue slid into my mouth, and I tasted her and smelled her scent and felt her firm curves pressed against me, and I folded her into my arms, and the beige room and the stifling heat and the fear all evaporated in a moment that was over all too quickly.

She pulled her face away, so that our lips parted but our breath still mingled.

'I'm sorry I took it out on you,' she said.

'For Christ's sake, stop apologizing,' I said.

'Give McGovern the message and get out of there, OK? And be careful. I . . . don't want to lose you.'

'You'll always have Patrick,' I said.

'Oh, Finn,' she said. 'Don't be so bloody stupid.'

TWO

Amobi checked his mirrors, indicated – he drove as fastidiously as he dressed – and pulled over to the kerb, carefully avoiding a bus stop. He kept the engine running; the car was a bland and anonymous Ford, but I got the impression there was serious power under the hood if it was ever needed.

It was a sweltering afternoon in London's East End. I'd spent the previous night back in my own bed, wired and sleepless – not from the sticky heat, or trepidation at the task that faced me, but with thoughts of Zoe and how we'd parted. Right now I just wanted to get the Turk's stupid errand over and done with so I could get back to Zoe and pick up where we'd left off.

'The pub's called The Horsemonger,' said Amobi.

'It's five minutes' walk straight down this road, right-hand side, on the corner.'

'The Horsemonger? Seriously? What's the food like?'

'I wouldn't eat anything they cooked up in that place.' He looked across at me. 'Good luck, Finn. Be careful. And call me as soon as you get the chance, OK?'

'Yeah, OK,' I said, trying to sound as if this was no big deal, largely for my own benefit. 'See you around.'

I stepped out, shut the door and walked on without looking back. Amobi hadn't wanted to drop me too close to the pub itself, for obvious reasons, so I tried not to draw attention to the fact that we were together. I wondered for a moment if it was paranoid to imagine that my every move was being monitored; then I figured that in the circumstances a little paranoia was probably healthy.

But I soon wished Amobi had been a little less cautious. The street was broad and hot and noisy with traffic, running north–south with no shelter or shade from the sun. My shirt had glued itself to my skin as soon as I stepped out of Amobi's car, and now I felt rivulets of sweat running down my sides. The heat was getting to everybody – I could hear voices raised in anger, and from the corner of my eye I saw the traffic start to slow and circle cautiously around some obstruction.

Across the road two police patrol cars, lights flashing, had swerved round to box in a knot of black kids who'd been hanging out on some park benches. It looked like another of those stop-and-search operations the cops were entitled to use on any civilian who looked suspicious but only ever seemed to use on black teenagers. Usually the kids being detained simply tolerated it, with sullen resignation, but today it felt different: tempers were flaring like gas off an oil rig. These kids were crowding the pavement, arguing loudly with the cops – four burly constables in stab vests and shirtsleeves, all of them pasty white, with faces flushed by heat and righteous exasperation – and for a moment I thought the cops would snap and pull out their batons and pepper sprays. But the shouting and waving and finger pointing went on, and I remembered I didn't have time to stop and gawp like the pedestrians around me – I had to keep going and find the Guvnor's pub.

How long had I been walking? I looked to the corner on my right, but I couldn't spot any pub, and I briefly wondered if Amobi's information was up to date. Half of London's boozers had closed in the last

few years; drink was so much cheaper in supermarkets that people preferred to get pissed at home
in front of their tellies, and a lot of former pubs had
been converted into offices or flats. The place on the
corner ahead of me, for example – that looked like it
had once been a pub; it had a tiled exterior and
frosted windows like an old-fashioned saloon bar,
but there were none of the signs you'd associate with
a boozer – no tables outside, no blackboards advertising karaoke or cheap cocktails. Looking closer,
however, I noticed a discreet signboard hanging over
the door at right angles to the front wall, showing a
badly painted horse's head, and olde-worlde gold
lettering underneath so small it was barely legible,
even if you weren't as dyslexic as me.

The Horsemonger.

It wasn't exactly inviting. It looked like a 'local'
pub, the sort that only locals knew about – and where
only locals were welcome. The door onto the street
was solid, heavy and painted black. I half expected it
to be locked, but it gave when I pushed it, and I
caught a whiff of old beer. When I pushed harder the
door swung open. I stepped into the stale, stuffy dimness, and the noise of the street died away behind me.

Inside, pop music burbled from a blown speaker
system, so distorted it was hard to tell what the tune

was or even what era it was from. The ceiling and walls were nicotine-yellow, the luridly patterned carpet was sticky underfoot, and a one-armed bandit bleeped and flashed in the corner, ignored by the handful of customers I could see. There was one middle-aged bloke lost in a newspaper at a side table, fumbling in a bag of pork scratchings, and in the far corner to the left of the bar two men in their late twenties – one big and bearded, the other short and wiry – sat with their heads close together, conferring solemnly in a way that suggested they weren't here to relax and get pissed.

The blonde, blousy woman behind the bar was displaying a lot of pale wobbly cleavage as she wiped down the beer taps. She worked at it listlessly, as if to give herself something to do while she half listened to an old man perched on a tall stool at the bar telling her some story that probably didn't end. He was in his mid-seventies, I guessed, and lean, with thin black hair slicked down and grey hairs sprouting from his big fleshy ears. Like most old people he wore too many clothes for the hot weather: a cosy cardigan, a collared shirt and even a tie. He looked as if he lived here; in front of him a half-pint glass of lager was slowly going flat, and he squinted as he took a drag from his cigarette. Smoking had been banned in pubs years ago but nobody here seemed bothered about details like that. I wondered how such a dump stayed in business, until I remembered it belonged to the Guvnor. Most likely its main function was to launder money, not serve customers. McGovern usually preferred more upmarket investments – I'd worked in his fancy Pimlico restaurant, till it had been redecorated with blood and brains – but maybe he felt sentimental about The Horsemonger. Or maybe he'd forgotten it existed.

The old man's mumbled monologue dried up as I stood at the counter. The barmaid glanced at me and stifled a sigh, as if I was someone who'd wandered in by mistake and would soon wander out again.

'Yes, love?' Her voice was flat, bored and devoid of welcome.

'Could I get a . . . half of lager, please?' I glanced at the old bloke in the cardigan, who ignored my existence and tapped his cigarette into his personal ashtray. I expected the barmaid to ask me to choose a specific lager, but she merely picked up a glass, tilted it under the nearest tap, flipped the serving lever and watched the glass slowly fill. I opened my mouth and closed it again; I had thought of making small talk to break the ice before I dived in, but the ice in here felt about a metre thick. I head-butted it instead.

'I was hoping to talk to the boss,' I said. No reaction at first. Maybe she thought I was looking for a job.

'You're talking to her,' she said, as she scraped the foam off the top of the lager with a wooden scraper that looked like it was also used for cleaning the floor.

'No, I mean the boss. The governor,' I said.

No sudden silence; no one dropped a glass, and the muzak didn't suddenly stop. Old Cardigan sucked on his cigarette, his wrinkled cheeks pulling tight against his cheekbones, but still he didn't look at me or betray the slightest interest. That was what told me how closely he was listening. The barmaid plonked the lager in front of me, with some irritation; the beer slopped over the rim to make a piss-coloured puddle on the counter.

'Like I said, you're talking to her. That'll be two pounds fifty.'

I dug in my pocket for coins, expecting her to ask what it was I wanted, but she said nothing more. I slapped the coins on the counter. I didn't ask for the Guvnor again, because there was no point – she'd heard me, and the old man had heard me, and Little and Large in the corner had stopped chatting and were studying their drinks, so I was pretty sure they'd heard me too. I picked up the beer with my left, shoved the cash across the bar with my right, and raised my glass.

'Cheers,' I said, and took a sip. It was sour and stale, but it was cold and wet, so I gulped it anyway, and stood there and waited.

The barmaid sighed so I could hear her this time, turned to the till and punched in the sale, dropped the money into the cash register and wandered off to the other end of the counter. There were no customers up there to serve, so she started to rearrange her packets of snacks instead.

I wondered how long I'd have to wait. At this rate I'd still be here at closing time – if this place ever closed – skint and full of rancid beer. Those guys in the corner, maybe I should sit next to them, start a conversation. Or maybe I should skip the formalities and knock their drinks over. I had to make some sort of noise, create a ruckus big enough to come to the attention of McGovern.

The old man screwed his cigarette out in the ashtray and slipped off his stool. He wobbled slightly as he straightened his cardie, and I wondered if he was drunk or just really old, but then his glance met mine. His eyes were a frosty bloodshot blue, and there was something in them that looked like pity. He flicked his head almost imperceptibly – *this way* – and headed towards the rear of the bar, towards the door that led to the toilets. I didn't really want to follow him in there – if the public bar was this grim, God knows what the loos would be like – but I didn't have many options. The old man was spry for his years, and though his spine was a little bent he moved quickly, and the door had shut behind him before I finally decided to go after him, leaving my drink on the bar.

Beyond the door a long smelly passageway led to the toilets, but the old man had pulled open another door off to the left, and was vanishing through it. Following him I found myself outside again, in the pub's back yard – a fenced-off patch of concrete at the end of a long grimy alley lined with battered metal bins and wheeled plastic skips that hummed with flies and stank of hot, festering garbage. I glanced up; a dozen windows overlooked the yard, every one of them dusty and disused. A good place to have a private conference, or to discourage nosy visitors.

Old Cardigan had paused by the rear fence, with his back to me, and as I watched he reached into a pocket, pulled something out and unfolded it. When he turned round I saw it was an old-fashioned razor, and now it hung loose in his hand like it was part of him, like he used it every day. But not for shaving.

Behind me the door burst open again, and the two blokes I had last seen staring down into their pints emerged, their faces hard set and their fists clenched. I raised my hands to calm them down and got as far as saying, 'Wait a minute—' when the shorter of the two of them charged up and threw a punch in low to my stomach. I blocked it but didn't counterpunch – I was hoping we could still talk, but that was a mistake, because they weren't interested in conversation. The larger bearded one had ducked behind me while I was parrying his little mate, and now he threw his arm round my neck and closed his elbow on my windpipe.

'You know what gets my goat about kids these days? They got no sense of history,' said the old man as he walked slowly towards me. I held still, keeping my eyes on the blade that glinted in his hand. The shorter guy backed aside, grinning, looking forward to the show. 'They know nothing about the men who made this country great,' the old man was saying. 'Nothing about showing respect. About speaking when you're spoken to, about minding your own business. I mean, how hard can it be to teach this stuff?' He waved the razor in mild exasperation. 'Kid sticks his hand in a fire, he gets burned – lesson learned, he doesn't do it again, does he?' He smiled as he came to the point; he had old-fashioned British teeth, blackened and yellow and pointing in all directions. He raised the blade to the level of my chest, and I knew that in the next instant it would flash across my face and open it to the bone. 'A scar is a lesson. It goes deep enough, you'll never forget it.'

'For God's sake, you don't even know why I'm here—'

He grinned. 'I don't give a shit.'

One brisk kick sent the blade flying over his head. It bounced off a wheelie bin behind him and went skittering off across the concrete. I heard Old Cardigan curse, and glimpsed him turn to go after it, but at that moment I was busy piling backwards towards the wall behind me, making sure the large guy with his arm around my neck slammed his big beardy head hard against the iron drainpipe.

He grunted in pain and his grip weakened, and I grabbed his wrist and twisted his arm, holding his hand locked back while I turned to his pal, Little, who was piling towards me in fury, his right fist pulled back over his shoulder. I let him throw the punch, dodged to my right, and slammed my free fist square into his pockmarked face, feeling the gristle crack and flatten. He yelped and clutched his nose as blood and mucus squirted through his fingers.

It gave me time to push Large away, far enough to land a hard kick to his solar plexus with the ball of my foot. While he staggered, wheezing and gasping for breath, I swung him round in a circle, hoping to drive him headfirst into the brick wall, but he collided heavily with a dustbin instead. The clang was gratifying, but it meant he wasn't out of the fight just yet – and now Little had recovered, wiping blood and snot off his face and onto his pastel-green polo shirt, and he came back at me twice as hard.

The lid of the dustbin had come to my hand as Large slammed into it, and now I grasped the handle almost instinctively and raised it like a rusty metal shield, diffusing Little's flurry of punches. He snatched at the rim, hoping to wrench it out of my hands, so I let him have it, in the nose again to start with, then ramming it against his cheeks and jaw as he stumbled backwards.

By now the old man had found the razor and was cleaning it on an old tissue. Little had fallen back against the pub's back door, his legs liquefying, while Large was slowly getting to his feet. Grasping the handle of the bin lid firmly I slammed it down on the back of his head a few times to encourage him to stay on the floor.

Old Cardigan was smiling his ghastly black smile;

he was crouched, the razor once more in his right hand, circling it slowly, inviting me to come and try my luck. I didn't need luck; I didn't even need the dustbin lid. Chucking it aside I strode forward, seized the old man's razor hand in my left and grabbed his thin bony old face in my right.

'You know what gets my goat about old people these days?' I said. 'They think they have nothing to learn and they never sodding listen. I came here to talk to the Guvnor, not listen to some nasty old fart witter on about his childhood.' Old Cardigan was still grinning, and he hadn't dropped the blade. His bony left hand had closed around my right wrist, as if to pull it off his face, but his grasp was light and feeble as a cobweb. I forced his right wrist upwards until the cut-throat razor was a finger's breadth from his eye, and all he did was twist his head to the side and offer me his jugular. He had balls, for an old bloke, but I noticed he'd missed a bit when shaving that morning. Ironic.

'What the fuck's been going on here?'

I looked behind me. Large was on his hands and knees, shaking his head; Little had slumped away from where he'd fallen against the pub's back door. Standing in the open doorway was a heavyset guy in his late twenties with a golden tan and thick black hair cut so short it stood up. His clothes were expensive and well-cut, concealing the extra bulk he carried around his shoulders and midriff. He struck me as a man used to giving orders, and from the look on his face he wasn't impressed by the scene that greeted him – Little and Large stunned, bleeding, and daubed with blood and filth, and some sweaty over-grown teenager he'd never seen before mugging Old Cardigan for his razor.

I shoved the old man's face away and wrenched the razor from his bony fist. Bending down I stood on the blade and twisted the handle until the blade snapped off. Then I straightened up and tossed the stump at him. He made no move to catch it, but just let it bounce off his cardigan and rattle onto the concrete.

'I've another dozen like that at home,' he sneered.

'Go and fetch one then, and try again. I've got all week.'

'Get inside, clean yourselves up,' the new arrival grunted at Little and Large. Both men stumbled meekly back into the pub, Little wiping his hands on his polo shirt, making the stains worse. Ignoring me, the new arrival turned to Cardigan with a scowl of contempt. 'What did I tell you about playing vigilantes, Eric? You too senile to remember, is that it?'

Odd, I thought. I'd expected him to challenge me first and bollock the old man in private later, but the new guy must have really hated Old Cardigan – Eric.

The old man was shaking now, with rage rather than age, and I saw his fingers twitch for his razor before he remembered I'd disarmed him. His rheumy old eyes blinked. 'Don't you talk to me like that, you little prick,' he protested. 'I was sorting out proper hard men when you were still pissing your britches.'

The big guy leaned in and fixed the old man with a steady stare from icy-grey eyes that didn't water or blink. 'Eric, you can't even bloody shave yourself any more, so stop trying to scare people with that razor, it's embarrassing.' I'd seen that stare before: it looked like I was in the right place. Eric's saggy jaw was working away in furious humiliation, and his fingers twitched again, longing for the feel of the blade. But he said nothing more, and the younger guy turned to me. 'And what do you want?' He was my height, but heavier, and his cold stare was drilling into me in a way I remembered all too well.

'The name's Finn Maguire. I have a message for your dad.'

It was a gamble, but it paid off. McGovern Junior smirked, intrigued. 'What message?' he said.

'I'd rather deliver it in person.'

'I'm sure you would.' Junior frowned, as if my name had rung a bell. 'Hold on – Finn Maguire?'

'I used to work for your dad. In that restaurant in Pimlico.'

Another gamble, with higher stakes. In that restaurant I'd seen the Guvnor's second-in-command murder a cop, a fact I'd never admitted to anyone. I was pretty sure the Guvnor wouldn't have talked about it either: everybody in his clan would be curious to hear what had really happened. Curious enough to take their time and ask nicely, I hoped, rather than by shoving needles up my fingernails until I was screaming the truth to anyone who'd listen.

I saw calculation flicker in McGovern's eyes, then he grinned like a wolf and squinted up at the sun.

'Christ, it's hot out here,' he said. 'And it stinks. Eric, go change your Y-fronts, I think you've shat yourself again.' He turned back and offered me his hand to shake. 'I'm Steve,' he said. 'Let's get a pint.'

Steve made a quick muttered call on his mobile in a quiet corner of the pub, his glance flicking over to me every so often, while I stood at the bar gulping down lemonade. I'd expected him to take the mickey when I asked for a soft drink, but he'd merely nodded to the barmaid, who went scurrying off for my pint of lemonade. The lager I'd abandoned earlier sat on the bar getting warmer and flatter still, but I left it there – I wanted to keep my wits sharp, or at least not blunt them any further. Old Eric had followed us in, and now he clambered back onto his stool at the bar and lit himself a new cigarette, squinting into the smoke. Young McGovern returned, tucking his mobile phone away, apparently satisfied, and started telling me what a player Eric had been in his prime; about how much the Krays – or was it Jack the Ripper? – had feared that razor, and how Eric had slashed faces to order and got paid by the length of the wounds. 'Three farthings a stitch, wasn't it?' snorted Steve.

The old man sipped at his lager, stony-faced. I felt a twinge of pity for him, having to sit there and be sneered at by the boss's son, when all he'd been doing was defending their turf. Then I remembered the vicious old bastard approaching me with his razor open. He probably deserved all of it, and worse.

Eventually Junior grew tired of baiting Eric and turned back to me. 'So how'd you find this place then?' I'd expected him to lower his voice, but he didn't seem to care who heard him.

'I asked around,' I said.

'Who'd you ask?' Young McGovern's grin had hardened.

'It's in *The Good Pub Guide*,' I said. Junior laughed, as I'd hoped he would, and I tried to steer our conversation in a less risky direction. 'I need to speak to the Guvnor. I have a message for him.'

'Yeah, you said,' said Junior.

'So can I meet him?'

'What's it about, exactly?'

Why don't I tell him? I wondered. Let him give the Guvnor the message, give him the Turk's phone number, let them sort it out between themselves?

Because appealing as the impulse was to blurt out the Turk's demands and do a runner, I didn't trust anyone to deliver the message but me. Yes, it was dangerous getting involved, but Zoe and I were already involved; I was alive right now because the Turk wanted to use me as an envoy, and if I wanted to stay alive I had to deliver the message in person and see how the Guvnor reacted. The more I knew about each side, the more clout I'd have with the other, and with Amobi.

'The Turk,' was all I said.

It was all I needed to say. Junior nodded thoughtfully. Picking up his pint he sank the rest of it in one gulp, then slammed the glass down. 'Turn out your pockets,' he said.

It didn't take me long: a handful of change, a

wallet with a bank card and a travel card, my house keys and my phone. McGovern slid the phone across the counter to where the blousy barmaid rematerialized.

'Lose that for us, Michelle,' said Junior. Wordlessly she picked up the handset, flipped the back off and lifted out the battery, then started to work the SIM loose.

'Oi, that's my phone,' I protested.

'Tough,' said Junior. He was flicking through my wallet, feeling in the seams and corners – for bugs presumably – while Michelle wrapped up my mobile in a sheet of foil.

'Don't I even get the SIM back?'

'Phones can be traced, SIMs can be traced,' said Junior. I felt a flash of hope: if they were taking me somewhere I couldn't be traced, maybe it was to meet the Guvnor. Then it struck me how incredibly naive that was. Maybe Junior was just humouring me so I'd go quietly; maybe the Guvnor already knew what the Turk wanted and wasn't interested in talking, in which case I was surplus to everyone's requirements. I wondered how many people had entered this pub and never been seen again: somehow I didn't think Amobi would bring an NCA unit to raid this place, kicking over tables, roughing up the punters and demanding to know what had become of me; more likely his department would just look for a new snitch and start over.

'Derek, frisk him,' said Junior. I glanced over my shoulder and saw Large looming behind me, but he waited until I'd had placed my hands on the bar and spread my legs a little before he started patting me down. Large Derek was cautious – probably worrying that if he did find anything I'd elbow him in the face – but he was thorough. Down my arms, all over my torso, my front pockets and rear; from the tops of my trouser legs all the way down to my ankles. I was wearing light trainers with thin soles, where it would have been nearly impossible to conceal anything, but he kneaded each foot in turn.

Junior slapped my wallet back down on the bar. 'Properly,' he grunted to Derek. What the hell, I thought – is he planning to stick a finger up my arse and root around for a tracking device? I sensed Derek hesitate, before his big beefy right hand cupped my balls and gave them a good kneading. My eyes watered and I nearly did slam an elbow into his face, but I held back: better to be groped than forced to drop my trousers and show everyone that the only weapon I had tucked away in there was standard issue.

'I usually don't go this far on a first date,' I said.

Derek snatched his hand away, more embarrassed than I was, and I saw Junior catch his eye, nod and turn to Michelle.

'Is he there yet?'

'He's just bringing it round,' she said.

'You're lucky I called in today.' Junior smirked at me. 'I don't normally. Prefer places with a bit more life, to be honest. And a lot more fanny. It's like a geriatric ward in here, except the food's worse.'

I saw Michelle's glance flick to him, in her eyes a tiny spark of resentment that she snuffed out instantly. Her over-painted face resumed its bored, vacant expression. She was scared of Junior, I could tell, and I suspected his jolly, sardonic exterior was a thin layer of hardened lava over a volcanic temper; the same temper I'd seen in his father.

'Oh, and I'll need a carrier bag,' Junior told her, as an afterthought. Michelle rooted around under the counter – I got the impression she was rummaging in a dustbin – before she finally produced a thin plastic carrier bag, the sort you get from all-night no-name supermarkets. She shook some dubious liquid off it and handed it to Junior. I thought he'd insist on a clean one but he didn't seem bothered, and when he rolled down the rim and turned to me with the bag held in two hands I understood why.

'You're not going to suffocate,' he said. 'It's only until you're out in the car.'

'I could just shut my eyes—' I started to say, but he'd already started pulling the bag down over my head and neck, so I couldn't even see out of the bottom. I heard Eric pipe up, with a snort of sarcasm, 'You going to spin him round and round as well? Like in Blind Man's Buff?'

'No, I've got a better idea,' I heard Junior say, an instant before his fist crashed into the side of my head. I staggered, lights flashing behind my eyes, and my knees went a little. Or rather I let them go a little, so Junior wouldn't feel it necessary to hit me again. He'd been aiming for my face, I knew, hoping to knock a tooth loose or split my lip, but as soon as he'd spoken I'd heard his intentions and turned my head. It still felt like I'd been whacked in the skull with a frying pan, and the cut to my temple had opened up again, but the blood trickling down my neck below the bag's rim seem to satisfy Junior for now.

A hand under my armpit hauled me upright and dragged me forward, back towards the passage that led to the toilets, and out again into the hot still air of the stinking yard. I heard an engine running, a quiet purr of power, and knew I was being dragged towards the boot of a big car before my thighs collided with a rear bumper, the tow hook nearly taking my kneecap off, and a hefty hand between my shoulder blades pushed me forward and bent me down.

I let my balance go and fell into the open boot, raising my fists and pushing my chin into my chest to shield my face as I landed. Somebody hauled at my legs and I pulled them in only a moment before the boot lid slammed shut, locking me in darkness. Instantly I felt like a spud left to bake in a slow oven. Sweat gushed from my pores, soaking my shirt, and I tasted the blood from the cut to my temple as it changed direction and trickled down into my mouth.

Well, at least I'm getting somewhere, I thought. And my hands were free. I hooked the rim of the bag with my thumbs, pulled it off my head and gasped for air – I'd been running so low on oxygen even the hot, stuffy boot was an improvement. The Guvnor's people had locked me in a trunk once before, but that car had been a rustbucket in a breaker's yard, and this one was luxurious by any standard – thickly carpeted, with a tiny cool air-conditioned breeze leaking in from the passenger compartment. Rumpled underneath me was what felt like a woollen picnic blanket.

I tried listening for conversation from the passenger compartment, but if anyone was in there they weren't talking. I had nothing to eavesdrop on, no idea where I was headed or how long it would take, and nobody to call, now my phone was sitting at the bottom of The Horsemonger's trash bin. I shifted my feet, my hip and my shoulders in turn as I pulled the picnic blanket from underneath me, rolled it up into a long, squishy pillow and tucked it under my head. It smelled of stale wine and rancid strawberries.

After ten minutes or so the car was stopping and starting less, making fewer turns, and it had picked up speed. That suggested we were on a main road heading out of the city – from the regular thump of the tyres one of those concrete roads with seams every hundred metres; soon that noise transitioned into a quiet smooth roar, and we picked up more speed. We were on a motorway, and it occurred to me that if I counted one beat a second I could maybe work out the distance between junctions . . . but then it might be twenty minutes to the next junction, and I didn't know if I could count that high. I decided to take a nap instead.

I was woken by a jolt, a speed bump or something.

I'd been out for an hour or so, but I couldn't be sure. Since my last place had burned down with most of my belongings in it I'd been using my phone for a watch, and that was gone now. But beyond the stale blanket and the smell of the leather seats I could now smell something else – freshly mown grass, and the faint whiff of cow dung. We were in the countryside, on a narrow twisting road that must have had a problem with speeding traffic, judging by the frequent speed bumps. The commuter belt around London?

Abruptly the car slowed again, swerved to the left and pulled up, the engine running. I heard a faint electronic tinkle and a distorted voice – an entry-phone. Then an electric whine and the metallic rattle of automated gates opening. The car moved forward, gravel crackling under the tyres for thirty seconds, then a gentle turn to the right, and suddenly the sound of the engine was folding back on us, echoing off hard walls up close – we were in a garage. Two doors opened, the car eased up on its springs, and the lid of the trunk popped open. I looked up, only to be dazzled by a strip light on the ceiling high above, and two bulky silhouettes appeared, one from each side. On the right was McGovern Junior; on the left, so massive he made Junior look like a flyweight, was

Terry, the Guvnor's driver and minder. Last time
we'd met had been at that bloodbath in Pimlico.

'Tel!' I flashed him a grin, absurdly relieved to see
a familiar face. 'Long time no see.'

I should have known better than to expect a
response. Terry just stared down at me, huge and
impassive as an Easter Island statue. Come to think of
it, had I ever heard him talk? Maybe the Guvnor had
had his tongue cut out.

Junior jerked his chin at the thin plastic bag lying
crumpled behind me. 'Put that back on.'

I obliged, then felt Terry's massive paw grasping
my arm, and I scrambled to get out of the car on my
own two feet in case Terry dropped me face first onto
the concrete floor. He kept one massive paw under
my armpit as he hopped me, not especially gently,
through a doorway along a hall with cream carpet
underfoot – I could just see it under the rim of the
bag. I hoped my shoes were clean. This was going to
be a delicate enough interview without me trampling
dogshit into the Guvnor's rug.

Through another door, and now I could smell a
slightly acrid, old-fashioned tang – mothballs?
Suddenly Terry was walking me backwards, and I
felt the backs of my legs hit a low couch. I sat, my
hands by my sides, and felt the smooth shiny leather

of a deep-buttoned cushion. A fist closed on my scalp – I grunted in pain – and the plastic bag was yanked off my head, taking some of my hair with it. I looked around, blinking.

'Christ, what a sodding mess,' said Junior.

I rubbed my cheek and realized the trickle of blood from my temple had dried in a streak down the length of my face. Between that and the fading bruises it must have looked as if I'd been dragged behind the car rather than carried in the boot.

Junior clicked his fingers at Terry, and held out his hand. Terry turned to him – was that a flash of irritation on his scarred face? – and looked blank. 'Fetch him a hanky, or some tissues or something,' snapped Junior. Terry turned to a low wooden coffee table behind him, picked up a box of tissues and handed it to me. I pulled one out, spat on it, and started to dab the dried blood off my face while I checked out the room.

I remembered the Guvnor's house up in North London. Modern, sleek, if a bit busy. This place looked like it had been furnished by his auntie – lots of thick, expensive fabrics, heavy curtains and ornate old-fashioned chairs with curved, knobbly legs, all in fussy patterns that didn't quite match. Unlike the Guvnor's lounge, this room didn't centre on a huge

TV, but on a massive marble fireplace that looked old but wasn't, with an empty hearth concealed by a tapestry screen in a curly wrought-iron frame. The whiff of mothballs was getting right up my nose, but underneath that smell the air was stale anyway, as if the windows hadn't been opened for years. It was a hideout, I realized; a mansion owned by someone with too much money that had been sitting empty until the Guvnor had rented it under a fake name. Out here in the commuter belt, sandwiched between golf courses, big cars with tinted windows came and went all the time, high fences and electric gates were commonplace, and no nosy neighbour would ever pop round to borrow a lawnmower or suggest a car-share for the school run.

'Finn Maguire, back again. You're worse than sodding herpes, you are.'

The Guvnor had emerged from a door behind me, and his greeting sounded almost affectionate. He was casually dressed in chinos and jumper, the only hint of gangster bling a chunky gold watch on his wrist. Two men had followed him in, both in their thirties, muscular and grim; one had thinning red hair shaved close to his skull and a nose squashed flat against his broad pale face; the other was taller, tanned and windburned like a gardener, with greasy black hair and bulging eyes. McGovern didn't introduce either of them.

The Guvnor had lost a little weight; maybe Russian food didn't agree with him. He was slimmer than his son, but his blue-grey eyes were as piercing as ever and he had lost none of the menace he radiated even when he smiled. Especially when he smiled. He was smiling now, extending his hand to shake. I stood and shook, and his grip was familiar – muscular and cool. But when he saw my face close up his face darkened and he turned to Junior. It was the first time I'd seen Steve McGovern blink. He stood his ground, but I thought I saw the flicker of a sulky teenager expecting to get slapped, and when he spoke he sounded like one.

'He was like that when he turned up.'

'It's true,' I said. I glanced at the blood and spit mingled on the tissue in my hand. 'This was the Turk. His minders, anyway.'

'You've met him?' McGovern grabbed a few pistachios from a bowl on the table and sat down opposite me in a winged armchair. He looked relaxed and cheerful; not much like a gangster whose empire was under siege. His two companions remained standing, observing silently from a distance.

'Yeah,' I said, easing myself back onto the sofa. 'I've met him.'

'Where are my manners? Steven, fetch Mr Maguire here a drink.' Steve twitched; he didn't look happy about playing the skivvy.

'I'm fine,' I said. I wasn't thirsty, or hungry, I realized: I just wanted to deliver the Turk's message and get out of there. Only . . . how was I going to get out of there? I'd been so intent on finding the Guvnor I hadn't considered what might come after. His people had gone to a lot of trouble to keep me in the dark about where I was – if I played nice, would they drop me back where they'd found me?

'And?' said McGovern. I snapped back into the present.

'When I first met him he called himself Bruno,' I said. I told him the same story I'd told Amobi: how the Turk had grabbed my lawyer because she was about to blow a huge scam he'd set up at a City bank, and how I'd managed to find her. She'd left the country and the Turk had come looking for me, but he'd left me alive so I could deliver his message. 'Bruno's not his real name,' I said. 'Nobody knows his real name. Everyone just calls him the Turk.'

'His real name's Rebaz Pirbal,' said the Guvnor, 'and he's not a Turk.' He spat a pistachio shell onto the carpet. 'He's a Kurd. From Western Anatolia.'

'Where's that?' interjected Junior.

McGovern didn't look round. 'Who gives a shit?' he replied.

I said nothing, but sat there trying to take this in. I'd thought if Amobi and the NCA didn't have any details on the Turk, no one would; but I should have guessed McGovern had sources the cops didn't.

'His dad ran heroin into Germany all through the nineties, sent golden boy to a posh boarding school in Switzerland,' McGovern went on. 'Old man died last year, and the son took over. He's trying to diversify, into girls and money laundering, and now he wants into the UK market, except he won't go through the proper channels.' By which he meant that the Turk should pay the Guvnor a percentage of his turnover, I guessed. 'Fancies himself as the CEO of a multi-national,' said McGovern, 'when in fact he's a cocky little wog too stupid to know when he's out of his depth.' He cracked another nut between his molars, picked it out of his mouth and pulled it apart, flicking shards of shell onto the floor. He must have seen the look on my face.

'What?' he said. 'Don't like me calling him a "wog"? How about "darkie"? Didn't take you for one of those PC dickheads.'

SHREDDER

'That's not it,' I said, although it was, partly.
McGovern's casual bigotry was bad enough, but it
struck me as stupid to judge the Turk by the shade
of his skin. 'The Turk – Pirbal, I mean – he's clever.
He takes his time and he does his homework.'

'If he'd done his homework, he wouldn't be
picking a fight with me,' said the Guvnor.

'What I mean is, when you think you've got him
sussed, that you're one step ahead of him, he's
already figured out all your options and which one
you're going to choose.'

'Didn't stop you screwing up his City deal, did it?
Or blowing a big hole in his white slave business,'
said McGovern, with a hint of amusement in his
voice. He had a point: I had already proved the Turk
wasn't invincible. 'So what's this message?'

'He wants a meeting,' I said. 'With you.'

'Cheeky bollocks,' said McGovern. 'As if I'd go
on a blind date with every bloody Arab who thinks
he's a player. Did he say where?'

'No,' I said. 'He gave me a number to call.'

McGovern considered a moment, then raised a
hand and clicked his fingers. One of the silent
observers – the red-headed guy with the flat nose –
stepped forward, reaching into his pocket, and produced a slim, basic, old-fashioned phone with no

touchscreen. A burner, I realized: a handset with no registered owner or address, disposable and untraceable. McGovern's team must have had crates of the bloody things.

'What's the number?'

I recited it from memory. I never have any problem keeping information like that in my head – it's getting it in there to start with that takes the effort. McGovern punched the numbers into the keypad with his thumb, put the phone to his ear, and we all waited.

'Pirbal, you prick,' he said. 'I hear you want to talk.' He rose from his chair, listening intently, and strolled out of the room.

I sat there for a while. Nobody spoke. Between the immobile, impassive Terry, and McGovern's two deputies, standing there with their arms folded, it was like after-hours at Madame Tussauds. Junior, clearly desperate to know what was going down, drifted towards the doorway his dad had disappeared through, but soon realized he wasn't going to overhear anything. He muttered a curse under his breath and looked at his watch as if wondering if he had time to go grab a sandwich. I reached for a handful of pistachios – with all the sweating I'd done I needed the salt – and the four men in the room all looked at me as if I was taking a dump on the rug.

'Chill,' I said. 'I'll leave some for the boss.'

The door I had entered by opened again, but no one appeared at first. 'This is my dad's meeting room,' said a small voice. 'I'm not allowed in here when he has visitors.'

'You are with me,' I heard a gruff reply.

I'd recognized the boy before he even entered: Kelly, the Guvnor's youngest son, the six-year-old I'd dragged out of the family swimming pool back in the spring. Now when he looked around his big brown eyes widened in alarm at the sight of all the grim-faced grown-ups – he knew this was one of the times he wasn't supposed to be in here.

But the man whose hand he was holding didn't want to retreat. He was a burly, white-haired bloke of sixty-something, in a pink shirt with a lot of buttons undone, grey chest hair poking through the gap like from a burst sofa, and buried in the grey a flash of gold. His hands were studded with jewelled rings, and when the old man grinned around the room, I thought I saw a diamond embedded in one of his front teeth.

Then little Kelly's look latched onto me, and he beamed and tugged at the old man's hand. 'That's

Finn!' he said. Caution forgotten, he ran across the room, and to my amazement threw his arms round my neck. I hesitated for a second, then wondered why I was hesitating, and hugged him back.

'Kelly, hey,' I said. 'How are the swimming lessons going?'

'Kelly, buzz off, we're busy,' said Junior, before his little brother could reply. He threw an anxious glance at the old man, who I noticed now was staring hard at me. Aware of a sudden tension in the room I peeled Kelly's arms from round my neck as gently as I could.

'Are you staying?' Kelly asked.

'I don't know,' I said. I checked the faces circling me for clues, but found none. 'I don't think so. But we'll talk soon, I promise.' At that moment McGovern re-entered, the burner phone dead in his hand. Seeing the old man he grinned, but there was a hard cold edge to his smile. 'Hey,' he said. 'You need something?'

The old man shrugged, held out his hands in apology. 'Kelly, he want to explore. We go,' he said. He beckoned to the little boy, who threw me another big smile and scampered off to take the old man's hand. The door clicked softly shut behind them, and Terry strode across to stand in front of it and prevent any more interruptions.

Who the hell was that? I thought. His accent sounded East European – Russian, I guessed, though I hadn't heard many Russian accents outside of movies. With all that bling . . . was he Russian mafia? Had it really been the kid's idea to go exploring? Or had that old man been curious to know what was being discussed – and to get a look at the messenger? For a moment I felt I was the centre of attention, like a rare medical specimen. Then I remembered what happens to rare medical specimens: they get dissected.

'He's very persuasive, this friend of yours,' said McGovern to me. He tossed the handset back to Red, who immediately started dismantling it.

'You're going to meet him?' I said.

'Yeah. Good old-fashioned face to face.'

'Where?' asked Junior. 'Somewhere neutral?'

I don't want to hear this, I thought. Screw Amobi and the NCA – I'd done my part, and now Zoe would be safe. Amobi might be pissed off that I didn't know the venue, but if the Guvnor never told me it wouldn't be my fault.

'Trafalgar Square,' said the Guvnor. 'Noon to-morrow.' He scooped up another few pistachios.

The rest of the room fell silent for a beat, taking that in, while I thought, Oh shit . . . because now I could feel myself being sucked into that swamp.

'You must be kidding,' said Junior. 'Out in the open? All that public, all that CCTV?' The Guvnor's two wingmen were still silent but the look on their faces spoke volumes – they agreed with his son.

'There is nowhere neutral, is there?' said McGovern. 'There's nowhere in this town we don't control, he knows that.'

'Send someone else, then,' Red piped up. His accent was South London, his voice calm and even, calculating. 'Send Steve.'

'Why send anyone?' said Steve. 'Why are we even negotiating with this piece of shit?'

'Who said anything about negotiating?' said the Guvnor. 'He thinks, Trafalgar Square, all that public, all that CCTV, we'd never pull anything there. He thinks it's safe.' He tossed the empty nutshells back into the bowl. 'Scum will never know what hit him.'

There was another moment of silence. They were going to murder the Turk in the middle of Trafalgar Square? If anyone else considered the idea insane, they didn't say so. I suddenly remembered a story I'd come across when I first learned about the Guvnor: that he'd once gone to an underworld conference to bury the hatchet with a rival firm. All weapons had been checked in at the door, but as soon as he'd come face to face with other firm's boss the Guvnor had strangled him with his bare hands. After that there was peace. McGovern got away with the most outrageous shit: that's how he got to be the Guvnor.

'Still no need for you to be there,' said Red.

'He knows what I look like,' said McGovern. 'If I don't show, he's not going to sit down.'

'But we don't know what this Turk looks like, do we?' said Junior.

'One of us does,' said the Guvnor. And he grinned at me.

THREE

'You're in here.' Gary opened a door and stood back. I stepped into a small, neat, white-painted room with a single bed, a washbasin in one corner, a built-in closet and a flimsy white dressing table. A small old-fashioned TV on an extending arm faced the bed, and the only window was a long narrow one at high level – too narrow to climb through – and all that showed beyond were thick thorny bushes. It had once been a staff bedroom, I assumed. Gary nodded up the corridor. 'There's a kitchen up that end. Make your-self something if you're hungry, have whatever's in the fridge. Anything you need?'

A phone, I almost said, but I knew there'd be no point. 'A toothbrush?'

Gary frowned. He was one of the Guvnor's side-kicks, the one with bulging eyes and the gardener's tan. The other one, the ginger guy with the shaved head, was called Martin, and he was the senior of the two, which was presumably why Gary had been detailed to show me to the room where I'd be spending the night. He didn't seem to mind, until I asked for the toothbrush – now he seemed to be figuring out if it was worth the effort, when he wanted to get back to the Guvnor; there were plans being laid.

'I'll find out,' he said, and he strode off down the corridor the way we'd come.

I'd noticed as we entered that there was no lock on that door, but I'd seen half a dozen other heavies lurking in the hallways beyond – this wasn't a house where I could creep about unseen, looking for a phone or an unlocked laptop; there was no way I'd get a message to Amobi tonight. I decided I might as well make myself something to eat, as Gary had suggested.

The kitchen, like my bedroom, was neat and compact with high windows, but it wasn't empty. At the small round laminate table in the centre two kids were eating pasta, supervised by a girl not much older than me. She had thick, wild golden hair woven into an old-fashioned plait that sat on her shoulder, and she was laughing as I entered, her laughter tinkling like a crystal bell; but when she saw me her laugh died away, as if she was frightened or embarrassed.

'Hey,' I said.

'Hello,' she said cautiously. That one word was enough to tell me where she was from – Glasgow, or thereabouts. Her voice too had a crystal ring, and her eyes were big and brown in her almond-shaped face. She was really quite beautiful, I realized; this brief confinement might be bearable after all.

'Finn!' The Guvnor's son Kelly clambered down from his seat opposite the girl, abandoning his bowl of pasta. Grabbing my hand he dragged me over to the table. 'This is Finn,' he announced loudly. His younger sister – I'd never learned her name – was sitting between Kelly and the older girl, who I presumed was their nanny; recognizing me, the little girl smiled but said nothing.

'Hey,' I said. Then realized I'd said that already.

The nanny looked up at me. 'You want some pasta, Finn? There's plenty to go round.'

'I'd love some,' I said.

'It's got sausages in it,' said Kelly, clambering back into his chair.

'My favourite,' I said.

'I'm Victoria, by the way,' said the nanny, as she

brought out a bowl from a high cupboard and reached for the pan of pasta on the hob. 'Bonnie, eat up now,' she told the little girl. 'I don't want you asking for biscuits later.'

'I told them you were here – they didn't believe me,' said Kelly, twirling a fork in his spaghetti with slow concentration.

'Yes I did,' said Victoria, plonking the bowl in front of me. 'It's just, you weren't supposed to go wandering round the house, you know that.'

'But Dimitri was with me!' protested Kelly.

Victoria's smile concealed a wince. 'And we're not supposed to talk about your daddy's friends, or his business,' she said.

There was a moment's awkward silence; I pretended not to have heard the old Russian bloke's name, while Bonnie looked down into her bowl. I'd guessed that after Kelly had taken Dimitri on his guided tour someone had administered a bollocking to Victoria, and the kids hadn't quite understood what had been going on. Kelly was frowning now, puzzled, as if he didn't know what he was and wasn't allowed to talk about.

'This pasta's lovely, thanks,' I said to Victoria. She smiled at me so warmly I suspected I'd done something stupid, and sure enough, I'd managed to flick a dab of sauce onto the end of my nose. Kelly squealed in delight.

'Kelly, that's not nice,' scolded Victoria, so sweetly I wished she'd been scolding me. It was incongruous, finding a girl this angelic in the Guvnor's basement, while upstairs some horrendous violence was being plotted. I remembered the hug Kelly had given me when he found me upstairs, and wondered if it was this girl who'd taught him to be so warm and open with his affection. Hugs didn't seem to fit in with the Guvnor or his circle – a handshake was as physical as they ever got, if you didn't count the violence. Junior hadn't come across as the touchy-feely type when he punched me in the face.

'How come your brother doesn't eat with you?' I asked the kids.

Kelly looked baffled. 'My brother?' he said.

'Steve,' I said. I saw Victoria glance at me, suspecting my motives for asking, but I didn't have a motive, apart from being nosy.

'Steve's not my brother!' snorted Kelly. 'He's only half a brother.'

'We've got a different mum,' said Bonnie.

'Have you got a brother?' Kelly asked me.

'Naw,' I said. 'No brothers, no sisters, no folks, just me.'

'Oh,' said Bonnie.

'It's fine,' I said. 'Mostly.' I could tell that like most kids they found the thought of being all alone in the world quite scary. So did I, sometimes. I glanced at Victoria, but she didn't ask any questions. Just as well: I didn't really want to explain in front of Bonnie and Kelly how my parents had been murdered. 'You a friend of the family?' I asked her.

She hesitated. Maybe I should have asked her something harmless, rather than put her on the spot; but tomorrow the Guvnor was taking me to an execution, and I might end up being one of the bodies left behind. I didn't feel like discussing the weather.

'My dad ... he knew Mr McGovern back in ... they were business associates.' She floundered to a halt, blushing. So her father was a gangster too? I thought. A dead one, by the sound of it. Amobi had warned me long before that the Guvnor was dangerous to know, and I'd ignored him. And now here I was.

'Don't suppose I could borrow your mobile a minute?' I asked.

This time when Victoria looked at me there was a steely glint in her eye, as if now I really was taking the piss. 'I don't have one,' she lied.

'Hey, you two! Have you been good?'

We looked up from our food to find the Guvnor's young trophy wife Cherry entering. She still looked like a supermodel, all dangerous curves and golden skin, but her glance slid off me as if she didn't want to acknowledge my presence.

Her kids leaped in delight from their chairs to greet her, and while Victoria explained what they'd been doing that day – playing and watching TV, mostly – I took in the minder who had entered with Cherry. He was a tall tanned bloke in his mid-twenties, with curly dark hair and flashing brown eyes. Like most of the Guvnor's retinue, he wore a suit, but he wore his better than any of the others wore theirs. He looked at me, reached inside his jacket, pulled out a toothbrush in a cellophane-sealed packet and tossed it to me. 'Thanks,' I said. He grinned, cocky as a rock star.

Cherry was collecting the kids to take them home, letting their nanny have the night off; they said noisy goodbyes to Victoria, embracing her while Cherry looked on, obviously keen to get the hell out of the house. I knew how she felt. Finally she led them away up the corridor, leaving just me and Victoria and the tall tanned minder. Now he reached into a side pocket and produced a DVD in a clear plastic sleeve, labelled with a marker scribble.

'I got the next few episodes,' he said to Victoria, as if I wasn't there.

'Great,' she said, blushing sweetly. She didn't bother introducing us, which was fine, because I really didn't care who this guy was. She just said, 'See you later, maybe. Finn—' and went off with him down the corridor to a bedroom opposite the one Gary had shown me, closing the door behind them. It didn't look like they were going to spend their evening watching a pirated DVD: I hoped the walls had decent soundproofing.

Then I thought of Zoe, and felt a twinge of shame for leching after some girl I'd just met when I'd only left her that morning. But she was in a safe house, I knew, surrounded by cops, while I was banged up here – pretty much the exact opposite of a safe house – for what might be my last few hours on earth. And anyway, she'd never have found out . . .

I left the scattered dishes in the kitchen – Victoria was being paid to tidy up, I wasn't – headed back down the hall to my cell, and unwrapped my tooth-brush. Sod it, I'd forgotten to ask for toothpaste. I scrubbed my teeth with water, tossed the toothbrush in the sink, pulled my clothes off, lay on the bed and stared at the ceiling.

* * *

I wasn't aware of having slept, but when the knock came I suddenly realized my eyes were closed and I was still fully dressed.

'Yeah?' I said.

Gary opened the door. 'We're leaving in fifteen minutes,' he said. He waited till I nodded to demonstrate I'd understood, then shut the door again.

I swung myself out of bed and sat on the edge of the mattress for a moment, trying to clear the sleep from my brain and figure out what I should do. Get to a phone somehow, obviously, and warn Amobi what was going down. But that had been impossible last night, and this morning would be no easier. What about doing a runner? If the Guvnor needed me around to make this meeting happen, maybe I could scuttle it, or at least delay it, by not being around. I glanced up again at the window. It was no wider than it had been the night before, and though I was pretty sure I could run faster than any of the Guvnor's goons, I had nowhere to run to. I could feel the adrenalin building up in my system; maybe it would be better just to duck through the ropes into the ring and get this confrontation over with.

Gary returned as I was polishing off a bowl of cornflakes. I left the bowl on the table and he walked me back through the house to the garage. I didn't head for the boot of the car parked there – a sleek silver Jag with darkened windows – because I didn't fancy being brought to this fight like a dog in a cage. But that didn't seem to have been Gary's intention. He merely grunted at me to hold still, pulled a black cloth bag from his pocket and dropped it over my head. I didn't resist but I didn't offer to help, either. The hood was of a soft, thick material that allowed me to breathe but made it impossible to see my surroundings or even tell day from night. I heard a rear passenger door open and felt Gary's hand on the top of my head, pushing me downwards, and I went with it. I shuffled along and settled into the seat; he bent over me, pulled the seatbelt round my body and clicked it home.

I sat there for five or ten minutes, wondering who the last person was to have worn this hood. It smelled of soap, mostly, but there was also a subtle hint of vomit that the soap had failed to wash away. That wasn't a pleasant or useful train of thought, so I focused instead on the meeting about to happen. If it was out in the open, in public, that meant I too would be out in the open, in public. I might get a chance to grab a passer-by's phone, call Amobi and raise the alarm ... except of course it would be too late to summon the NCA by then. I still had the Turk's number in my head – maybe I could call him at the last minute, and warn him he was walking into a trap. But why the hell would I do anything to help the Turk?

I heard the connecting door to the house open again, and soon the garage was filled with a bustle of bodies, but there was little talk – no last-minute recaps or changes of plan for me to overhear. Everybody knew the strategy and understood their role. The driver's door and the other passenger doors opened, and someone got in beside me. I knew instantly it was the Guvnor himself, from that expensive-smelling aftershave he liked to splash on. I heard the whine of the garage door opening and felt the gentle shudder of the Jag as the engine fired up, then we rolled out into the glorious morning I'd glimpsed earlier through the windows of the kitchen. I presumed it was still glorious – I couldn't see a thing through the hood.

'Sleep all right?' the Guvnor grunted.

'Fine, thanks. You?'

He snorted at my familiarity. 'Like a baby,' he said. 'When we hit the M25 you can lose the hood. Won't be long.'

We rode together for a while in silence, the car

weaving, stopping and starting as it followed the lanes out towards the main road. Then we picked up speed and soon I could hear the hiss and roar of other vehicles we passed. I was about to ask for the radio to be turned on, but it didn't seem appropriate somehow; listening to some cretinous DJ wibbling on about this hot and sticky weather was the last thing I wanted to hear. Especially as it might well be one of the last things I heard.

McGovern said nothing, but I wasn't picking up any tension from him; on the contrary, the mood was relaxed and mellow, like were heading to a picnic in Hyde Park. I wondered why I had been given the honour of riding with the Guvnor himself, and it occurred to me I might as well make the most of it.

'Why are you doing this, Mr McGovern?'

'You what?' His voice suggested he'd been lost in thought.

'It just seems so risky. I mean you've been in' – I was about to say 'in hiding', but I reconsidered at the last minute – 'incognito since you came back. And now you're meeting up with the Turk in public, in broad daylight, as if you don't mind who sees you. Especially when . . .' *Especially when you're planning an ambush*. It seemed unnecessary to finish the sentence.

'It's about face,' said the Guvnor. 'This guy's

dissed me, and he's made sure everybody's seen him do it. This way everyone gets to see what happens to him. It's like what the government says when they bung a quid on the price of a packet of fags – it's all about sending a message.'

Who to? I thought. Not the Turk – his death would be the message. The Guvnor's London rivals, maybe? But this seemed way over the top for a local audience – surely they'd be more impressed by a discreet assassination than a messy public execution? Then it came to me: his guest Dimitri. The Russians were the ones the Guvnor wanted to impress – he must be going into business with them. I'd heard about the Russian mafia – how they owned Moscow, bought all the cops they needed, and weren't afraid to settle their arguments face to face, in public. The Guvnor wanted them to see he had clout enough and balls enough to do the same in London, and screw the consequences.

'What about the CCTV?' I asked. 'All those tourists with cameras?'

'Forget 'em,' said McGovern. 'If they don't know what to look for in advance, they don't see shit. You can take that bag off now.'

I hooked a thumb under the hem and pulled the hood up over my head. Even through the tinted windows the mid-morning sun was searingly bright and I blinked, my eyes watering as they adjusted to the dazzle. We were just coming off the M25, I realized, heading for central London. Gary was riding in the front passenger seat; the driver I hadn't seen before. Beside me McGovern was wearing big Ray-Bans with lenses so dark his eyes were invisible, and in his lap sat a cream-coloured Panama hat with a wide brim, the sort old blokes wear to keep the sun off their balding scalps while they watch the cricket. Of course: even if surveillance cameras zoomed in on him, the footage would be useless as evidence – not enough of his face would be visible. I on the other hand had no way to conceal my face. By the time this was over I would be more deeply implicated than any of the Guvnor's crew, unless I could get a message to Amobi in the next thirty minutes, and that didn't seem likely.

I glanced over my shoulder. On the slip road behind and ahead of us were two more expensive, powerful cars, four-by-fours with tinted windows. The Guvnor was travelling in convoy, I realized, and he had probably sent some more people ahead to stake out the rendezvous well in advance. This was going down like a military operation and I was the only one who hadn't been given any orders.

'What exactly to you want me to do?' I said.

'Stick with me,' said McGovern. 'And when you see him, and you're sure it's him, you give me the nod. We'll do the rest.'

I took a deep breath and looked out the window, trying to keep my pulse steady and my mind calm the way I used to do before a big fight. We were making good time: the schools had broken up by now and a lot of Londoners had abandoned the city to escape the muggy polluted air, so the traffic was light, and before long we were heading over Westminster Bridge, past the golden gothic spires of the Houses of Parliament, and on up Whitehall towards Trafalgar Square. When the Jag pulled up on the south-east corner we all clambered out, and it drove on up St Martin's Lane.

I hadn't walked through Trafalgar Square since I was a kid. Like most Londoners I took it for granted, and left gawking to the tourists, but today it felt as if I'd never seen it before. Its broad paved plain was ringed with granite bollards and overlooked by stately buildings of grey and golden stone; to the east and west, lines of plane trees sagged, unbothered by any breeze. For about a hundred years fat, flea-bitten pigeons had crowded this square, pecking at litter

and crapping on everything and everyone, but now
the stalls that had sold bags of breadcrumbs had been
banished, and with them had gone most of the
pigeons. Instead of feeding the flying rats,
the throngs of sightseers contented themselves with
staring at the sculptures, taking grinning selfies on
their smartphones, or merely lolling on the steps that
led up to the National Gallery on the northern side of
the square.

The sun was beating down on all our heads like a
hammer and I could feel the heat of the granite
paving slabs through the soles of my shoes. The
tourists didn't seem to mind the heat; kids were
clambering up onto the bronze lions at the foot of
Nelson's Column and a good-looking couple in their
twenties were splashing about fully-dressed in one of
the fountains to our right, hooting at each other in
Italian. Two shirtsleeved coppers were heading
in their direction, determined to get them out of the
water before everyone else decided to follow their
example. Unlike the police I'd seen at King's Cross
these two were unarmed, and that was probably a
good thing – when the Guvnor made his move they
wouldn't be tempted to wade in spraying bullets
everywhere like action heroes.

McGovern looked every inch a tourist himself,

strolling along in his shades and his Panama hat and his lightweight summer blazer. At his other elbow Gary was already starting to perspire. Mirror shades concealed his eyes, and he wore a leather bomber jacket, far too hot for this weather. He wasn't going to take it off, I guessed, because it concealed a gun. I found myself irritated by how tense and conspicuous he appeared, and realized with some surprise that for my part I was totally calm. Maybe my mind had gone numb with fear, but somehow I found it no effort to relax and glance around, as if I was just another gormless grockle with nowhere specific to be and nothing specific to do. In fact, I was scanning the crowd for the rest of the Guvnor's crew, but I couldn't see any of them. Was that good or bad?

At the centre of the square, in the narrow shade of Nelson's Column, a temporary pavement café was doing a brisk trade. It was operating out of a classy dark-red pavilion, surrounded by heavy mosaic-topped tables and light aluminium chairs, the whole enclosed by the black railings that ringed the foot of the column. It was a very European scene somehow; all it lacked was parasols, which seemed a daft over-sight in this heat, but maybe the café management wanted the customers to keep moving rather than hang around sipping coffee all day.

Ignoring the waiting queue the Guvnor sauntered over to a table in the corner and plonked himself down, taking a seat that faced north across the fountains towards the National Gallery. A waitress glanced our way and frowned, pondering whether to tell us off for not waiting to be seated, but then seemed to change her mind. Maybe she was intimidated by the Guvnor's presence, or maybe all of this had been arranged – the table, the seating and the view of the square. I sat myself down at McGovern's left hand, and Gary took the chair to his right. Gary watched the bustling crowds, inscrutable behind his aviator shades; the Guvnor picked up the menu and studied it, as chilled as a British pensioner sitting in an English bar in Spain.

'Yes please?' The waitress was at my elbow, pad and pencil in hand. She looked harassed and nervous, but then it couldn't have been easy, scuttling about in this bustle and heat.

'Two Cokes, an espresso, and a bloody umbrella,' said the Guvnor.

The waitress scribbled quickly on her pad. 'Sorry, we don't have any parasols – they all got vandalized last night,' she said.

'You're kidding,' said McGovern. He sounded disgusted at the casual drunken hooliganism of today's youth. Gary ignored the whole exchange, I noted, scanning the crowds around us like a CCTV camera himself.

'Slashed them to ribbons,' explained the waitress. 'Really stupid – people have been complaining all morning. Just the drinks, yeah?'

'Yeah,' said McGovern.

Thanks for asking what I wanted, I thought, although there was so much adrenalin pumping through my system I wasn't sure I would even be able to swallow the Coke. I found myself scanning the crowds too, wondering when I'd see the Turk's slight figure strolling towards us with his customary swagger. No – he wouldn't swagger, I realized. The swagger had been Bruno's, and Bruno had never existed. He was a fiction Pirbal had created, then discarded once it had served its purpose. I wondered if I would even recognize the Turk when I saw him again, or whether he'd be right on top of us before I'd even realized it.

But surely that was Pirbal on the western edge of the square: that dark, slight, self-possessed man in his mid-twenties, graceful and dangerous as a leopard. I'd been right – there was no swagger; in fact, in his baseball cap and shades I might not have recognized him had it not been for the stumpy gait of the man trying to keep up – my old friend Dean. Dean's Elvis quiff had gone and his hair was cut short, but I knew that rat-like face, even though I'd changed its shape during our last encounter, when I'd managed to break it and knock out two of his molars.

'That's him,' I said. 'In the red baseball cap and sunglasses.' I was surprised how steady and clear my voice sounded, when deep down I felt anything but.

The Guvnor turned to his left and tilted his head back to get a good look through his shades: Gary got up and stood back, vacating his seat for the Turk, his hands hanging loosely at his sides; but I noted the tiny tremble of tension in them, and guessed he was mentally rehearsing reaching under his jacket for his gun. At the same time an uneasy thought stabbed into my mind like a thorn in my sole.

'Wait a minute,' I said. 'Kemal's not with him.'

McGovern glanced at me, expressionless.

'The Turk's right-hand guy, his fixer, he's not here,' I said. There was no way the Turk would come to a meet like this without Kemal . . . so where was he? But it was too late now to wonder.

Trafalgar Square was smaller than I'd remembered, but it seemed to be taking Pirbal and Dean a long time to cross it. I realized time had slowed down, like it used to in the boxing ring, when adrenalin would heighten all my senses. I could make out every face in the crowd around me, and even see the hi-viz jackets of the coppers by the fountains behind us, somehow; I could smell lemon in the glass of the woman sitting at the next table, and hear the jingle of her bangles as she rooted in her handbag.

And off to my right, skipping down the steps from the National Gallery, I could see pale, broad-nosed Martin, in short-sleeved shirt and sunglasses, carrying a folded newspaper and strolling nonchalantly south, his path destined to pass behind the Turk and Dean just before they reached our table.

I didn't turn my head towards him, but kept my eyes focused on the Turk, and noted the twitch of his lips as he saw me, seated there beside the Guvnor. He was smiling, apparently unaware of Martin, now twenty paces away, slipping his free hand into the folded newspaper. I guessed the paper concealed a pistol, and saw now what was about to happen: the Turk and Dean would each take a bullet to the back of the head before they'd even reached our table, and the Guvnor would walk away, unscathed and uninvolved.

Now Martin was eight paces away.

Seven.

Then the right side of his head exploded.

Blood and brains and bone sprayed over half a dozen tourists beside him, and under the roar of the traffic and the chatter of the crowds I heard a distant *crack* echoing faintly around the square and dying. Slowly Martin's legs shuddered and folded, and his lifeless body fell forwards, and the stunned, gore-spattered tourists looked at him and each other, and the screaming started.

The wave of panic was small at first, but it rippled outwards across the crowds like flames on petrol. Around me I saw people turn, and frown, and stare, and I felt their curiosity turn first to recognition, then to terror – but all that was on the fringe of my awareness, because I was scanning the skyline to the east, where the bullet had come from. I saw what I was looking for – a rounded shape on the hard edge of a rooftop, a hint of movement, and a tiny tinted flash as sun glinted off the glass of a scope. *Sniper.*

I don't even know where the thought came from, unless it was playing too many console war games, but I dived for the floor. The quickest way down brought me piling straight into McGovern, still sitting there motionless until my body slammed into his, and we both went down in a rattling tangle of

91

chair legs. A second *crack* snapped hard in my ear, and I swear I felt the cool draught of the bullet's passing, and then the hot granite paving under my hands.

Behind us Gary had ducked, his fist already under his jacket, and then he was up again and there was a gun in his hand. The Guvnor grunted and gasped as I squirmed around on top of him, braced my foot underneath a table and heaved. It toppled slowly, like a falling tree, the solid slab of its mosaic top slamming against the pavement, its metal legs resounding like a bell, glasses and saucers smashing and a steel serving tray ringing and rattling as it settled on the stone. McGovern scrambled for cover behind it, just in time – a third shot smashed into the table top with a bang so loud it rattled my teeth in my head. But we still weren't safe, I realized; the Turk and Dean were behind us, and I scuttled round, expecting any second to feel bullets rip into my belly.

But the Turk had vanished. Only Dean remained, squatting with a revolver held in two hands, blasting shots at Gary, who blasted shots back, while pandemonium broke out all around them – some tourists trembling face down on the ground, scream-ing and weeping, others running in all directions, carrying or dragging hysterically shrieking children, dashing out into the traffic that was somehow still moving round the square. Gary and Dean were only a few metres apart and I was wondering how the hell they were managing to miss each other when a bullet caught Gary in the chest and spun him to the floor, yelling and cursing. Which left Dean, striding towards us, his revolver outstretched, hoping to take McGovern and me at point-blank range.

I felt the rim of the toppled serving tray under my hand, and without thinking I picked it up and flung it hard as I could straight at Dean's face, frisbee style. And just like a frisbee it went veering wide, but it was still enough to make Dean flinch for a split second, and in that split second I managed to cover the distance, slap his gun hand with my left so his shot went wild and grab his face with my right. I kicked his legs from under him so hard he was practically horizontal before he dropped, and I kept my hand on his face to make sure he took plenty of the impact on the back of his head. Grabbing his gun I flung it away.

How many seconds had passed? Ten? Twenty? Someone behind me was shouting instructions – 'Get down, stay down—!' and when I looked over my shoulder the two foot-patrol cops I'd seen earlier were headed towards us, one stooped, babbling into his lapel radio, the other with his baton extended in one fist and a taser in the other. Who the hell brings a taser to a gun battle? I thought, and I was about to yell at him to follow his own advice and get down when from the south of the square, out of the traffic, came a long rattling clatter of shots so close together they were almost a buzz. The copper with the taser fell to his knees, then to his side, and lay there, writhing, his yells of pain mingling with the screams of the crowd.

While the second copper dashed over to help his colleague I scrabbled for cover behind one of the stumpy granite bollards, and peered round it long enough to see a tall skinny man in a hoodie and sweats approaching from the south clutching a machine pistol. He was switching magazines as he came striding over towards us, implacable and so utterly focused he was oblivious to the screams and the distant sirens and the blaring car horns – and to the roaring engine of the Range Rover that had mounted the kerb behind him. He didn't see it accelerate towards him before it slammed hard into his back, tossing him into the air over the hood to tumble down out of sight beyond.

The driver slammed on the brakes, his door flew open, and Terry clambered out. I'd never seen him move so fast, but he took no evasive action at all –

maybe he knew he was so huge it would be impossible to conceal himself, or maybe he reckoned he could absorb a few bullets before he had to slow down. I was half expecting to hear another rifle shot, but nothing came, and when I glanced at the eastern skyline the bulge I'd spotted before had gone. Terry walked right past me, stepping over the bawling, hysterical bodies all about, grabbed McGovern and hauled him to his feet. There was blood running from the Guvnor's ear and he was so groggy he could barely walk. For an instant I thought he'd been hit, but no – the impact of that last bullet on the table had stunned him. As I watched them stagger towards the waiting Range Rover I realized this was my chance to run, to get the hell away from the Guvnor and the Turk and this bloody insanity. I could hear the shriek of sirens heading up from Whitehall – armed response units were on the way. All I had to do to be safe was lie down.

I didn't see where it came from or who threw it; I just saw it skittering along the paving slabs – a grenade, spinning round like a bottle at a drunken teenage party, rolling to a halt right in the path of Terry and the Guvnor, three paces away from me. I covered the three paces in half a second and booted the grenade hard, aiming for a gap in the traffic. It flew off like a bullet under the Range Rover, and it must have been right under the petrol tank when it blew, because an instant later the whole car leaped into the air, consumed in a fireball, and the scorching blast blew me clean off my feet. My ears were ringing, I was half blinded, and there were shards of broken glass in my hair and mouth, but someone was hauling me by the collar, dragging me stumbling forward through the smoke and the heat and the screaming, before throwing me down on a hard rubbery surface . . . the floor of a cab, I realized, as it lurched into motion, toppling me onto my side. I lay there, barely conscious, too weak to do anything but curl up into a ball and cough, as I felt myself speeding away.

FOUR

'It was a massacre,' said McGovern. 'We had our fucking arses handed to us.'

Someone had given me a cold bottle of beer. I threw my head back and chugged half of it down in a few gulps, as thirsty as if I'd been lost in a desert for a month. I'd just about stopped shaking from the adrenalin rush, but my throat was still raw and every so often a crumb of windscreen glass would fall out of my hair. I suspected my face was blackened with smoke, but I hadn't looked in a mirror yet. I wasn't even sure I still had eyelashes.

We were back in the Guvnor's borrowed mansion, sitting around the musty lounge that smelled of mothballs – what was left, anyway, of the crew that had set out that morning. Martin was dead, we all knew. Gary was reported to be in intensive care with a punctured lung and two cops stationed outside his door waiting for him to come round. Two other guys I hadn't known about, sent out in advance as scouts, were missing, presumed dead. New faces had filled the room now – second-string hoods abruptly promoted, most of them trying hard to conceal their shellshock. The Guvnor, their invincible, untouchable Guvnor, was apparently neither.

The black taxi Terry had thrown me into had been arranged as an emergency backup – an inconspicuous getaway vehicle. It had driven away at speed from the chaos, mounting the pavement twice to get round cars that had slewed to a halt in the road from panic or to make way for all the emergency vehicles that were converging on Trafalgar Square from every direction. I'd been dimly aware of the driver shouting at someone – a copper that tried to flag him down, I think – that he had to get his badly wounded passengers to hospital and couldn't wait for an ambulance. Of course, he hadn't gone near any hospital; a few minutes later he'd pulled up in a back street, and Terry had hauled me out by the arm and pushed me towards a people-carrier with tinted windows sitting on a double yellow line with its engine running. I was racked with coughing from the smoke I'd inhaled, and my eyeballs felt scorched, but

I managed to glance around; we were in the City of London somewhere, it looked like, in a side street lined on both sides with scaffolding sheathed in plastic . . . of course – no CCTV coverage here.

Terry had folded himself in with us and the minivan had headed east, past St Paul's and the Tower of London. Every few seconds another cop car – every cop car in London, it felt like – would come screaming past us, blue lights blazing, heading for the West End. The three of us – McGovern, Terry and me – stared out the windows in silence, and slowly the ringing in my ears subsided. There was no talk now of putting a hood over my head; me knowing the location of the Guvnor's base was the least of his problems, and I was too shaken to trace our route anyway. I glimpsed signs on the motorway and the roundabout junction where we came off, but I couldn't have read them if I'd tried.

And now the post-mortem was starting.

'We were set up,' said the Guvnor's son. 'Had to be.'

When I looked up Junior was staring hard at me. It was pretty obvious he wanted to blame me for the bloody rout in Trafalgar Square, but I said nothing – partly because my throat still felt like sandpaper and partly because anything I said would sound as if

I was making excuses. But then, it had been Steve's decision to bring me to meet his dad, so he was guilty by association. He had to shout and point the finger to take the heat off himself, especially as he had stayed back here, safely out of the line of fire.

'Whose bloody idea was Trafalgar Square anyway?' said Junior. Still staring at me.

'Mine,' said McGovern. He was clutching a beer too, though not drinking it, and looking out through the French doors at the monotonous green expanse of the golf course next door. I could see him replaying the events in his head – that phone call to the Turk, the encounter in the square – and analysing them, to figure out where he'd gone wrong and what to do next. And I could see Steve didn't give a toss about analysis or strategy – he wanted revenge, the more brutal the better.

'You sure about that?' I croaked, looking at McGovern. I was ignoring Steve; nothing I could have said would change his mind. The Guvnor came out of his reverie to stare at me coldly. 'Maybe the Turk wanted you to think the location was your idea,' I went on. 'I told you, you think you're playing him, he's playing you. He made sure the café parasols were vandalized so Kemal could get a clear shot.'

'Who the hell is Kemal?' said Junior.

'I think he was the one up on the roof with the sniper rifle,' I said. 'I knew he had to be there some-where.'

Steve's face twisted in furious disgust. Reaching into his jacket he strode over to where I sat, pulled out a sleek pistol and pointed it at my head. 'You knew what was going to happen, didn't you? You're working for him, you little shit.'

I could have slapped it out of his hand but I didn't move, partly because I was knackered and aching, but mostly because I reckoned it was stupid macho bluster – if he hadn't shot me straight away he wasn't going to. I was beginning to downgrade my opinion of Steve; he was doing a good impression of a panicking idiot.

'Leave it,' growled McGovern.

I stared up at Steve, whose face was burning now. He lowered the pistol and tucked it away again, but reluctantly, as if he was over-riding his instincts with a massive effort of will.

'Finn warned us about the Turk. And his fixer Kemal. And I didn't sodding listen,' said McGovern. 'We got a good kicking and we deserved to. If it wasn't for Finn I wouldn't be standing here.'

He was right: I'd saved his life in that shootout, twice. Mostly by accident, it was true – I'd been trying to save myself – but I wasn't about to admit that and squander any advantage it had won me. And then I found myself wondering, was it really accidental, what I did? When I dived to the ground, why had I dived onto McGovern? If I'd let him get killed this war would be over by now and I could have gone home. I remembered that uniformed copper, that idiot who'd waded into a shootout armed only with a nightstick and a taser. Why the hell hadn't I tried to save *him*?

'We have to hit these wogs back, hard,' said Junior to his dad.

'For Christ's sake,' I said, before I could stop myself.

'What?' snapped Junior. 'You want to fix up another meeting?'

'It's not about hitting the Turk hard,' I said. 'It's about hitting him where it hurts. It's about using your head.' When I heard myself talking I clammed up. Why the hell was I telling him his job?

Steve went pale with fury, but the Guvnor actually laughed. 'Enough,' he said. 'Today was my fault. I got lazy and I got complacent. It's not going to happen again.' He finally turned from the window. 'Right, I want intel – proper intel this time, not just the frigging headlines, and I want it double-checked. I need to know everything: who Pirbal's friends are, where he operates, how he makes his money, who works for him, where his family lives.' He looked at his son. 'Talk to McKenzie, and Pete, and our people at the Border Agency.'

'We shouldn't be discussing this in front of him,' said Steve, nodding at me, but McGovern ignored him.

'I'm going to ring round, let our friends know the score, call in some favours,' he continued.

And let them know you're still alive and still in business, I thought.

'We're going to shut down Pirbal's businesses and take out everyone who works for him. Then we're going to find his family, his mum and his dad and his brothers and sisters, and we're going to skin them and mince them and feed them to pigs, right in front of him.'

He said it without relish, without rancour – a simple statement of intent that everyone there knew he meant literally, and meant to fulfil. There were no cheers from his fresh young crew, just quiet smirks of anticipation at the fun and games ahead. Of course, this was exactly the sort of thing these guys had signed up for. 'Any questions?' said McGovern.

'What about . . . our guests?' said Steve. He meant

the Russians, I assumed. It was a good question; if McGovern had wanted to make an impression on them, he had – but not the one he'd intended.

'What about them?'

'What do we tell them about today? They'll have seen all that shit on the telly.'

'They're Russian,' said McGovern. 'They don't believe anything they see on telly. I'll sort them out. Anyone else?'

'Yeah,' I said. 'Can I go home now?'

Everyone in the room, not just Junior, turned to scowl at me.

'You wanted me to finger the Turk. I did,' I told McGovern. 'I'm finished here.'

'Unbelievable,' said Steve. 'He's actually volunteering to get whacked.'

'I helped out today,' I went on, 'but I'm not going to fight for you, and I'm not going to kill anyone.' I nearly added 'Sorry', but stopped myself just in time.

'Nah, I don't think so,' said McGovern. 'Fact is, after today, you're with us – like it or not. You might not think so, but that prick Pirbal does. And that African copper from SOCA you've been cosying up to.'

I stared, trying not to react, but even not reacting was a giveaway. That morning my faith in the

Guvnor had been shaken, as it had been for everyone else here. I'd temporarily forgotten how connected he was, how his influence had rotted SOCA and the Met police from within like a cancer. Pirbal might be smart, I saw now, but McGovern was older, with more experience, more allies, more influence and more muscle. The Turk had hurt the Guvnor, but he hadn't taken him out, and that had been a big mistake. This war had barely begun.

'Don't worry, you won't have to fight,' McGovern went on. 'You can't drive and you can't shoot, so you're sod all use to us anyway. What I need right now is a babysitter. Richard?'

One of the new faces stepped forward, a face I'd seen before – the slim, handsome heavy in the designer suit who'd hung out with Victoria the night before, slipping his pirate DVD into her entertainment centre. 'Take Finn up to the house in Maida Vale,' said McGovern. 'The two of you can help look after Cherry and the kids till this is sorted. There's a team up there already, but from now on we're taking nothing for granted.'

'Got it,' said Richard. 'Let's go.' He flicked his head at me as if I was his trained Alsatian. I didn't want to stick around, but I took my time getting up all the same.

'And Richard,' said McGovern. 'You're on duty, all right? So no shagging the nanny.'

Richard grinned.

I liked McGovern's kids, but I'd never done any babysitting. Even if I'd volunteered, none of my neighbours would have hired a convicted drug dealer to read their precious darlings bedtime stories, especially one who couldn't read. I could have played computer games with them, I suppose, like I did that afternoon with Kelly, slouched on a beanbag in his playroom in front of an enormous plasma screen. His mother had banned him from playing war games, shoot-'em-ups or LA hoodlum simulators – I suppose she thought he'd get enough of that when he was older – so we spent a lot of time racing virtual go-karts and breeding candy-coloured virtual monsters. That was fine by me; after seeing Martin lose half his head that morning, playing at urban warfare wouldn't exactly have been escapism.

Months ago, when I'd decided to ask McGovern if he'd had my dad murdered, I'd headed up to North London and sneaked through the Guvnor's gates to find this place: a huge glitzy palace with deep-pile white carpets and TVs the size of tennis courts in every room. At the time I'd wondered why McGovern needed so many rooms for one small family and their nanny, but now I knew. The house was a fully-serviced fortress with its own power supply and a panic room with a solid steel door. The extra bedrooms were for the private retinue who'd move in at times like this. For all I knew there were escape tunnels out of the basement and a hidden arsenal of rocket launchers, but I wasn't encouraged to go exploring.

When Kelly and I got bored with gaming we went for a swim in the Guvnor's pool, the same one where I'd found Kelly drowning, back in the spring. He'd taken lessons since then, and both he and his sister Bonnie could easily swim a length underwater. Even so, they were constantly watched by Victoria.

McGovern didn't need me to babysit, that much was clear; in fact, *I* was the one being supervised. With Richard and the half-dozen other heavies patrolling the house and grounds, I'd never get a chance to scale the three-metre walls surrounding the mansion. I couldn't even use Kelly's games console to send an email to Amobi – it had no Internet connection. There was no landline to the house either, presumably because it would have been way too easy for the authorities to bug. I kept an eye open for any mobiles lying about, but nobody ever left theirs unattended. The Guvnor might have been grateful to me for saving his life, but not so grateful that he trusted me.

I wasn't sure if there was any point in contacting Amobi anyhow: there was nothing I could tell him he hadn't already found out. Late on that first night, after the kids had finally gone to bed, I caught the TV news. The fiasco in Trafalgar Square was the second item: one man had been shot dead, another man plus a copper injured by gunfire, and twelve people had been hurt in the stampede. The official line was that a drug deal had gone wrong; Martin's blurry grinning face flashed up, seated in a pub that looked very much like The Horsemonger, while the reporter listed his previous convictions for cocaine smuggling and GBH. The second victim – I presumed that was Gary – was still in intensive care, to be interviewed by detectives when he recovered. The copper they described as 'critical but stable', whatever that meant. There was no mention at all of the Guvnor, I noticed, or of any gangland war. Amobi and the NCA must have known the real cause – why were they keeping it quiet?

The news ended with a reprise of the lead item – yet another terrorist outrage. A bomb had gone off on a coach headed for Liverpool, killing two passengers and maiming six. It had used some new hi-tech liquid explosive, concealed in a backpack, and all that was left of the man carrying it was embedded in the other victims' bodies. No warning, no claim of responsibility, no kamikaze video where the bomber explained his motives; this was terrorism at its purest, just random carnage and cruelty, followed by shrill demands from the media and MPs for the authorities to crack down – on what or whom exactly, no one seemed to know. The failed bomber Amobi's people had caught in Bristol was still being questioned, but reports suggested he was merely a courier who couldn't speak English and had no idea what had been in his bag, and the police were making no official comment.

I switched the telly off and headed for the bedroom I'd been allotted, next door to Richard – presumably so he would notice if I tried sneaking about at night. I took a bath, as hot as I could bear, to ease the bruises and the stiffness that had set in since that morning. There were still a few crumbs of grit in my hair that I'd missed when I'd showered earlier, and on impulse I put them to my nose and smelled them. They were scorched rubber, I realized, from the tyres of the car that had exploded, and the acrid stink set my eyes watering. Or maybe that was shock;

when I shut my eyes I could hear screaming, see Martin's lifeless body take its last tottering step, see panicking parents dashing for safety with their kids in their arms.

Alone in my bed I wished Zoe was there, and was grateful she wasn't. Amobi would keep her safe, I knew, until this war was over – and if I survived it, maybe she'd forgive me for involving her, in person. That reminded me how she'd said goodbye at the NCA offices, and how she'd slipped her tongue into my mouth, and thinking about that helped to take my mind off everything that had happened since, and what with one thing and another I managed to sleep.

I wasn't the only bloke longing for female company, I realized over breakfast, when I joined Victoria and the kids for a bowl of cereal and a glass of orange juice. Richard appeared, keen to know if we'd slept OK, but it was obviously only Victoria's sleeping arrangements that interested him. He flirted with her shamelessly, staying just this side of obscene for the sake of Kelly and Bonnie listening, and she lapped it up, her face going pink, giggling so much it drew puzzled looks from the kids.

The two lovebirds kept up the accidental encounters and the whispered innuendo all day.

Richard was always loitering within earshot, Victoria throwing him distracted glances. I didn't know if the kids minded, but before long it was getting right on my wick. How long was I going to be banged up in this high-security nursery watching these two make cow-eyes at each other? What if the Guvnor's struggle with the Turk went on for months?

I'd done what the Turk had instructed. For all I knew Zoe might already have gone back to York, while I twiddled my thumbs in McGovern's protective custody. I tried to work out some of my frustration on the running machine in the Guvnor's home gym; Cherry had set it at a decorous speed barely faster than a jog, but I cranked the revs up to maximum and ran at full tilt for thirty minutes, then hit the weights. But it soon felt like I was working out in one of those cushy prisons where they send rich fraudsters and disgraced politicians, and I gave up in bored disgust.

I took a walk around the gardens instead, pretending to admire the roses while checking to see if there really was no way of getting over the walls. The kids had a trampoline, I discovered. Maybe I could drag it over to the foot of the wall and bounce my way to freedom, if I didn't mind breaking both legs when I landed on the road outside. The Guvnor's guards didn't seem to be paying me much attention; they were too busy conferring in grim knots of two and three. They didn't look happy. Maybe they thought they weren't getting enough overtime, or maybe they were as pissed off as me at being confined in here missing the action . . . or maybe there was bad news they didn't want to discuss out loud. When I strolled over and tried to eavesdrop on their conversation they clammed up, glaring at me like a basket of snakes.

The TV news that evening was the same as the day before, in a slightly different order, with more detail on the victims of the coach bombing. The reporters were playing up the pathos and the dashed hopes, the way the media always do when they have nothing to offer as background or context or explanation, not even a gloating statement from some religious fanatic. They focused on the innocent victims instead, milking the tragedy until it got almost mawkish. For 'analysis' they wheeled on some expert who tried to make sense of the bombing campaign and couldn't, because the terrorists hadn't bothered to give their reasons, issue bloodthirsty speeches or make impossible demands. There was nothing to analyse.

I lay in bed, sleepless in the heat until the early

hours, thinking. I was going to have to do something
– write a message to Amobi in a bottle and throw it
over the wall, or pick someone's pocket for a phone.
As a brat running wild in West London I'd tried that
a few times. Drunks heading home in the evening
made easy targets, but scoring in the daytime when
the punters were alert? That was much harder. I still
remembered the basics – the stall, the distraction and
the dip – but most of those techniques needed an
accomplice. Without one, the best target had to be
Victoria. She was already distracted a lot of the time,
batting her eyelashes at Richard, and there was
bound to be a mobile in that big handbag she always
left lying about.

In fact, that sounded like Victoria's voice next
door, in Richard's bedroom . . .

At this time of the night, when the rest of the
house was asleep, that could only mean one thing.
She must have had enough of the wistful looks and
the smutty giggles and sneaked down to Richard's
room. Yes, the Guvnor had told Richard to keep his
pecker to himself, but if a girl as beautiful as Victoria
slipped into my bedroom in the middle of the night,
I too might have forgotten my orders.

Great, I sighed to myself. In that other mansion
there'd been two doors and a corridor between my

room and Victoria's. Here there was nothing but a thin partition, and I was going to hear everything. I was about to go find some loo paper to make earplugs when I realized there was something off.

I couldn't hear what the two lovebirds were saying, but I could hear tension in their voices: Victoria's was pitching higher and higher, Richard's sinking into a lower murmur – were they having a tiff? I knew it was creepy to listen, but I couldn't help hearing. Victoria's voice grew more and more shrill, and abruptly there was a thump of footsteps, then a door opening, and almost immediately being slammed again. Then a scuffle, and a squeak – or a gasp – and then . . . silence.

I pulled back the bedclothes, slipped silently out of bed and tugged on my jeans.

I opened the door to my room as quietly as I could and peered out along the landing. The only light came from a halogen spotlight recessed into the ceiling over the stairs. I caught the tail end of a movement there – someone heading up to the next floor where the kids slept. Victoria flouncing out on Richard? But I felt sure that what I'd heard had been more than a lovers' squabble. There was no point in me just hanging around wondering what was going on; I stepped out into the hall, clicked my door softly shut behind me, and padded along to Richard's. From the other side I heard a faint scratching, soft and subtle as a mouse gnawing on woodwork. Gingerly I tried the handle, composing an excuse in my head about going to find something to eat, and getting the rooms mixed up – but the door was locked. The scratching grew louder, becoming a frantic scrabbling, and I realized someone was fumbling at the lock from inside. I could sense their desperation, and I was just about to barge my shoulder into the woodwork when the lock clicked and the handle turned.

Victoria was standing there, clutching her head and looking up at me, dazed and pale with shock. Blood was trickling through her fingers and soaking into the sleeve of her white cotton nightdress. On the floor lay a heavy marble ashtray stained with red. Richard had bludgeoned her with it. She staggered as if she was about to pass out, and I dashed forward to catch her and help her back towards the bed – but weak as she was she resisted, plucking at the bare skin of my chest as if to grab the shirt I wasn't wearing, and muttered something.

'The k—' Her lips worked as if she was forgetting how to speak. 'The kids—'

I stopped and watched her eyes roll back into her

head as she lost consciousness. I eased her onto the bed as gently as I could, then turned and bolted through the doorway, heading for the stairs. I took them two a time, praying I was wrong about what was happening, praying I wasn't too late if I was right. None of McGovern's heavies were around now that I needed them – had Richard told them to stand down? How long had he been planning this?

There were low-level nightlights along the wall of the landing that led to the master bedroom where Cherry was sleeping. Halfway down was the bedroom Kelly and his sister shared, and Richard was the slim dark silhouette slipping through their door, something hard and narrow glinting in his hand. For an instant, absurdly, I worried about waking the kids – then I yelled, 'Richard!' as loud as I could. I had to wake the children – they'd be terrified, but at least they'd have a chance, and if the racket brought the Guvnor's goons running, all the better.

Richard stepped back onto the landing, saw me coming, cursed and ducked back into the bedroom, slamming the door behind him. I heard the crash of furniture being pulled over – with no lock on the inside he'd tried to barricade the door, but when I threw my shoulder against it, it opened a few centimetres, and the next shove knocked the obstruction back – a toppled bookshelf, I saw, as I squeezed through the gap, clambering over scattered storybooks that slid about under my feet.

The kids usually slept in twin single beds in opposite corners of the room, Bonnie's fluffy toys piled on one side, Kelly's robots and remote control cars on the other. Kelly, unbelievably, was still asleep, but not Bonnie – Richard had dragged her from her bed and was restraining her, one hand clamped over her mouth, the other holding a knife to her throat. Bonnie was squeaking in terror, her fine blonde hair tangled over her eyes. Richard grinned at me, but I could see from the way the blade twitched how wired he was. He was wearing gloves, I noticed.

'One move,' he said. 'One word, and I slit her throat.'

But he was going to do that anyway, I knew – now Bonnie was awake he had no choice. But how the hell did he plan to get away afterwards?

'You're too late,' I said. 'Cherry will raise the alarm. You're not getting out of here.' Immediately I wished I'd kept my mouth shut. I sucked at negotiating – all I'd done was remind him he had nothing to lose. The Guvnor would show no mercy to someone who'd threatened his children.

'No she won't,' said Richard. 'Silly slag necked

half a bottle of wine tonight. And I threw a couple of bennies in, just in case.'

'How long have you been working for the Turk?' I said.

'Me?' smirked Richard. 'I'm not working for him. You are.'

Then he snapped Bonnie's head back, exposing her pale white throat, and her mouth opened to whimper as the blade bit into her skin, and his little finger slipped between her teeth, and she bit down hard. He flinched in agony and I was on him before he even had time to yell, grabbing his wrist and wrenching the blade up and away.

Bonnie writhed, squealing, and Richard let her go so he could punch me in the face – and he did, hard, twice. I slammed my body up against his to close the range, and felt his hand crawl across my face like a spider, before he hooked two fingers up my nose and wrenched my head back. It was bloody agony, but I had to hold onto the hand that grasped the blade. I shook my head, twisted my body round and backed him up against the wall, folding his knife hand forward, trying my best to break his wrist. The blade fell from his fist and he ducked to scrabble for it with his left, and when I went for it too he jumped up and kneed me hard right on the nose.

Stars exploded behind my eyes and I staggered backwards, nearly stumbling over the fallen bookshelf. I blinked and shook my head, my vision clearing just in time to see him stoop and grasp the knife, then hesitate, scowling – I'd wrenched his right wrist so badly he no longer had the strength to hold it. I saw Bonnie beyond him, blood streaming down her neck and staining her pyjama top, shaking Kelly and shrieking in his ear. Richard tossed the blade from his right hand to his left, while I grabbed at the chair that stood at the foot of Kelly's bed, still hung with his discarded clothes, and wielded it like a lion-tamer.

Richard snorted – it was a kid's chair and too small to be any use as a shield, but that wasn't what I'd been going for. When I flung the little chair at Richard's head he had to duck, so he didn't see me grab Kelly's jeans and flick them like a whip that tangled around his left hand and fouled the blade long enough for me to close the gap and punch him full in the teeth. A punch to the throat would have floored him, maybe killed him, but I wanted him alive – and that put me at a disadvantage, because Richard wanted me dead. He fell back spitting blood, raising his right arm to try and shield his head and body from my punches while he shook his left hand free of the jeans. Both the kids were cowering now on Kelly's bed, screaming, but still no one came.

'Run, you two!' I roared at them. 'Go get help!'

My sheer volume snapped them out of their terror and they scrambled down Kelly's bed, crying as they ran for the door. Seeing his last chance disintegrating Richard threw himself at me, swiping and slashing wildly with the knife, while I fell back, ducking and dodging to stay out of range, and failing – the razor point parted the skin on my chest like a scalpel, so cleanly I barely felt pain, but forcing me to step back, square onto a lump of Lego that crunched into the bones of my foot.

Richard glanced over my shoulder, and paused in his crouch, wavering, with the knife still primed and ready. I kept my eyes locked on him, and felt rather than saw McGovern's heavies piling into the room behind me. Richard smiled, then laughed, then straightened up. He held his hands wide open in surrender, but he didn't drop the knife; instead he gritted his teeth and held his breath, and with one swift movement drove the point into his own throat.

Blood spurted across Bonnie's bedclothes, and Richard staggered and collapsed in a heap. With a yell of anger and frustration I dived on top of him, grabbing Kelly's jeans and clamping them against his jugular where the knife still protruded, visibly twitching in time to his fading pulse. Nobody offered to help: his former comrades in arms stood around watching, probably figuring out who was going to cop the blame when the Guvnor heard about this. Soon the blood had soaked through Kelly's jeans and was staining my hand; it was spreading across the carpet – I could feel its warm stickiness under my knees. In less than a minute Richard stopped twitching and the light faded from his eyes.

Cherry was practically sleepwalking; she was still stoned and half drunk when she went to fetch the first-aid kit, and I told her not to bother trying to patch me up – I'd sort myself out. She didn't argue, but took the kids up to her bed to comfort them while I taped the slash on my chest shut with surgical tape. Without stitches I was going to end up with a spectacular scar, but I didn't think McGovern would let me go to A&E. It was too late for Victoria, the nanny. When I'd led the Guvnor's crew down to Richard's room we found her wide-eyed and staring, her golden hair matted with blood.

The Guvnor had arrived about an hour later, and went up to check on his wife and kids while I sat there waiting in their showroom kitchen with its granite worktops and hand-painted oak cupboards. I was too tired to go back to bed, anyway. I sat there cursing myself for not saving Victoria, even though I knew if I'd stopped to help her the kids would be dead. It didn't make me feel any better. OK, she was one of McGovern's employees, but she hadn't signed up for a war, any more than I had. She'd loved Bonnie and Kelly, and they'd loved her. I wondered how McGovern would get rid of her corpse. Bury it in the garden? No – they'd want to lose the body and make sure it could never be connected to the Guvnor. They'd smash her face and hands and teeth so she couldn't be identified, and dump her body in water somewhere to destroy any forensic or DNA evidence. Suddenly my stomach heaved, and only the burning pain of the cut to my chest stopped me from bending over and spewing.

Footsteps came striding down the hall: the Guvnor entered, looking scruffier than usual – he must have thrown his clothes on in a hurry – then stopped and peered at me with his chilly grey eyes. Steve was at his shoulder, pale and shocked, and behind them Terry filled the doorway.

'I was wrong about you, Finn,' said McGovern. 'Turns out you were some use after all.' He offered me his hand, and I took it. His grasp was cool and firm.

'How are they?' I said. 'The kids?'

'Shook up, but they'll survive,' said McGovern. He pulled out a kitchen chair and sat, weary and more drawn than I'd ever seen him. 'They been asking for Victoria. I told 'em she had to leave in a hurry.' I wondered how many previous employees of McGovern had had to 'leave in a hurry'.

'He told me I was working for the Turk,' I said. 'Richard, I mean. I think he was planning to pin all of it on me. Kill your family, then me, and tell everyone he'd caught me in the act. Make it look like Trafalgar Square was me setting you up as well.'

'That must have been the Turk's idea too,' said Steve. 'Richard was never the sharpest knife in the box.'

'How long had he been working for you?' I said.

'Seven years, on and off,' said McGovern. 'Two inside after a job went wrong. Done his bird, never talked, never complained . . . I trusted him.' He looked at Steve. 'If he's been working for the Turk all along, that explains a lot.'

'A lot of what?' I said.

McGovern answered me but ignored my question. 'Terry's taking the kids and their mum away to a safe house, a place nobody knows about but me and him. To keep them out of harm's way till this is over.' His pale eyes drilled into me as if he was trying to figure out my angle, like he couldn't understand why I'd risked my life to save his children. 'Thanks for what you did tonight. And in the square. I owe you.'

'Don't worry about it,' I said, and not just from politeness – I didn't want the Guvnor owing me anything. 'I just want to go home.'

'You sure about that?' said McGovern. 'When the Turk finds out it was you who stopped Richard, you'll be better off in here than out there.'

'So don't tell him,' I said. Just then a thought occurred to me, but I didn't voice it. If McGovern was willing to consider letting me walk away I wasn't going to distract him.

'If I'd let you go last time you asked, my kids would be dead.' McGovern grinned like a wolf. 'So let me think about it.' He turned to Terry and sighed. 'Search him,' he said.

Terry stepped forward, grabbed the back of my chair, dragged it back and tipped me out of it so I had to stand.

'What the hell—?' I said. Terry's meaty paws slapped me down: one trouser leg, then the other, and finally he took a good handful of my backside and crotch. 'You think I've been nicking the spoons or something?' I asked McGovern.

124

'If Richard was talking to the Turk he must have had a second phone,' said McGovern. 'Have you seen it?'

'Oh yeah,' I said. 'Just before he slashed my chest open he ordered a pizza with extra mushrooms.'

'We found his smartphone,' said McGovern. 'Nothing on that. So he must have used a burner.'

'If he did, I don't have it,' I said. 'Shall I drop my trousers? You can check up my arse.'

McGovern looked like he was considering it. 'Leave it,' he said to Terry finally. 'Go turn his room over.' He stood up.

'This needs stitches,' I said, pointing to the badly bandaged slash on my chest. 'I have to go to A&E.'

'No you don't,' said the Guvnor. 'One of the lads is good with a needle and thread, he'll sort you out. Steve, get Chris onto that.'

Steve nodded, and without another glance at me, McGovern headed off up the corridor.

'Chris?' I said to Steve. 'He a nurse or something?'

'Na,' said Steve, taking the seat his father had vacated. 'His dad was a vet.'

'Great,' I said. 'He can sort out my fleas while he's at it.'

'I wanted to say sorry,' said Steve. 'For everything earlier.' That shut me up. Steve was staring at the

125

table in embarrassment, clearly unaccustomed to apologizing. Then he seemed to realize that was rude, and with an effort he lifted his head and looked me in the eye. 'For smacking you about that time, and all the accusations, and waving that gun about . . . I've been a prick. You saved the kids, and my dad, and I appreciate it. It was me who shoulda been there, both times, and I wasn't, and I feel like shit about it, and took it out on you . . . bollocks, anyway, thanks, sorry.'

'Forget about it,' I said, and this time I meant it. Maybe he wasn't as big a prat as I'd thought. It must have been hard growing up the shadow of a dad like McGovern, constantly having to prove yourself vicious enough to be worthy of the family name.

'My dad's grateful too,' went on Steve. 'More than he let on. It's just, things aren't going our way. If that had gone down tonight . . . What a fucking savage the Turk is, attacking children.'

I wondered if he could hear what he was saying. Not two days ago McGovern had been demanding information on Pirbal's family, and it wasn't because he planned to send them a bouquet. Amobi had told me once how the Guvnor had had enemies and even former friends maimed and raped and blinded – for him there were no innocent bystanders, and no act was too atrocious. That was what had won him his reputation, and had made him untouchable, until now.

Now he had an opponent ruthless enough to play by the same rules, and smart enough to strike first.

'Your dad said Richard working for Pirbal explained a lot,' I said. 'What was that about?'

Steve glanced at the door to check if anyone there might overhear. 'His name's not Pirbal,' he said at last. 'Everything we thought we had on him was bollocks. We don't know who he is, who's working with him, nothing.'

'What about your contact at the Border Agency?'

'He's been nicked,' said Steve. He dug a packet of cigarettes out of his pocket, flipped it open and muttered a curse – it was empty. He crushed the box in his hand, kicked his chair back and went wandering round the kitchen, looking for the bin concealed behind one of the dozens of identical exquisite hand-painted cabinets.

'That's one hell of a coincidence,' I said.

'Two of our contacts in the Met have been busted,' went on Steve. 'Another one's suspended from duty. Our people hit a warehouse he was supposed to have been using, turned out to be an abandoned chicken shed, nothing there but shit. Meanwhile a lorryload of merchandise we were bringing in from Austria got hijacked and burned, driver got his legs broken.' He finally pulled at the right handle and a rubbish bin slid silently out from under the counter. He tossed the empty fag packet in and slammed the door shut again with his knee. 'And Gary died,' he said. 'My dad and him knew each other since they were kids.'

Gary? Sunburned Gary, who'd been shot in Trafalgar Square? I'd liked him. He'd been helpful and polite and considerate, for a thug.

'I thought he was recovering,' I said.

'He was,' said Steve. 'He's not any more.'

'If that was the Turk's lot, how the hell did they get to him? There were cops outside his door.'

Steve shrugged. 'You can say it.'

'What?'

'*I told you so.* You tried to warn us. This Turk is the worst thing to come out of Europe since the frigging Common Market. He turned Richard, shopped our contacts, fed us duff intel. We've been fighting in the dark. But now Richard's been nobbled – thanks to you – all that's going to change.'

The thought that had bugged me earlier while I'd spoken to the Guvnor came back to me, and this time I voiced it. 'If the Turk got to Richard, how do you know he hasn't got to anyone else?'

'We don't,' admitted Steve. 'From now on we're taking nothing for granted.'

'What's your dad going to do?'

Steve pulled his nose. 'Let's just say, we have foreign associates who are very keen to protect their investment. Between them and us, we're going to send this towelhead back to Crapistan or wherever in two-gram plastic bags. Apart from that – sorry, kid. After tonight, it's strictly need-to-know.'

Fine by me, I thought. I didn't need to hear details, and I didn't want to. I wasn't running any more errands for the Turk or trying to gather intelligence for Amobi, and I wasn't going to risk my neck for the Guvnor again. When Steve had mentioned 'associates', I'd guessed he was talking about the Russians, but I said nothing. Sometimes it's safer to be taken for stupid; I wished I'd remembered that earlier.

'Steve,' I said. 'Ask your dad to let me go. I've must have done my bit by now. I'm not going to talk to the Turk or the cops. There's nothing useful I could tell them even if I wanted to.'

Steve studied me and sucked his teeth. 'All right,' he said finally. 'I'll see what I can do.'

He strolled out, leaving me alone in the kitchen. I waited a beat, listening to his footsteps fade, then quickly reached under the table, retrieved Richard's phone and stuffed it down the crotch of my jeans – I wasn't likely to get frisked again.

When I'd led the Guvnor's guards to Victoria's body, still sprawled across Richard's bed, they'd been too disgusted and upset to notice the cheap flip-phone lying on the bedside chest of drawers. But I'd seen it, and immediately knew it must be Richard's burner, and I'd slipped it into my pocket unnoticed. I'd guessed the Guvnor would tell his people to find it, so when Cherry had left me alone with the first-aid kit I'd stuck it to the underside of the table with surgical tape. It was my insurance policy: if they didn't let me go, I'd call Amobi to bust me out of there, and if they did . . . they owed me a phone any-way, since the barmaid at The Horsemonger had trashed my old one.

I had a good idea who'd answer if I pressed redial, but I wasn't going to do that – I never wanted to talk to the Turk again. I wasn't even going to switch the phone on until I had to; then I'd make one call and drop it down a drain somewhere.

Steve returned. 'My dad says yes,' he said, jerking his chin at me. 'Go.'

'So how did this happen?' asked the A&E nurse. He

was a bit old for a nurse – fifty-something – with a scruffy greying beard and an Ulster accent like my father's.

'DIY,' I said. 'I was mending a broken window, dropped a piece of glass.'

'At this time of night?' The nurse peered at me over his rimless glasses. 'Looks more like a knife cut to me.' I didn't answer, and he didn't ask again, but turned to the white metal trolley beside him. 'I'll give you something for the pain,' he said. 'Otherwise this will sting a bit. A lot, actually.'

'I'm fine,' I said. 'Just get on and do it.'

It was five by the time I left A&E and emerged onto the empty street, under an inky blue sky slowly being bleached by the dawn. It had been a long night, but the air was still as hot and motionless and clammy as it had been the day before, and the day ahead promised to be yet another scorcher.

Unknown to the cops at the safe house, Zoe had taken her mobile phone with her into protective custody. For safety's sake she kept it switched off, but she'd promised to switch on at six each morning for fifteen minutes so I could contact her if I had to. And now I had to. I punched her mobile number into the keypad of Richard's burner. I told myself I was calling to let her know I was all right, but deep down I knew that was just an excuse; I wanted to hear her again, however briefly, to remind myself why I'd been going through all this. As the connection clicked through and the ringing tone warbled I could already imagine her voice in my ear, husky and half asleep. I heard an electronic bleep – she'd picked up.

'Zoe? It's me, it's Finn,' I said.

'Hey, Finn,' said a male voice. My mouth went dry and my pulse pounded in my ears.

'We need to meet,' said the Turk.

FIVE

The instructions the Turk gave me were straight-forward enough: walk south for five minutes, wait by a certain bus stop outside a burger joint, and give my phone to the guy who turned up to meet me. At this time on a Sunday morning the streets were still half asleep; a few partied-out revellers were shuffling home, past traders setting up their stalls for a street market, and the only traffic was a clutch of cyclists in lurid shirts and shades taking advantage of the empty roads to bomb through red lights without even slowing.

I found the burger joint, and through its tinted windows I watched the staff getting ready to open up. A kid my age in a shit-coloured nylon uniform was wiping down tables with pink disinfectant and a rancid grey dishcloth. He had a long sweaty day ahead, I knew, in a boiling kitchen, flogging greasy junk food to ungrateful punters – and for a moment I envied him. Then I remembered Andy, that fake-tanned skidmark I used to work for at Max Snax, and I realized I'd rather be back in Trafalgar Square getting shot at.

Reflected in the window I saw a white van pull up at the kerb behind me. The driver hadn't been dumb enough to park on the bus stop itself and risk being photographed by 24-hour traffic cameras. It was Dean, I saw now, at the wheel, and when he smirked at me his nicotine-yellow grin seemed more crooked than ever. I smirked back, looking hard at his wonky teeth so he'd know what I was thinking – *I did that*. He didn't get out, but merely held out his hand through the driver window. I tossed the phone to him.

'In the back,' he said, as he stripped the handset down.

It was a bog-standard white Ford van, a few years old, the sort a plumber or decorator might use. I glimpsed the ghost of signwriting under the patchy paint job, but I didn't stop to try and read it: I hauled open the rear door and clambered in. The rear compartment was separated from the front by a ply-wood board and the floor was bare metal, dented and stained, with nowhere to sit and nothing to hang onto. When Dean abruptly pulled away from the kerb, I slid backwards and slammed into the door I had just shut, but luckily both doors held and I didn't tumble out into the road, as Dean had clearly been hoping I would.

Another mystery tour. The rear windows had been whited out with emulsion at some point, but even though the paint was scratched through in some places, I didn't bother trying to peer out and track our route; I just leaned up against the steel wall, spread my legs to brace myself against the van's movement, and tried to figure out my next move.

Was the Turk looking for vengeance? Because I'd saved the Guvnor from the sniper, and the Guvnor's kids from Richard? I knew how the Turk repaid anyone foolish enough to oppose him or betray him or just disappoint him, and I wondered if I should have run instead of meekly climbing into this van; but that had never really been an option. If the Turk had Zoe's phone, he had Zoe too, and if she was still alive, there was a chance we might survive this. Might.

Twenty minutes later the van pulled to the left and stopped, its engine running. I heard a chain rattle and the deep screech of a huge metal roller door being hauled open, and suddenly we were off again, bumping up a short ramp and into a vast building, judging by how the roar of the van's engine echoed. The ride was smooth and steady – no more potholes: we were in some sort of factory or warehouse with a concrete floor. When the van drew to a halt and the doors were pulled open, I saw a huge barn of a place, with steel pillars supporting a high sloping roof of wrinkled tin, and bare walls lined with wheeled metal hoppers piled high with pulverized metal and plastic. Suspended from the roof gantry were sodium lights the size of dustbins, bathing everything below in cold white.

As I climbed out I clocked the man holding the van door open: I hadn't seen Kemal close up in a while, but his moustache was still long and bushy and streaked with grey, and his huge muscular hands still glittered with studded rings, worn less for show than for the impression they made when he punched you in the face. His eyes were black and unblinking and cold; when last we'd met I'd split his bald scalp and tried to break his knee, but he looked at me with no emotion, the way a cat's owner might inspect a flea before cracking it with a thumbnail. He nodded to indicate the way I had to go.

Dean had parked the van with its nose pointing towards a massive metal cube raised on steel stilts, with a conveyor belt running underneath. I thought it was another waste container until I saw how, at the top of the cube, the four walls splayed outwards to make a square vertical funnel. Along one side of that funnel ran a metal walkway, and I felt Kemal's hand in the small of my back shoving me, almost gently, towards the metal staircase that led up to it. I was suddenly reminded of an old engraving I'd seen, of the public gallows that once stood at Marble Arch; of the thousands of ghouls who gathered to stuff their faces with mutton pies and watch men and women being dragged to the scaffold, draped with nooses and dropped through a trap to dance and twitch. I cursed myself inwardly for coming so obligingly to this place, but there was nothing I could do about it now. I wasn't going to face death snivelling, and if it did come to that, maybe I could take a few of these bastards with me. I grabbed the handrail and took the steps two at a time, aware of Kemal's heavy tread stomping steadily up behind.

As I'd expected the Turk was waiting on the walkway, in a cream linen suit and a crisp white shirt that was open at the neck. No bling, no gold teeth, no oversized designer watch; he didn't need to advertise his status. He had his arms folded, and in the crook of his right elbow lay a young cat with ginger and white fur. The Turk was tickling it behind one ear, for all the world like some cheesy Bond villain, but from what I could see the cat wasn't happy with its role; it looked desperate to spring from his arms, but could see nowhere to go. On one side was a sheer drop to a concrete floor, and on the other the metal funnel gaped, leading downwards, I could see now, to four massive interlocking camshafts of hard, dull steel. This was an industrial grinder, I realized – the sort that could reduce an engine block to shreds of tinfoil in the blink of an eye.

'I wanted to show you something,' said the Turk, without ceremony. I didn't see him make a signal, but somewhere below a piercing bell rang out, and with a grinding metal roar the machinery underneath us shuddered into life. The four metal camshafts started to spin, each in the opposite direction to its neighbour; raised spurs on the massive metal discs swept towards and past each other, steadily and implacably. Not so fast that they blurred: this machine was all about power, not speed. The Turk glanced down into the massive metal maw and grinned, and with one swift, fluid movement he grabbed the cat by the fur at its neck and tossed it into the funnel.

Tense as the cat had been, the Turk had taken it by surprise, and it didn't even get a chance to lodge its claws in his sleeve. I felt a jolt of horror as it flew through the air, almost in slow motion, but I knew better than to turn my head away. The cat twisted in flight to land, as all cats do, with all four paws downwards, but that did it no good; almost instantly its legs were caught in the rotating cogs, and it barely had time to struggle or screech before it was dragged downwards into the interlocking camshafts, to disintegrate in an explosion of blood and guts and fur. From the corner of my eye I could see Kemal's massive shoulders shaking with laughter; with an immense effort I kept my own face impassive and my eyes locked on the shredder's roaring toothed wheels, smeared now with gore and clotted hair. Had the Turk done this as a warm-up? To intensify the terror I'd feel before it was my turn? As horrible as the cat's fate was, for a grown man it would be worse – maybe a whole minute of terror and agony and vain struggling to escape before the machine sucked me down, mashed me up and finished me off.

But somehow I sensed that wasn't going to happen, not right now, not today. If the Turk wanted to kill me this way I reckoned he'd do it slowly – have me lowered into the grinder on a rope or a chain while he looked on. But there was no sign of any chain, or any hoist. And he'd kill me in front of Zoe, to double the fun – but there was no sign of Zoe here either. Whatever the Turk had in mind for me today, I decided, it wasn't death: nothing so simple. This had merely been a demonstration of what was in store if I dared to defy him again.

Still smirking, the Turk caught my eye and jerked his head towards the steps. He didn't try to shout over the roar of the industrial shredder, but his meaning was clear enough. He crossed – behind me, he wasn't stupid – to the stairway and skipped lightly down; I followed, all the while closely watched by Kemal.

Someone shut off the power to the shredder, and the whining roar of the engines that powered the camshafts lowered in pitch and volume and finally sank into silence, leaving my ears ringing. Not far away, in a space uncluttered by waste hoppers, a table had been set up, the sort you might find in any canteen – a laminated surface mounted on slim grey metal legs. Two standard grey plastic stacking chairs stood facing each other on either side. As the Turk approached the table, Dean pulled one chair back and stood aside, in a scruffy imitation of a butler. The Turk settled into his seat, shuffled it forward and gestured for me to sit in the one opposite.

I plonked myself down, Kemal looming behind me. The Turk was leaning back slightly, one hand on the table, the other on his lap, utterly relaxed; I forced myself to relax too, slouching in my own chair to mirror his posture.

'Where's Zoe?' I said.

The Turk grimaced and smiled at the same time, as if I'd barged straight to the point without observing the necessary formalities. I had, on purpose: I knew he'd wanted me to ask about the shredder – whose it was, whether he'd often used it on his enemies. He wanted me to haggle and bluster and plead, but I wasn't going to play that game. He couldn't mention the shredder now without making it sound like a clumsy threat, and he fancied himself as too cool for that. He claimed he wasn't vain, but I knew that was just another aspect of his vanity ... although the way things had been going for him, he had plenty to be vain about.

'You were required to deliver a message,' said the Turk. 'That was all. Instead you decided to choose a side. The losing side.' I tried in vain to place that mid-European accent of his, but it was like trying to nail down smoke. 'I know you are not as stupid as I first thought,' the Turk was saying, 'but I really cannot see what you were hoping to achieve.'

'If you're talking about that meeting,' I said, 'someone started shooting at me. I didn't have time to think it through.'

'He was not shooting at you,' said the Turk. 'Kemal was the finest sniper in the Hakkari Brigade. In Kurdistan, for a bet, he shot a baby off its mother's breast from two thousand metres. He would not have missed McGovern if you had not intervened.'

Christ. My guess had been right – it had been Kemal up on that rooftop looking down at us through a sniper scope. Why hadn't he taken his shot while we crossed the square? I supposed that with McGovern in that panama hat and sunglasses, Kemal had to be sure he wasn't a decoy. If only the Guvnor had been that subtle.

'I had no way of knowing that,' I said. 'I was trying to stay alive. It was kind of an accident I kept the Guvnor alive while I was at it.'

'And his family? Was that too an accident?'

'No,' I said. 'But I wasn't going to stand around watching Richard slit their throats. Why did you order that? Those kids were no threat to you.'

'In war,' said the Turk, 'it is not enough to kill a man. You must first enter his house, eat his food, defile his wife, and slaughter his children, while he watches. When he knows that he has lost everything, then you have won.' He sounded like one of those billionaires who keep working even when they own so many yachts and mansions and tropical islands they can't ever visit them all. Such possessions are just trophies – what those guys really enjoy is the business; and the Turk's business was butchery. 'Thanks to you,' he went on, 'that pleasure has been denied me.'

'Richard was going to kill me too, wasn't he?' I said. 'So he would have someone else to pin the blame on.'

'What can I say?' The Turk shrugged. 'You're dispensable.'

'Not any more, obviously, or you wouldn't have brought me here.' The Turk smiled, as if he was enjoying the banter. I wasn't – I just wanted him to get to the bloody point.

'You are telling me you are not on the Guvnor's side?' he asked.

'I don't think it matters what I tell you,' I said. 'But no, I'm not on his side. You two can kill each other for all I care. And the sooner the better.'

'But he thinks you are on his side. You saved his children. He trusts you now.'

'He knows I'm not on yours. Apart from that, he doesn't trust anyone any more.'

'That will be enough for my purposes,' said the Turk. 'Go back to him. Tell him I have threatened to kill you for saving the lives of his children. He owes you a favour, and he pretends to be a man of honour, so he will say yes. And shortly after he takes you in, you will kill him for me. I will forgive your . . . interference, and you and the lovely Zoe can go free.'

Free for the sixty seconds you'd let us live, I thought. 'And if I fail?' My glance must have strayed to the massive shredder behind him, because he grinned in satisfaction.

'If you fail, I won't punish you,' said the Turk. 'McGovern's people will kill you. And Zoe . . . Zoe I will hand over to our old friend Dean. He has disposed of one or two people for me already, but frankly' – he grinned at Dean, who looked uncomfortable at being singled out – 'he lacks . . . finesse. He needs to learn how to prolong the pleasure, how to make each moment more exquisite than the last. He can practise on your girlfriend. And if he . . . peaks early, well – so much the better for her.'

There was nothing to say in reply that would not have sounded like empty threats and bravado, so I said nothing; I simply stared at the Turk. In the past it had sometimes felt as if he could read my mind, and right now I was counting on that, and thinking hard about what it would be like to stamp on his face until it caved in – the sound it would make, and the mess.

I was pleased to see the Turk's eyes widen, and his

self-satisfied smile flicker slightly. He licked his lips and sat up with an abruptness that bordered on irritation, and I saw him collect himself before he pulled something out of his pocket and tossed it onto the table. It was a memory stick, and it lay there between us like a gauntlet.

'Something extra to motivate you,' said the Turk. I didn't move.

'She is counting on you, Finn.' His smug smile was back. 'I told her what I would ask you to do. She knows you are the only one who can save her. That little flame of hope is the only thing keeping her going.' He leaned across the table towards me. 'Honestly?' he said. 'Part of me wants you to fail. To see the look on her lovely face when I tell her you are dead, and that her hope was all for nothing. Before I give her to Dean and Kemal.' He pushed the stick towards me.

'You have two days,' he said.

Back home – in the desolate empty house that passed for home – I plugged the memory stick into a laptop. It held a single video file; my hand hesitated on the trackpad, afraid of what I was about to see, but I knew I had no choice. I double-clicked on it.

The footage that first appeared I'd seen before,

on the Turk's phone: Zoe pulling her bike down the steps of her house; with a bagful of books bustling across campus; gossiping in the canteen with a friend. The camera zoomed in so close at one point you could see the stud glinting in her nose, but she seemed blissfully unaware and utterly unself-conscious. Maybe with her looks she was so used to being stared at and ogled she didn't even notice any more; for once I wished she hadn't been so blasé and laid back, that she'd been paranoid enough to look about her. If she'd spotted the surveillance guy she could have gone to the cops, had him picked up for harassment, told her friends, taken precautions . . .

What was I saying? We *had* taken precautions – we'd gone to see Amobi. What had gone wrong with that safe house? Had she got fed up with the confinement and walked out on them?

This footage had been cut, I noticed; it wasn't just shots snatched by a smartphone and strung together. Beginnings and endings – the places you'd expect to see camera-shake or auto-focus kicking in - had been edited out. There was more where this came from that they weren't showing me, and I wondered why; had the cameraman made it look slick to impress the Turk, or to intimidate me?

Suddenly I was watching footage I hadn't seen

before, and it wasn't so slick any more. The camera was in a dimly lit room and jumping about all over the place. I could hear laboured breathing, and yelps of pain that sounded like they might be Zoe's. The lens was hoovering up shots of wallpaper and crumpled bed sheets, then a blurred close-up of a girl's hand being roughly gripped, as her wrist was bound to a slatted bed frame with a length of cheap blue nylon cord. Whoever was filming this girl was also helping to restrain her.

The person holding the camera stepped back; yes, it was Zoe, gagged and bound to a wooden bed in a corner of a dingy room – a first-floor room, judging by the level of the street lights I could just make out through the net curtains. She was in a grey cotton T-shirt dress that had ridden up her thighs as she struggled and thrashed about; Dean stood by the bed, leering and winking at the camera, and he reached out to stroke her face. I heard him tell her, 'Say hello to your friend Finn,' as he tugged down the bandanna tied tightly around her mouth.

She snapped at him with her teeth instead, and when that failed she spat at him, 'Fuck you!'

The watchers – three or four of them by the sound of it – jeered and tittered as she wrenched at the ropes, cursing. I could tell every move was agony for her, as the coarse cord bit into the flesh of her wrists. Dean giggled and hooted, and ran his hand up her thigh, pulling her dress up higher, over her hip, lingering on the hem of her panties—

I pulled the memory stick out. I'd seen enough. In a corner of my mind I'd been nursing one tiny sickly runt of hope – that the Turk had been bluffing, that he didn't have Zoe, that he'd been counting on me to panic and run to do his bidding. Now even that hope was dead. Why would he have bluffed, anyway, when I could call Amobi and find out the truth?

But what *was* the truth? Zoe wouldn't have walked away from the safe house – had the Turk's people snatched her? There was only one way I was going to find out, and only one way I could get Zoe back safely.

The landline in this house still worked, even though I'd never paid the bill. I dialled Amobi's number.

It was about noon when I found the dead-end side street off a busy main road, a few tube stops from my house, where we'd arranged to meet. His unremarkable Ford was neatly lined up in a parking bay and Amobi was a shadow behind the wheel. Even on a Sunday you had to pay to park round here; I noticed he'd bought a ticket and stuck it on his windscreen. He wasn't the sort of copper to wave his officer's ID at a traffic warden and tell them to sod off.

I pulled the front passenger door open and slid into the seat. Although the cul-de-sac was narrow and shaded from the blistering sun, the air inside the car was rancid and clammy, and I felt myself break out in a sweat before I'd even shut the door. I'd grabbed the chance to change my clothes and shower before I came out, but already I smelled of exhaustion and desperation. Amobi had hung his suit jacket up on a hook over the seat behind him, but he hadn't switched on his air-con or even opened a window, and when I saw his posture I decided not to ask why. He hadn't spoken or turned to look at me when I got in; now his left hand lay in his lap, and with the other he rubbed his mouth as if to stop himself blurting something out he might regret. It wasn't hard to sense his anger.

'Hey,' I said. 'Thanks for coming.'

Now he turned to look at me, then turned away again. 'Yeah,' he said.

I felt my own anger flaring up. *Yeah?* What the hell did that mean? When he'd answered his mobile his replies had been short, almost monosyllabic, but I'd thought that was him being efficient and business-like. If he was just going to grunt at me now I didn't know why he'd agreed to meet up.

'I'm sorry about Trafalgar Square,' I said. He fixed me with a stare that suggested he thought I was taking the piss. 'I wanted to get in touch,' I said. 'But McGovern's people took my phone, kept me incommunicado—'

'Forget it.' Amobi turned away again. 'It's all water under the bridge now.'

'He's got Zoe,' I said. 'The Turk. If I don't kill McGovern for him, his people will kill her.'

'Christ,' said Amobi, and he closed his eyes and shook his head like he was trying to shake out the words he'd just heard me say. 'Where are they holding her?'

'I don't know,' I said. 'A flat somewhere.' Amobi actually snorted. 'He gave me this . . .' I held out the memory stick, but Amobi didn't take it.

'What do you want me to do with that?' he said.

'I don't know!' I snapped. 'Analyse it – bloody look at it, at least—'

'For God's sake, Finn!' he snapped back. 'I can't get a sample of piss analysed!' I'd never seen Amobi lose control. Part of me was fascinated, while another part of me wanted to grab his shiny tie and strangle him with it. 'I told my people you would help me stop this gang war before it started. Instead, two men died, twenty tourists got injured – a police officer got shot, in the centre of London!' He held up two fingers in a pinch. 'I am *this* close to facing a disciplinary committee—'

'A disciplinary committee? God, I'm so sorry,' I said. 'What will they do? Shoot you? Throw you in a blender?' My own frustration was boiling over now. 'Or will they just pull a few bloody buttons off your uniform?'

Amobi turned away, trying to reassert control of himself, and I saw the muscles in his face clench as he ground his teeth. He rubbed his face again, the other hand gripping the steering wheel till the colour bleached out of his knuckles.

'You told me you'd keep her safe,' I said. 'You promised me – you promised *her*. What the hell happened?'

'Orders happened,' snarled Amobi. But he couldn't look me in the eye – he was ashamed of betraying Zoe, and I was angry for letting him, and furious at myself for ever taking the word of a copper. 'After that shootout the word came down – shut the safe house, send Zoe back home. And what the hell could I tell them?'

'You could have told them she was still in danger,'

I said. 'You could have told them she was the daughter of a copper you used to work with—'

'I did tell them!' yelled Amobi. 'Of course I told them! And they said none of that mattered, to shut down the operation down, let the Turk and McGovern settle their shit between themselves, without involving innocent passers-by—'

'Zoe and I are innocent, for Christ's sake!'

'Look, the NCA has its hands full trying to shut down a terrorist network slaughtering people all over the UK – we need all the help we can get—' Amobi cut himself off abruptly, as if he'd said too much.

'*Help?* What the hell does that mean?'

'What it means,' he said, more quietly now, 'is we're way overstretched. We have to – make the most of our resources.' But he was avoiding my eye again, and now he'd started spouting bureaucratic jargon I knew he was hiding something.

When I realized what it was, I gasped. 'Holy crap – the Turk is *helping* you people? How?'

'That's not what I said!'

'That tipoff you got the other day – was that from him?'

'Finn, just stop with the questions, OK? This country is at war, and we need allies.'

'But the Turk's a gangster, a psychopath—'

'And so is McGovern.' Amobi knew he'd as good as admitted it, and there was no point in any more evasions. 'Right now we have to choose the lesser of two evils,' he said.

'The Turk's taken Zoe,' I said. 'He says he's going to torture her to death.'

'I'll try to help,' said Amobi.

'How?'

'I'll make some calls.'

'Are you fucking *kidding* me?' Suddenly I understood what he meant, and it hit me like a bullet to the belly. 'You can't do anything, can you? That's why we're meeting in secret like this. Zoe and me are on our own.'

'I'm sorry, Finn,' said Amobi, 'I really am—'

There was a sharp rap of knuckles on his side window. We'd both been so engrossed in yelling at each other we hadn't noticed the two uniformed coppers approaching. They'd parked their patrol vehicle across the neck of the alley so Amobi couldn't drive off if he tried, and now they were standing one on each side of his car. All I could see was their midriffs – the white polycotton shirts tucked into black serge trousers, the stab vests and the belts groaning with handcuffs, truncheons and pepper spray. Amobi cursed and fumbled for the electric window switch. The window went halfway down, then stopped, jammed. Amobi stabbed at the button, muttering, but it wouldn't budge any further. The copper at his door leaned down and peered through the gap, clearly suspecting Amobi of playing silly buggers.

'May I ask what you're doing here, sir?' said the copper. His 'sir' was a flimsy pretence at politeness, a paper flower poked into a turd. He had a hard, chiselled face, buzz-cut hair and eyebrows so blond they were barely there. His pale cheeks glistened with sweat.

'Sorry, Officer, we're just about done here,' said Amobi. He reached for the keys hanging in the ignition and started the car.

'Would you mind switching your engine off, please?' The copper gripped the window rim as if he could hold the car back with one hand if he had to. I glanced over my shoulder and watched the other cop – skinny, spotty, younger than the first – stroll round to the rear of the car and stand muttering into his lapel radio, reading out the numberplate. I was waiting for the moment when they'd realize their mistake and back off, grovelling to Amobi, but that didn't seem to be happening, and Amobi for some reason didn't seem in any hurry to enlighten them.

Instead, he meekly switched his engine off as instructed.

'Officer, we're minding our own business, and we're not committing any offence—'

The copper stood back and beckoned Amobi out with a crook of his finger. 'Step out of the car for me, please.' The 'sir' had disappeared, I noticed, and I could hear that familiar authoritarian tinge creeping into the copper's voice – that smug, supercilious tone that dares you to answer with sarcasm or a smart remark, if you like the taste of pavement.

Sighing, Amobi opened his door and clambered out, leaving his jacket hanging in the rear, and shut his door carefully, so as not to appear to be slamming it in irritation. All of them seemed to be ignoring my existence; I wondered if the plods had even noticed I was there.

'Now I'm asking you again,' the first copper was saying to Amobi, 'to tell us exactly what you're up to here.' *Up to . . .* typical copper question. No matter how you replied to it you'd sound guilty and defensive.

'I was conducting some private business,' said Amobi. 'Having a private conversation, that's all.'

For Christ's sake, I nearly spluttered, *just tell them who you are!* But Amobi, professional to the point of absurdity, seemed determined to maintain his cover.

'Not on the PNC,' said the second cop to the first.

'Might I suggest you check again, Officer?' said Amobi, but the guy ignored him, droning like a droid into his lapel radio, conferring with his nick about a male IC3 in a blue Ford saloon – IC3 was Met police code for black, I knew – and requesting backup. I'd been stopped and harassed by surly cops myself enough times to know this encounter wasn't going well – and unlike Amobi, I'd never made the mistake of having dark skin.

'Thing is,' said the first copper, with that same fake-friendly sing-song tone in his voice, 'there seems to be a problem with your car's registration. It doesn't appear to be on the DVLC database, which suggests it's a false registration. So I need to see some ID from you and a V5 for this vehicle.'

'For goodness' sake—' I could hear the exasperation creeping into Amobi's voice, and so could the copper, because he didn't wait to hear Amobi's explanation.

'Word of advice, calm down, all right, and we'll get this straightened out. Now I've asked you twice—'

'I'm a police officer, OK? This is an official vehicle,' snapped Amobi at last, struggling to keep his voice low and even. 'Detective Sergeant Philip

Amobi, seconded to the NCA, and I'm actually on a case—'

'Seconded to who?' said the first copper, as if he couldn't decipher Amobi's faint Nigerian accent.

'The NCA – National Crime Agency—'

'You mean SOCA?' said the first cop. They'd clearly never heard of the NCA.

'Yes, SOCA!' replied Amobi, at the end of his tether.

'Well that's not the NCA, is it?' snorted the spotty copper.

'Look, I'm going to get my ID out, OK?' I saw both coppers tense as Amobi raised his hands from his sides.

'Slowly, all right?' said the first copper.

Amobi brought his right hand down to his rear pocket, dipped his fingers in and rooted about. 'Damn it,' he said, 'it's in my jacket – in the back of the car—'

'No, step away from the car, all right, mate?' said the spotty copper. 'I'll take a look.' He pulled open the rear door, unhooked Amobi's expensive suit jacket, tugged it out and started patting it down for a wallet, letting it dangle inside out and drag along the gutter. Pens and papers started falling out of the pockets.

'Oh, for God's sake, let—' Amobi reached for his

jacket, and the first copper grabbed his arm and Amobi pulled it free, and an instant later he was slammed face down onto the bonnet of his car with his right arm up in a lock behind him, the first copper pinning him down with all his weight while he yelled in indignation, 'I'm a police officer! I'm a police officer!'

I pushed my own door open and climbed out. The first copper glared at me as he tried to control the writhing Amobi. 'Back in the car, sonny, all right? We'll come to you in a minute.'

'Forget it,' I said. 'I don't do guys in uniform.' From the look on their faces I could tell they'd already leaped to the wrong conclusions – that I was a rent boy and Amobi was a john – just as I'd hoped they would.

Amobi raised his head. 'For God's sake, Finn, tell them who I—' was as far as he got before the first copper slammed his head down again so hard it bounced off the bonnet. Amobi roared, incoherent with fury by now, and the second copper waded in too, ratcheting a handcuff tightly round one of Amobi's wrists and fishing for the other wrist with the hook of the second, all the while shouting at me, 'Don't you move, all right? Get back in that car – now!'

I tilted my head to meet Amobi's eye. 'Really

sorry, sweetie,' I said. 'But you're on your own.'

And I started to walk away. The second copper left the cuffs dangling and his mate wrestling with Amobi while he scrambled to grab me, but I ran for it. He was young and fit, but I was younger and fitter, and I wasn't weighed down with half a ton of blunt weaponry, a stab vest and a bellyful of doughnuts. I avoided the crowds of pedestrians by running up the middle of the street, dodging the roaring buses and blaring cars, making sure I was heading in the opposite direction from the approaching sirens. Before I'd gone half a block a glance over my shoulder told me the copper had given up the chase and was bent over panting in the heat, ready to collapse. As I rounded the next corner I slowed to a walk, then immediately ducked into the blissful cool of an air-conditioned shopping mall, where I wandered for the next few minutes among cable TV sales stands and perspex racks of fluorescent jelly sweets. I kept checking around and behind me to see if any would-be vigilantes had taken up the chase, but there was no one. Making my way through a side exit I emerged into a bus station where the hot stale air shook with the steady throb of huge diesel engines. A litter bin nearby overflowed with plastic bottles and greasy sandwich wrappers, and I paused, took

Amobi's NCA ID out of my pocket and tossed it in.

I'd filched it from Amobi's jacket when he'd climbed out of the car to reason with the chisel-faced cop; I'd been hoping to cause him trouble somewhere down the line, but as things turned out I'd succeeded right away. I could guess what would happen now: those two plods would frogmarch Amobi to their car – cracking his head on the edge of the roof as they shoved him into the back seat – and on arrival at the nick they'd drop him as they helped him out again, maybe standing on his hands accidentally-on-purpose. He'd be banged up in a cell for an hour or two while his story was checked out, and then the horrified duty sergeant would dash to unlock his cell door and the woodentops who'd busted him would be crawling to Amobi on their hands and knees, pleading with him not to make an official complaint.

The thought of it gave me a warm feeling of achievement, but that didn't last very long. The Turk was still holding Zoe, and I had no idea where, and Amobi had been my final hope, and now he'd cut us both adrift.

There was only one person now who might be willing to help me, and that was McGovern. I was going to have to go back to him, ask him to take me in, and accept his hospitality and his protection. And then, at some point, I was going to have to kill him.

I headed back home the same way I'd come, by tube and bus, racking my brains all the way to try and figure out my options. There was no point in queuing up at the local nick to report a kidnapping. Even if they believed me, I'd never trusted cops to do anything competently apart from batter drunks and claim overtime. Seeing two plods work over one of their own officers for being the wrong colour in the wrong car hadn't done much to change my opinion, even if I'd helped to make it happen.

And this time it was worse – it wasn't that the cops would wade in and make a mess of it, but that they wouldn't wade in at all. The Turk's information had already foiled one bombing – he'd proved his worth. The authorities were so desperate for leads on the terrorists, of course they'd turn a blind eye to his dodgy business dealings. Why would they break up a gang war in order to save McGovern? They'd been trying to nail him for years, and got nowhere; if the Turk could do it for them, the war would be over that much sooner and the cops would only have one villain to sort out instead of two. Zoe and I would merely be collateral damage.

What if I could tip off the terrorists somehow, let

them know that the Turk was grassing up their operations? For once the Turk would be facing an enemy even more vicious and demented than he was. Yeah, great idea – I just needed to find the terrorists' website, or their email address. Maybe they had a Facebook page I could post on.

I felt bad about stitching up Amobi and getting him arrested, but not that bad. He hadn't even looked at that video of Zoe. He must have known that if he did, he would have had to get involved – at least get the footage analysed somehow. Everybody knew how the government was keeping tabs on the public these days; they probably had the technology to identify the smartphone that had taken that video, right down to the model number and the IMEI. There might even be a location tag embedded in the footage – but outside of GCHQ the only person I knew with that sort of IT genius was Zoe herself. Maybe if I watched the footage again . . . I'd seen a movie once where the cops traced a phone call by analysing the sounds they could hear in the background. Perhaps there'd be something in the footage I hadn't noticed – a glimpse through the window of that room where she was being held, a distinctive noise . . . It had to be worth a go.

Alone in my musty kitchen I plugged the memory

stick into the laptop again and took a deep breath. The prospect of sitting through the footage again made me feel tainted somehow, like the sort of sicko who slows down at motorway pile-ups in the hope of catching a glimpse of a corpse. But Zoe wasn't dead yet, of that much I was sure. And I was being prissy and pathetic – she was the one who actually had to go through the ordeal of being pawed and groped and God knows what else by Dean and the Turk's other gorillas, and she wouldn't give a toss right now how guilty or creepy I felt watching it. If there was any chance at all it could help her, I had to take it. I opened the memory stick's folder, navigated to the video file, and clicked 'play'.

The footage of Zoe on campus at York I'd already seen – it would tell me nothing about where she was now. I slid the cursor to the fast-forward button, then hesitated. Could there something in there I'd missed all the other times? I'd never made myself scrutinize it properly, I'd been squirming too much. I clicked on 'play' and forced myself to concentrate, to focus on the moving image, to try and stay cold and analytical somehow. There was Zoe dragging her bike down the steps of her shared house . . . strolling through the campus . . . chatting to a girl . . . I'd seen that girl tagged in a Facebook picture – Molly somebody . . . ?

I hit 'pause' again. I opened up a browser and rooted around for the bookmark I'd set for Zoe's Facebook page.

With dyslexia as severe as mine, just trying to read postings in that tiny little text gave me a migraine, so I hardly ever used Facebook. That had been my excuse anyhow – I didn't need to read her posts to know that Zoe was having a ball up there, far away from me. There were endless low-light pictures of her laughing at parties or moshing at gigs, and she always seemed to be among a crowd of hot girls and cool blokes, all at various stages of leglessness. And lately Patrick Robinson's languid smile had been beaming through more and more of her pictures like a smug little crescent moon. There he was beside her, picnicking in a summer meadow, one arm draped across her shoulders – pulling her close, or trying to. Here was a moody black and white one of the pair of them hunched on a park bench in the rain, sharing what looked like a spliff.

It seemed all the more odd, then, that I hadn't seen Patrick in the video footage.

I jumped back to the start of the video, clicked on 'play'.

Zoe dragging her bike down the steps. The camera was on the far side of the road, opposite Zoe's house.

As I watched her yet again emerge and wrestle with her bike, I noticed again the guy coming in, who had to dodge out of her way – and there he was tagged on her Facebook page: Sunil, from her IT course. Now Zoe was chatting in the canteen, the camera zoomed into the stud glinting in her nose – that girl she was giggling with, that was Molly again, with her hair pinned up, maybe because she hadn't washed it that morning . . . still no sign of handsome Patrick anywhere.

What was that? The video had cut from the college canteen to Zoe in what looked like the library, but something had snagged on my consciousness, something so subtle I wasn't sure I hadn't imagined it. I hit the 'pause' button, found the control that moved the footage forward in tiny increments, and clicked on 'reverse', moving backwards one split second at a time.

Now we were back in the canteen. The image tight on Zoe's face . . . I found the button to creep forward, and clicked it, once, twice . . .

There.

An instant before the cut, Zoe's eyes flicked to the right, and she looked straight down the lens, and on her lips was the beginning of a smile.

SIX

I rang the doorbell of Zoe's shared house in York and waited. And waited some more. Standing back I squinted up at the windows, but there was no way of telling which of the residents were in or out. Maybe they'd split for the summer, maybe they were still asleep in bed at four in the afternoon. Either was possible – these were students, after all. I didn't even know which room was Zoe's, and it didn't matter anyway – I wasn't here to turn the place over for clues: I was here to talk to Patrick.

I took a seat on the cracked stone steps under the front door. Although it was old and crumbling, the house was pretty enough in its own way, with big sash windows that let in lots of light, and a long garden out the front that soaked up the noise of passing traffic. The grass was shaggy and full of dandelions – obviously none of the residents was into gardening – but it was thinning now and going yellow, longing for the rain that never seemed to come. As the grass died back an old bicycle was emerging from its depths, rusty and decaying, like a skeleton exposed on a dried-up lake bed.

I'd prepared a cover story in case any of Zoe's other housemates turned up – that I'd come to visit Zoe, that I hadn't known she'd left, had she and Patrick had an argument? I needed to speak to him ... hopefully they would take it for a lovers' tiff, some melodramatic triangle, and leave us to it.

If I was right about Patrick – that he had taken that footage of Zoe and passed it on to the Turk – it would take all my self-control not to leave his perfect smile looking like a row of broken bottles. He might hesitate before calling the cops, but his flatmates wouldn't, and if I got done for assault up here in York I could end up remanded in prison for a week with no friends to bail me out. I did have a lawyer once, but after tangling with the Turk herself she'd fled to South America. And I'd pretty much burned my boats with Amobi that morning.

I'd been staring into space while all this went through my mind, and Patrick was halfway up the path with his door keys in his hand before we saw each other. Even on this hot sticky day he radiated cool – designer shades, loud baggy shirt, baggy cargo shorts exposing muscular tanned legs – but when he saw me he froze. For a second or two I could see him wondering how to play this – innocent, baffled, bored, amused? He had to assume I knew nothing about his sideline doing surveillance for the Turk; he'd pretend to be the broken-hearted boyfriend abruptly abandoned by his sweetheart after I'd come up to visit, and that he had no idea where she was now. He wouldn't invite me in – he'd ask me sullenly what I wanted.

'Hey, Finn. What can I do for you?'

'He's got Zoe,' I said.

'Who has?'

'The Turk,' I said. Patrick had decided to go for baffled, I could see, and I made an effort to hold onto my patience.

'I haven't seen Zoe since she ran after you,' said Patrick. 'If you don't know where she is, I sure as hell don't. Excuse me please, I'd like to go in.' He made to walk past me, but I didn't shift from the step.

'He said he was going to—' I stopped. I really didn't want to explain everything all over again, especially to this tall, handsome, treacherous smart-arse. But then, how much did he actually know?

Maybe he'd never met the Turk in person. Maybe he hadn't known who or what the footage was for. Maybe this whole trip would turn out to have been for nothing.

I had to start with what I knew.

'The footage you shot of her,' I said. 'Who did you give it to?'

'I don't know what you're talking about, and I'd really like to get into my bloody house now,' he said.

He tried to squeeze past me, practically shoving his crotch in my face, making my choice pretty straightforward. No room to swing a punch, so I just grabbed instead. Good thing he was wearing those baggy shorts – if he had been wearing tight jeans I would never have found his scrotum first time. If big Terry and the Guvnor's other gorillas could overcome their qualms about handling another bloke's tackle, so could I. I grabbed the ballsack beyond Patrick's dormant prick and held it firmly, without squeezing it. Yet.

His first reaction was gratifying – he let loose a high-pitched yelp, dropped his keys and clawed at my hands – and I squeezed, just a little to let him know this wasn't a mistake and it wasn't going to end anytime soon. He went for broke, and back-handed me across my bruised face with the bones of his wrist – a fancy fighting move I'd never encountered before, which hurt like hell. I'm not the best fighter I know, but one skill I do have is the ability to take a beating. Pain drains your strength and your spirit unless you can set it aside; it's a handy trick, and somehow I doubted Patrick had learned it. When he whacked me again across the mouth I held firm, stood up, and twisted his nuts, just a little. He squirmed and yelled and danced on the spot, and he stopped trying to hit me.

There's this medical condition called torsion of the testes where the tubes and veins feeding a man's testicles get tangled. It's excruciating, apparently, and sometimes the only cure is amputation. I wasn't planning to go that far with Patrick – the amount of pain he was in right now was plenty for my immediate purposes. He quickly stopped squirming and yelling and tried to hold still, scrabbling at my hands again. I was right up close to him – I had to be – and I could literally see beads of sweat oozing from his pores and trickling over his lovely tanned cheekbones.

'Jesus, please—' he whimpered. 'Oh Christ, please stop—'

'Who did you give the footage to?' He still hesitated. I gave my wrist a tiny flick – just enough to remind him of his immediate priorities.

'The Turk, the Turk – I gave it to the Turk,' he babbled. He looked at the house, then over his shoulder down the path, wishing someone would come to his rescue. It was very likely someone would, and soon, and I couldn't let that happen. I held on, counting on him to keep babbling. 'He never told me what it was for – he didn't want her to know about it—'

'How do you know him?' I said. 'How did the Turk find you?'

'I did some coke,' gasped Patrick. By keeping my fist high I was making him teeter on the balls of his feet, his arms held out rigid by his sides, his fists clenching and unclenching uselessly. 'The guy who sold me the stuff, he told the Turk about me. I'm studying law, if I get done for drugs—!'

So he'd been blackmailed, and he'd sold Zoe out to save his own skin. This guy was a real prince. I just hoped I'd get the chance to let Zoe know.

'Did you take that last shot?'

Patrick frowned and opened his mouth and shut it again, clearly confused.

'The shot of Zoe being tied to a bed and felt up by Dean and those other guys. You were there, weren't you? You didn't just watch – you joined in.'

He looked appalled and terrified. 'No! No, I swear

171

to God, they told me they weren't going to hurt her, or do anything to her! I just shot the stuff up here, I never – please, I can't—'

Dammit. This had been a fool's errand after all – Patrick couldn't tell me anything I didn't know already. At the thought of failing, of having to leave Zoe in that cesspit, my fist closed tighter, without my even being aware of it.

And Patrick screamed. 'Oh God oh God please stop I just took her there I didn't talk to anyone they didn't tell me oh Jesus PLEASE!'

I loosened my grip – in fact I was so surprised and relieved I nearly let go altogether.

'She needed a place to stay in London, and she called me—' Interesting: relief from pain was as great an incentive to talk as the pain had been ... I'd probably make a good torturer. I shoved that qualm aside – there'd be plenty of time for guilt later.

'The Turk told me to bring her to this flat in Clapham,' Patrick groaned. 'I can give you the address.'

'Sod that,' I said. 'You're going take me there.'

I had intended to make him come back to London with me on the train. But after I'd let go of his scrotum and let him bend over and gag, and walk up and down for a bit, Patrick picked up his keys and led me to an old but shiny soft-top Mini parked on the street outside. He unlocked it with a remote, pressing the button twice – once for each door – and we both climbed in.

Travelling by car to London would make my task a lot simpler; on the train I would have had to stick by him all the way to ensure he didn't call the Turk with a warning, and that would have been tricky. I couldn't confiscate his phone either – he might call a cop over and make up some story that I'd robbed him, and if I had his handset in my pocket it would have been hard to deny. And with his own phone he could have gone to the loo at any time and made that call, unless I followed him in there, and I'd had enough intimate contact with his genitals for one afternoon. Sitting in the passenger seat while he drove down to London would present far fewer problems.

Except, of course, York was hundreds of miles from London. On the train it took roughly two hours, but even at eighty m.p.h. it was going to take us about four to get as far as the North Circular. His convertible was comfortable enough, but kind of cramped. I imagined the female students Patrick gave lifts to enjoyed rubbing thighs with him, hoping eventually to help him get his top down. I didn't, and

I wasn't, and as we headed south an awkward silence settled over us. I stared out the windows at the endless flat northern vista of scorched crops wilting for want of water and sheep slowly cooking in their woolly coats, while Patrick stared impassively ahead at the motorway unrolling before us. Normally I fall asleep on long car journeys but there was too much tension in that tiny space to let me relax. Patrick's face was half hidden behind mirrored shades, but the half I could see looked sulky and bullied, rather than guilty. I could imagine his growing indignation at finding himself obliged – forced, even – to drive Zoe's violent thug of an ex-boyfriend, two years younger than him, all the way down to London.

'This is so stupid,' he said eventually. 'I mean, what do you hope to achieve?'

I hadn't thought that far ahead, but that was none of his business, so I just looked at him.

'For Christ's sake,' said Patrick, 'it's a bluff. The Turk's not actually going to do anything to her, he told me.'

This guy's too stupid to be a lawyer, I thought. He's too stupid even to be a cop. 'Shut up and drive,' was all I said.

'He just wants you to think that, so you'd do a job for him.'

'When he told you he'd shop you to the cops for snorting coke,' I said, 'did you think he was bluffing then?'

He rolled his eyes like I was being stubborn for the sake of it. 'Either way,' he said, 'this, what we're doing now, this is just stupid. When he finds out I've taken you there, maybe he really will hurt her, and me and you, and it'll be your bloody fault.'

I wanted to thump him just to stop the snivelling self-justification, but at eighty miles an hour that wouldn't have been a good idea.

'Seriously, Patrick, just shut up and drive,' I said.

And he did, mostly. Two hours past Leeds he grunted he was hungry and pulled into some services. When he went for a piss I took one at the next urinal, and when he went to buy a sandwich I stuck to him like a shadow and bought the same thing as him. Stuffing our faces we headed back to the car. He pulled the keys from his pocket.

'Gimme those,' I said, spitting crumbs.

'You're not insured to drive it,' he said. I held out my hand and he sighed impatiently. 'Have you even passed your test?'

'Not a driving test, no. But I got a medal once for punching people in the face.'

He tossed them to me, sulkily. I hit the unlocking blipper on the fob, once for the driver's door, a second time for mine. 'Just in case you were planning to drive off without me,' I said. When I saw him clench his jaw, and the muscles flexing in his lovely sculpted cheeks, I knew that was exactly what he'd been planning. I clambered in, and he folded his long limbs into the driver's seat, and I passed the keys back to him. He snatched them from me and started the engine.

It was nine in the evening by the time we hit the North Circular, and coming up to ten when we crossed Battersea Bridge heading towards Clapham. We'd missed the worst of the traffic; the roads were quiet, but the pavements outside pubs were crowded with men in shirtsleeves and women in skimpy dresses, clutching drinks, hooting and sniggering in the hot night. Patrick seemed to know exactly where he was going – I didn't see him check any road signs or look at a map on his phone – and when he stopped in a shopping street, shifted into reverse and slipped neatly backwards into a parking spot it took me by surprise. He pulled on the handbrake, switched off the engine and sighed as some of the tension of the long drive subsided.

'Where?' I said.

He'd taken his shades off two hours ago when dusk fell, but he was still avoiding my eye. He nodded at a row of shops up ahead. 'The electricals store at the end,' he said. 'The flat upstairs.'

'You took her there?'

'She called me, told me she'd been staying in a safe house, but that the cops had called off the operation and told her to go back to York. Asked me if I knew a place she could crash in London.'

'And you called the Turk?'

'He told me to take her here. I didn't know what he— He promised me she wouldn't be hurt, it was only going to be for a day or two—'

'Yeah, yeah, you said. How many guys did you see? When you delivered her?'

He shrugged in clueless exasperation.

'OK, how many rooms are up there?'

'I didn't go in,' he said. 'Look, this is insane, why don't you just do what he says, do this fucking job, whatever it is? If Zoe gets hurt, it'll be your fault, not mine—'

His words were abruptly cut off, because I'd grabbed him by the throat. I could feel the blood pulsing through his carotid artery, urgent and pressured, and the air rattling through his windpipe as he struggled to breathe and fumbled at my fingers.

'Sit still and shut up,' I said. 'I'm going to let go in a minute, and then I'm going to get out of this car. And you're going to drive straight back to York, and you're not going to call anyone. You're not going to tell anyone I'm here or that I know about this flat. If you do, and the Turk's people catch me, I'm going to say you brought me here because you were worried about Zoe. And they'll cut your face off and feed it to you, and God knows what else, because they don't need you any more, and that's the sort of thing they do to anyone who pisses them off. Do you understand?'

With my thumb digging into his larynx, all Patrick could manage was a tiny flick of his head. It was enough. I let him go and he clutched at his throat, gasping, and trying to curse, but no words came out. I heaved open my door, climbed out, slammed it and walked away. Behind me I heard the Mini's engine fire up and roar as Patrick cranked the steering wheel, pulled out of the parking space into a tight U-turn and roared off into the night, heading north.

I'd forgotten about him already; I was surveying the flat where Zoe was being held prisoner, the shop below it, the other shops in that block and the flats above them. I strode down the street, trying to look as if I was headed somewhere, trying not to make my reconnoitre too obvious. As I passed on the far side of the road I raised my hand to scratch my forehead, to hide my profile in case anyone was watching from the flat. A hairdresser's nearly opposite had a deep unlit doorway piled with litter; they'd gone out of business months ago, by the look of it, so there was no light from inside to silhouette me. I stepped into the doorway, pushing myself back into the shadows, and took a good look.

The Turk's place was on a corner where a smaller road joined the main shopping precinct; the junction was a mini-roundabout. The flat took up the top two floors of a three-storey building, and its lower windows were nine or ten metres above the level of the street. To the front, facing the main drag, were two windows on each floor; round the corner, three more on each floor, plus small frosted panes that must have been bathrooms. A big flat, then, five or six bedrooms at least. Were they all occupied? I knew Zoe could be a handful, but surely she didn't need six guards, especially when she was lashed to a bed?

Unless this flat was a lodging-house for some of the Turk's heavies, and they had bunged Zoe in one room there rather than find a new place just for the purpose of holding her ... That made depressingly good sense.

The electrical goods shop on the ground floor was a small independent, not part of a chain; its windows were piled high with assorted toasters, microwaves and hoovers, and even the odd laptop and music player. It was probably struggling – didn't everyone buy that sort of stuff online these days? – but the owners weren't going down without a fight. The place was neat, secure, and well-maintained. The double gates onto the side street were freshly painted, massive and solid, set into a brick wall. No weakness there. The door to the stairs up to the flat opened onto the main street, and it too was solid and forbidding. One way in, one way out, unless I climbed onto the roof and squeezed down the chimney. Absurd as the idea was, I checked out the roofline. The building didn't even *have* a chimney.

I was bone-tired, I suddenly realized, and ravenous. It had been hours since that service station sandwich. I needed to eat and I needed to rest and I needed to think. Stepping quickly out of the shop doorway I looked up and down the street. There was a greasy spoon about five doors down, warm yellow light spilling onto the pavement.

I scurried up to it and shoved at the door, but it was locked. I didn't have to decode the red notice hanging behind the glass from a plastic suction hook to know it said CLOSED. Of course the café was closed, at this time on a Sunday. All the same it looked so warm and inviting the sight of it made my stomach rumble and my bones ache. The plastic tables had been wiped clean and were neatly laid ready for Monday morning, with pots holding packets of sugar, and salt in old-fashioned glass shakers, and squeezy plastic tomatoes filled with catering ketchup. It would probably open at six and immediately fill up with builders having huge fried breakfasts, reading the papers, exchanging dirty jokes and calling their clients to say they were stuck in traffic and would be there in twenty minutes, half an hour tops.

I glanced over my shoulder; the café offered a perfect vantage point to observe the flat. I'd come back first thing, settle in with a cup of tea, and I'd watch, and I'd think of something. I had to.

Eighteen hours later I still hadn't.

I hadn't gone home to West London; maybe it wouldn't have made any difference, but I couldn't leave Zoe in that place and slope off home to sleep in my own bed. If she *was* still in that place, and hadn't been moved . . . I pushed that thought away.

The night, like every night for the last month or so,

181

was warm and dry with barely a breeze to dispel the dusty, stagnant air. I wandered the local streets until I found a park. The gates were closed and locked, but it wasn't hard to scale the fence, and I went hunting for a bench to sleep on. The dark grass glittered with leftovers from the day's boozy picnics – crisp packets, doughnut boxes, and empty alcopop and cider bottles glinting in the hot moonlight. I caught a scuffle nearby, low down by the bushes, and in the blue shadows made out two foxes fighting over the carcass of a roast chicken. One panicked at my presence and ran, and the other glanced at me in contempt before picking up his trophy in his jaws and vanishing into the undergrowth.

I sat down on the first bench I came to, folded my arms, crossed my legs, bowed my head and tried to doze, but before very long I started to get shooting pains in my neck. I tried lying down instead, along the length of the bench. My thin clothes did little to blunt the hard edges of the slats, and I wished I had a blanket – even in that muggy heat, it was hard to sleep properly without the sense of something covering me – but from sheer exhaustion and willpower I managed to doze through the night and even miss the dawn.

I heard rather than saw the park workers un-locking the gates; if any of them saw me they ignored me. They probably hoped I'd wake up by myself and wander off, and that I wasn't another of those punters who break into parks at night just to top themselves – finding a dead body can't be the best start to anyone's day. I was stiff, even a little cold, but I spent a few minutes stretching, then jogged round the park twice to warm myself up and loosen my joints and tendons. I tried not to work up a sweat; I planned to spend all day in these clothes, and I didn't want to catch a chill from the damp of my own perspiration, or stink out that café.

It was already open by the time I got back to the shopping precinct, and two red-faced and fleshy women in butcher's aprons were hard at work cutting rolls and setting out mugs, while a chef in greasy whites clattered around in the kitchen beyond. I ordered a bacon sandwich and a cup of tea and made my way to a table by the front window. Some really early bird had already been and gone, leaving a smear of fried egg and a discarded tabloid on the table top. The newspaper was a good prop; I could hold it up and pretend to read while I observed the flat across the road, and it would make the staff less likely to wonder what the hell I was up to.

As it turned out, the morning rush was so frantic the waitresses had no time to wonder, and by ten, when the rush had died down, the place was so quiet they didn't seem to care why I was there or how long I was going to hog the table, provided I bought a cup of tea every hour or so. Maybe it would have been different if I'd been taking notes – that might have looked really dodgy – but I wasn't going to bother with that; my handwriting is so bad even I can't read it, so as usual I relied on my memory instead.

In the course of that morning five heavies I'd never seen before, plus one I had, came in and out of that street door, one at a time or in pairs, dropped off at the kerb and picked up again by two more guys driving unremarkable but powerful Merc saloons.

The one heavy I recognized was Dean; the others who came and went I nicknamed so I could keep track more easily: Swarthy was skinny and dark, with stubble so thick and coarse you could strike a match off his chin; Roly-Poly was as beefy as a rugby player, with hairy hands and an open-necked patterned shirt that strained to hold in his big belly; Blondie was barely twenty – nearly albino, with colourless skin, thinning blond hair and invisible eyebrows. And Popeye, and Blue Shoes . . . Two of them wore suits, three of them jeans and blazers, and Dean wore a leather bomber jacket that had seen better days, with spotless stone-coloured chinos.

Although he swaggered about like he was in charge, from the body language of the others it looked very much like Dean was an apprentice. For one thing, all the Turkish guys – as far as I could see – were armed. Four of them had a bulge under their left armpit and Blue Shoes a similar bulge under his right – he must be a southpaw . . . but although Dean had been packing in Trafalgar Square, he didn't seem to be now. Clearly he hadn't distinguished himself, if they'd taken his gun away.

I calculated I could take any of them one to one – close up, so they'd have no time to pull a weapon – but this wasn't one of those old kung-fu movies where the villains formed an orderly queue to have a go at the hero. Yeah, I could ring the doorbell, and maybe floor whoever answered it, but then I'd have to fight my way upstairs against five men, mostly armed, who knew I was coming.

Half an hour after noon I saw the door to the flat open again. This time no one came out. Instead another Merc pulled up at the kerb – a sleek modern one with darkened windows – and a slight, smart figure emerged, crossing the pavement and disappearing inside within a second or two. *The Turk*. I had only caught a glimpse, but I was sure it was him, and the sight of Kemal's massive muscular torso emerging from the car's other side and following him in confirmed it. He carried a small briefcase, I noticed, that in his huge paw looked the size of a paperback.

Tell the Guvnor. Of course, I could call him right now, hand him the Turk on a plate. Taking on this many men would need an army, and McGovern had one – even if his had lost the last few battles. The Guvnor wouldn't hesitate to use as much violence as necessary, and plenty more besides . . .

That was the problem. Even if I told him Zoe was being held inside, the Guvnor wouldn't give a shit. He wouldn't risk any men to save her – his crew would probably firebomb the place, and stand back laughing while burning goons jumped out of the windows, screaming. Zoe, tied to the bed, wouldn't even get that far.

By the time I'd thought all that through, the street door opened again and the Turk strode briskly across the pavement back to his car, weaving through shoppers who barely registered his presence. When Kemal lumbered after him, though, passers-by stopped in their tracks and parted to make way; he radiated such menace one or two even turned their heads to avert their eyes. The Merc's doors shut again and the car moved smoothly off.

Just like that, the Guvnor's chance had been and

gone. Even if I'd called him he wouldn't have had time to rally his troops, never mind get them down here.

A cold dark cloak of despair was smothering me: my options, if I'd ever had any, were fading fast. If I called the Guvnor I'd lose Zoe. If I called the cops, they'd nick me and ignore the Turk, because right now the government needed him more than it needed me or Zoe. I was back where I'd started, except now I'd wasted a day looking for a way out.

I'd never killed anyone – not on purpose, anyway. I'd never sat down and worked it out, never considered the million ways there are to stop a human heart, never chosen one, made the preparations. How would I kill the Guvnor? He was in his fifties, yes, but he was fit and strong, and now he was alert to the threat, and he trusted nobody. I couldn't shoot him; even if I got hold of a gun, I'd never used one, and Trafalgar Square had taught me you could fill the air with flying lead and still miss your target. What about a knife? From his kitchen maybe? When I'd been in that gang with Jonah, hanging out in that derelict house near the river, he'd told me a bit about knife-fighting, about the cut to the thigh that could kill in seconds. I hadn't been paying enough attention because the thought of it had made me sick. It still did.

I couldn't do it. I couldn't kill anyone in cold

blood. Yes, McGovern had murdered plenty of innocent people himself, if you believed Amobi, but I wasn't McGovern, and I didn't want to become like him.

I was going to end up in that shredder. In fact, between the Guvnor, the Turk, the Russians and the cops, I was already in the shredder, clawing at the sheer sides, dancing on the camshafts while the toothed wheels snatched at my feet.

And after me it would be Zoe's turn.

I'd missed lunch, I realized. One of the waitresses had said something to me, and I'd picked up a menu and stared at it, but the words made no sense and I had no appetite anyway. At one point three men in vests and hi-viz trousers – street sweepers, I think – sat down to share my table and yammered away in Latvian or something for half an hour, while I watched the Turk's men buzz in and out of the apartment across the road like sleek fat hornets, clutching sandwiches and coffee, laughing among themselves, exchanging cigarettes. I didn't realize the Latvian street sweepers were gone until they wheeled their bin-trolleys past my window and went off in search of litter.

Four o'clock. New serving staff had arrived: an older, chubby bloke and a young willowy girl with clunky glasses and a faceful of piercings. I caught shards of conversation – the two shifts conferring about whether I was worth the effort of throwing out. They decided to ignore me, and I was glad; it meant I could put off the inevitable just that little bit longer.

Five o'clock. I had to do it. Somehow I had to kill the Guvnor, or Zoe would die horribly. And I would have to do it without getting caught, and without getting killed, because the Turk wouldn't bother sticking to a deal made with a dead man. He wasn't sentimental, and didn't lie awake at night fretting about his personal honour, but if I did what he asked Zoe would at least have a chance. Now I felt that familiar feeling in the pit of my stomach, the adrenalin pumping through my system. My opponent was in the ring, waiting, slapping his gloves together, limbering up.

It was growing dark outside ... already? But it wasn't night falling – thunderclouds were gathering, shifting and towering overhead, thick and purple and heavy and menacing. I heard a distant rumble, then something else in the distance – a siren? London has sirens like most towns have birdsong, but this one was growing really loud, really quickly, not in fits and starts like ambulances do as they manoeuvre round traffic and slow down for red lights. Now the siren was mingling with the squeal of car tyres and the roar of engines, and shoppers in the street were looking about, half excited, half scared, to see what the commotion was and where it was coming from.

Up the side street leading down to the mini-roundabout a shiny black hatchback swerved into view, going far too fast for this busy suburban precinct. It fishtailed along the middle of the road as if the driver didn't know which side he was supposed to be on, then accelerated towards the traffic roundabout between me and the flat, clearly not intending to give way to anyone else. An instant later I could see why – a police patrol car came screaming round the same corner in the hatchback's wake, sirens blaring, blue lights piercing in the gathering gloom. It cornered smoothly, moving at speed but under perfect control, seconds behind the black hatchback.

Mere moments had elapsed since we'd first heard the siren, but already everyone inside the café had stopped talking and was jostling at the window for a better view of a real-life car chase. For an instant I thought the driver of the black car was going to lose control and come smashing through the plate-glass window where I sat, but he cornered hard on the roundabout, nearly clipping the kerb closest to us, and I could see him hauling on the wheel the same way Patrick had when he'd driven away the night before. He threw the screaming hatchback into a U-turn and gunned it back the way he'd come, hoping to speed straight past the police pursuers, but the cop car veered across its path instead, and kept coming when the hatchback tried to swerve round it. The two vehicles collided with a metallic bang and an explosion of shattered headlamps, the hatchback skewing and rocking to the left, the cop car jumping up in the air momentarily before slamming down onto its wheels again. There was a vast collective gasp from everyone watching, a moment of stunned silence, and then the shouting and yelling began, and passers-by came running to help.

The thin afternoon traffic had already seized up and car horns were blowing. A crowd of people – of all races and all ages – clustered around both cars, checking to see if any of the occupants had been injured. The doors of the hatchback were pulled open and I saw two people checking out the driver, a black guy, who from his bloodied mouth and nose seemed to have bounced his face off the steering wheel at the moment of impact. His three passengers, also black, hadn't fared much better, judging by the way they were staggering groggily out of their wrecked hatchback. It clearly had no airbags, but the cop car did, and the coppers had to struggle past the huge white sagging cushions before they could climb out of their vehicle.

The coppers were young and lean and hard – one a shaven-headed white guy, the other a wiry Asian – and they seemed to expect the crowd to stand back while they arrested the four suspects. But that wasn't happening; instead the crowd blocked their way – darting fingers at the coppers' faces and shouting angry defiance. From inside the café I couldn't hear what was said, but it looked like the cops were being accused of risking people's lives with a high-speed pursuit in a shopping precinct, of racism, and harassment and just being there. The coppers had already pulled handcuffs from their belts, and it looked like they intended to make their arrests regardless of what the crowd thought, but sensing the crowd's involvement might offer them a chance to escape, their suspects refused to be arrested, snatching their wrists away from the cuffs and joining in the shouting and protests.

I felt another rumble resonate in my chest, but was that the thunderstorm approaching or something else? Even from inside the café I could sense the shift in the mood of the crowd as the confrontation built up, smell something in the air – an intangible toxic cloud of anger and frustration and indignation that was seeping into the pores of everyone watching, like nerve gas. The hairs rose on the back of my neck. I'd felt this before somewhere, years ago . . . More passers-by, who up until that point had been watching the confrontation from the pavement, muttering disgust and dissent, started drifting closer – not only young black men like the guys in the hatchback, but Asians and white guys and even a few women, all young and overheated and pissed off, seizing the moment and the safety offered by numbers to have a go at authority figures in uniform.

I jostled my way past through the café's customers and staff, who by now were lined up at the window watching in a haze of fear and uncertainty, and hauled open the café door. Stepping outside I slammed into hot wet air and tension as solid as a concrete wall, and with every second the furious buzz seemed to be drawing in yet more indignant twitching teenagers from streets away. The men the coppers had been trying to detain had vanished, absorbed by the crowd, and now at last the coppers saw that they were way out of their depth. With barely a glance at each other they started to back off, tucking their handcuffs back into the pouches on their belts and heading back towards their patrol car – not so fast that it looked like they were panicking, but not too slowly either.

Wrenching open the doors they clambered back in, beating down the deflated airbags, clearly praying their vehicle hadn't been too badly damaged by the collision to get them out of there. But before they could even start the engine the furious crowd had ringed them in, open palms and clenched fists slamming onto the bodywork. The angry voices were rising to shrieks, demanding apologies or explanations, or simply spouting threats and abuse. The coppers fired up their siren and flashing blue lights, hoping to drive the crowd back with sheer ear-piercing racket and dazzle, but that seemed to aggravate the protestors even more.

From the fringes of the crowd I caught movement upstairs at the window of the Turk's apartment: a net curtain twitched and was pulled aside. I couldn't make out which of the Turk's men was watching, but suddenly I saw a possibility – a gamble on odds so long it seemed insane. But they were better odds than any I'd faced so far. The blasts of the cop car siren were making my eardrums rattle, and beyond its whooping and the angry shouts of the crowd I could hear more sirens in the distance, shifting and phasing. Police reinforcements were weaving their way through the stalled traffic and the clogged-up streets to back up their colleagues. It was now or never.

I looked around for something to use and saw nothing except cemented-down signposts and plastic litter bins bolted to the pavement. But stranded in the traffic a few cars back from the junction stood a skip truck, its horn blaring, its driver with his head out the window of his cab, banging on his door and shouting insults and complaints at anyone within range, demanding they shift their cars and get out of his bloody road. Turning away from the angry crowd at the junction I ran down past his truck on his blind side to check out the contents of the skip he was transporting, thinking, Please let it not be empty, please let it not be full of polystyrene blocks and flattened cardboard. I hooked one hand onto one of the massive pneumatic arms that hauled the loads on and off, planted a foot on the truck bed and heaved myself up, grabbing the lip of the skip to look in.

It was loaded with hardcore rubble and scrapped scaffolding poles, piled so high the end of one pole nearly poked me in the face. I grabbed that one, twisted it and pulled. It didn't budge. I chose a second, stubbier pole and tried again, heaving at it, and this time it shuddered and squealed in my fist, sliding out from under shattered bricks and lumps of concrete until it swung free and heavy in my hand. It was a steel tube about a metre long and twice the weight of a baseball bat, and it was just what I needed.

By the time I'd jumped down and started back for the junction other bystanders had already started to scurry down the street, away from the shrieking knot of chaos and the whooping police vehicle – pensioners hobbling along as fast as they could, mums with kids overtaking them in pushchairs, all of them clearly afraid that everything might get a lot worse at any second. I was hoping it would; in fact, I was planning to make sure it did.

I kept the scaffolding pole low, dangling it loosely from my hand as I pushed through the fringes of the crowd. By now the coppers were reversing, slowly and steadily, straight towards me, trying not to run anyone over, but all the same forcing the protestors behind them to step aside. I stepped aside too, took a firm grip with both hands on the scaffolding pole, and slammed it into the cop car's rear windscreen.

It imploded instantly, sending glass showering in silver crumbs into the car. I saw the coppers inside duck instinctively and the car leap on its springs as the driver stamped on the brake, and the crowd roared around me, and I felt the massed adrenalin surge and catch flame. In that instant the crowd became a mob, and their shouts became a cacophony – the massed screeching of a demon with a thousand heads that had scented human blood.

The cop car's engine roared, and it jolted forwards in a hard turn, this time knocking two people off their feet, but not stopping. I glimpsed the officer in the passenger seat screaming into his radio, head sunk into his shoulders and body hunched forward as from nowhere a brittle rain of bottles came down: milk bottles, beer bottles, water bottles – some smashing, some bouncing off the roof and bonnet. Then a massive lump of concrete – from the skip truck? – shattered the patrol car's light bar, and soon rocks and bricks were thundering on the bodywork and bouncing off into the crowd, sending us scattering. As the mob fell back the cop driving saw his chance, spun the wheel and gunned the engine.

At that instant beside me a stocky kid my age with a faceful of acne grabbed one fallen rock and pulled his hand back to hurl it through the crumbling ring of glass that had been the rear windscreen, right at the back of the Asian copper's head. In the chaos no one saw me knock the rock from his hand and kick his feet out from under him. It was the least I could do – these plods weren't the target, as far as I was concerned.

That reek I'd smelled earlier – of frustration and resentment and sheer mindless fury – I remembered it now. It was the stink of a rabid, unpredictable monster that lurked under the city pavements, and now I'd set it free.

Riot.

A few years back, while the world prepared to visit London for the Olympics, buses had burned in the streets, shattered glass had piled up on the pavements like drifting snow, and looters – their attacks coordinated on smartphones – had carried their booty away in vans. Hordes of hoodied teenagers with scarves for masks had run amok, chucking rocks at anything that moved and setting fire to anything that didn't. I remembered all of it, because I'd been there. Back then the cops, bewildered and outnumbered, had fled, sealing off the perimeters and waiting for the fury to burn itself out.

These cops were doing the same. The patrol car had pierced the gap in the crowd and was speeding away in the same direction it had come, trailing a battered rear bumper, its shattered lights flashing white and its siren blaring – only to very nearly collide head-on with a police van speeding round the same corner in the other direction, half full of blue uniforms but utterly unprepared for the frenzy that greeted them.

Both vehicles screeched and swerved to a halt, rocking on their springs for a few seconds, but in those seconds the mob roared and rallied and raced up the road towards the vehicles, hurling more bottles and rocks and bricks that showered down in a lethal hail, crazing two of the van's side windows before the crew inside even had a chance to drop their wire-mesh windscreen protector. The fleeing patrol car swung past the van and sped away round the corner; the driver of the minibus slammed his vehicle into reverse gear and screeched backwards after them, away from the crowd and clear of the fly-ing rocks, round the corner and out of sight, knocking the wing mirrors off two parked cars in his haste.

Now the police had been vanquished the mob surged and spun and seemed to hang motionless, the way I'd seen a tornado pause in one of those videos taken by kamikaze stormchasers ... and I remem-bered that when the vortex appears to be standing still, that means it's headed right for you.

This one exploded all around me.

SEVEN

Abruptly rain started coming down in hot torrents, soaking everyone, and to the crowd it was as refreshing and exhilarating as sprinklers going off at a rave. Windows shattered all along the street – the first targets were the shops selling booze – and the air quickly filled with shrieking sirens and clattering bells of burglar alarms, mingling with screaming and shouting and mad laughter and the roar of car engines as drivers trapped in the middle of the maelstrom tried to pull out of the stalled lines of traffic and somehow get out of there. One or two succeeded, bumping over traffic islands and even up along the pavement in their haste, while other drivers simply abandoned their cars in the street and ran.

The mob – blokes of any and every race, most of them in their twenties, plus a scattering of women, plus scores of kids barely into their teens – swirled and clustered and scattered again, seeking targets, egging each other on, swarming over the abandoned cars, dancing on their roofs, raking the interiors for anything nickable – sat nav units, sunglasses, CD players – only to dump their loot in the street and run on to their next target. One big shiny four-by-four, brand-new by the looks of it, the looters didn't even bother to ransack – they just ripped off its wipers, snapped and smashed its wing mirrors and crazed its windows and hacked at its bodywork with rocks and bricks and broken bottles and anything hard that came to hand. It was one of those huge ostentatious expensive cars whose only purpose in London was to inspire envy, and it was working all too well on this crowd.

The skip truck too had been abandoned, with both its doors hanging open, but now black smoke was drifting from the cab, and I could see an orange flicker from the footwell refracted in its windows. Someone had set it on fire. Other rioters were clearing its load of poles and rocks to use as ammunition. All of them were soaked and none of them gave a damn; even the fire seemed to blaze away more brightly in the rain.

I held back, fighting down the feelings of sickness

at the chaos I'd unleashed, trying instead to focus on how much time I had before the cops tooled up with riot gear and returned in force to drive us off the street. Last time it had taken them days; this time they might well decide to come back hard and fast, to snuff the riot out before it spread.

I had an hour maybe, at most.

All along the street shopkeepers were abandoning their premises, the braver ones risking the wrath of the rioters to haul down steel shutters in front of their windows; others – like the staff of the café I'd been sitting in earlier – merely bolting their doors, switching off all their lights, and retreating into the gloom at the back of their premises, presumably to escape through the service exits.

I was counting on the Turk's crew to panic too. Nothing could have prepared them for being stranded in a sea of burning vehicles and looted shops and flying rocks, and there was only so much they could find out by peering through their net curtains. Keeping the pole in my hand low and inconspicuous I ran across the street, treading carefully among the lumps of rubble the size of my fist that already dotted the tarmac, and stationed myself in the doorway next to the one leading up to the Turk's apartment. Pressing myself back against the door I waited.

I'd barely got into position when the door next to me rattled – at least two locks by the sound of it, heavy ones – and opened, and Dean emerged, looking around in amazement as if he'd stepped into a nightmare. I waited a beat to see who else came out, but he reached back and pulled the door shut behind him. *Damn*.

He was wearing an anorak with a hood pulled up against the rain. It restricted his peripheral vision, so although he had turned in my direction he still hadn't seen me before I stepped forward and drove the end of the pole hard into his belly. He doubled over with a gasping yell and I swung the pole up and over and down, hard on the back of his head – not hard enough to kill him, but enough to lay him out.

He dropped in a soggy heap of arms and legs, and in the chaos and the racket and the driving rain and the drifting acrid smoke nobody noticed us and nobody came to help, even when I bent over and started going through his pockets. A smartphone, a bunch of keys, a wallet thick with twenties, no gun. Those had to be the keys for that front door ... but how much good would that do me? There were still five men inside, whose nerves would by now be strung as taut as piano wire, with their eyes locked on the front door while they waited for Dean to report back.

When I realized what I had to do next I cursed, wishing I'd thought of it earlier. It's hard to lift a full-grown man who's out cold and lying slumped on top of his own folded legs. Setting the pole aside I stooped, grabbed Dean by his armpits and heaved, straightening my legs so they'd take the load instead of my back. More teenagers in hoodies, caps and scarves raced past me to join the riot, cackling and yelling, and jostled me so hard I nearly dropped him. But I gritted my teeth and kept going, and Dean slowly unfolded, leaving a shoe behind as I hauled him down the kerb and out into the road, among the abandoned cars.

When I was far enough out to be seen from the Turk's apartment, I let him fall, face down onto the soaked tarmac. I wasn't worried about being recognized by the crew upstairs; only Dean knew me, and I doubted he'd given them my description. In fact, I hoped one of them would see me – that was kind of the point – but I didn't glance up to check.

I simply stood back, took a deep breath, and thought about how Dean had helped to wreck my life and hurt my friends, and about Zoe tied to that bed, writhing, while he and his greasy-fingered friends felt her up, and raw fury flared up inside me. I raised my foot and brought it down hard, once, twice, three times on Dean's right kneecap, driving it down with all my weight and strength until I felt the joint crunch and the ligaments tear under my foot. Then I stood back. Dean would walk again without a stick, some-day. Not soon. I turned and ran up the road, a mugger done with his victim.

Come and get him.

Further along someone had rammed the front window of a phone shop with a stolen van, stoving in the steel grid shutter and ripping through the laminated glass beyond. The shelves inside had already been stripped, the locked cupboards forced open and emptied, and now the last of the looters were squeezing out under the wrecked grille, wading through glass fragments and discarded dummy handsets. I veered towards the mêlée as if to join in, then doubled back along the pavement, staying tight against the shopfronts so that no one watching from the flat would see me return.

I'd seen this tactic in a war movie: a German sniper injured an Allied soldier, leaving him lying out in the open yelling for help, waiting for his colleagues to go to his rescue so he could pick them off. It was sick and sadistic, but in the movie at least it worked.

Dean was lying crippled and unconscious in the street – it would take at least two of the Turk's crew to drag him back inside. I retrieved the scaffolding pole from where I'd hidden it, took up my former position next to the apartment entrance, and waited.

And waited. The rain was easing off; the riot was intensifying.

No one came out. They must have seen him lying there, but it looked like the Turk wasn't paying his men enough to risk their lives on a rescue, and they didn't care enough about Dean to do it for nothing. They might have tried to dial 999, but that wouldn't have done them much good – all the emergency phone lines would be jammed by now, and even if they got through to the ambulance service the paramedics would take their time coming. In a riot nobody is safe and nothing is sacred. Paramedics, firefighters, news crews, all of them risked being beaten and robbed and pelted with bricks. The mob was a rabid animal, unpredictable and merciless.

Two more guys jogging towards the riot stopped by Dean and stooped over him. One was twenty-something, the other a teenager, both mixed-race, one with big Afro hair, the other with dreadlocks. I half expected them to rifle Dean's pockets and lift his wallet and phone; instead, the dreadlocked one pressed a finger to Dean's neck and said something to his mate, who turned and ran back the way they'd both come. What the hell were they up to? I wasn't going to have to rescue Dean from them, was I?

Only when the younger guy reappeared, dragging a door that had been ripped off its hinges, did I grasp what they were planning, and all I could do was stand and watch. I knew mobs could be unpredictable, but ... As all around us more windows shattered and more wrecked cars burst aflame and more shops got looted – in one spot the pavement was strewn with musty old blouses and wrinkled shoes from a charity shop – these two rolled the unconscious Dean onto the splintered door, took a firm grip of each end, counted to three, lifted, and carried him off the way they had come, vanishing into the pall of greasy black smoke that billowed from the burning skip truck. I was stuffed, and Zoe was stuffed, thanks to those two noble, compassionate, interfering assholes. *Now what?*

A huge fat Indian guy in a sodden singlet and baggy tracksuit trousers suddenly jogged past me, hefting a fire extinguisher. I thought it might be another vigilante until he stopped in front of the electrical shop, planted his feet wide, pulled the extinguisher back and slammed it into the window. The first time it bounced off; the second time the plate glass shattered with an ear-splitting crash, sending razor-sharp shards falling like guillotine blades. Dropping his extinguisher the fat Indian guy danced back, dodging the fragments – the idiot was wearing flip-flops – and before he even had time to regain his balance the looters were stampeding past him, grabbing everything vaguely valuable in sight – toasters, microwaves, cordless vacuum cleaners – whooping and shrieking in excitement like contestants on some TV gameshow where you got to keep anything you could carry.

And I piled right in there amongst them.

I pushed past two girls fighting over a hairdryer – one of them was the face-pierced waitress from the café up the road – headed past the counter to the door leading to the back room, and tried the handle. Locked. I stepped back, preparing to kick it in, praying the shop owners weren't hiding in there, and wouldn't have a go at the looters if they were. I'd try to protect them if I had to, but even wielding a steel pole I would be as much use against a mob as a tinfoil hat.

The door flew open with one kick, and the room beyond was empty. Half a dozen looters followed me in, only to curse in disappointment; there was nothing in the little back office but a kettle, some mugs and a desk where an old video camera was lying in bits, awaiting repair. The rioters retreated in disgust – the rest of the shop had been stripped bare by now – but I headed for the rear exit.

The flat upstairs had two floors, which meant by law it had to have a fire escape, and that fire escape probably led down into the back yard. The door that led to the yard outside was huge and solid, reinforced with steel bars, but it had been designed to stop robbers getting in, not rioters getting out, and when I turned its two heavy latches and pushed, it swung open so readily I nearly fell face-first out into the back yard.

I'd been right – a black metal staircase zigzagged up the back of the building to a balcony that ran along the rear of the first floor. I wished some of the rioters had come with me – it would have helped to intimidate the crew upstairs – but the mob wouldn't bother with private homes, especially when there were still plenty of shops to pillage. I took the stairs as quietly as I could; if I couldn't bring a crowd along, better to let the guys inside think all the danger was still out front.

The apartment's back door was a flimsy plywood

number with a frosted-glass window and a tarnished silver handle. It opened inwards, so it would be easier to kick in, especially as it had just the one lock – the one built into the handle. It might be bolted on the inside . . . but then again, if there was normally no access to this door, would anyone bother? Sad grey net curtains drooped behind every window along the balcony, and that was a problem. The storm clouds were soaking up the sunlight but it was still plenty bright enough out here for me to be easily seen from inside, while the men inside the flat remained invisible. The windows were double-glazed, with modern PVC frames – hard to jemmy and nigh-impossible to break. It would have to be the door. Should I stand back and kick it? No – stealth first. Find out if it's even locked . . .

I moved quickly, stepping past the door's rippled windowpane and flattening myself against the red-brick wall beside it. The gutter overhead was overflowing, sending a steady trickle of muddy rain-water onto my head. That was bad – the water had been rattling loudly onto the steel balcony, and now it was splashing quietly, soaking into my hair. Anyone listening closely would have heard the change. I reached out, grasped the aluminium handle and turned it slowly.

The gunshot wasn't loud but it made me jump all the same. It was a short, muffled crack that punched a hole through the woodwork and sent a shower of splinters flying outwards. I snatched my hand back and froze; I'd been rumbled. I waited an instant for a second shot, or for someone to open the door, but heard nothing, and I made a dash for it, my feet a blur on the stairs as I fled. If the guys inside were using live rounds, that meant they were as strung out as I'd hoped they'd be. It also meant that unless that nearby charity shop stocked second-hand Kevlar vests, I wasn't getting into that flat alive.

I'd wedged open the rear door of the shop downstairs with a chair, and now the smoke from the cars and trucks burning in the street outside seemed to be blowing right through and billowing out in my face. The ceiling smoke alarms inside were screeching away, but no one was listening.

When I got inside I realized I was mistaken – the smoke wasn't blowing in from outside, it was coming from a pile of cardboard boxes – some still full of unused appliances – heaped in the middle of the shop and set alight. Already wild orange flames were licking the ceiling, warping the tiles, and the laminate on the counter was blistering in the heat. I looked around for the fire extinguisher the Indian guy had used to smash the window, but it looked like he'd taken it with him when he headed for the next shop.

Shit. My gamble had failed, horribly. I'd thought the mob might smash the place up – it made no sense to torch it. But then I should have known that nothing rioters do makes any sense. They don't set fire to shops and cars as a protest or as a tactic to block the streets – they do it for the fun of watching things burn. The five armed men upstairs were going to panic and clear out, and either they'd bring Zoe with them – meaning I'd have to take on all five at once – or they'd leave her behind, tied to the bed. It was one thing to escape from a burning building – I'd managed that a few weeks ago – it was another to get into one and get out again.

They weren't going out the back, I was sure – the yard gates were still locked. That meant they'd come out the front door, and they'd do it quick, before the stairs caught fire. I skirted the bonfire, feeling the heat from the flames scorch my skin and singe the hair on my arms, and climbed out through the shattered window. There was a knot of rioters across the street, attacking a jeweller's shop that had somehow resisted every attack so far, thanks to heavy steel shutters and pavement bollards designed to foil ram-raiders. I ran across to mingle with them, planning to hide in plain sight so the Turk's men wouldn't spot me the moment they emerged.

The door to the apartment opened, and the guys I'd nicknamed Popeye and Blue Shoes appeared. Flames were starting to gush from the ground-floor shop, lapping at the windows of the flat above, veiling the facade in black choking clouds. Grey smoke billowed out the door that led up to the flat – it looked like the stairs were already burning. The two men hung around the doorway, glancing up and down the street as if waiting; and when I followed their look I saw what they'd been waiting for.

The Merc with the tinted windows was back, cruising through the chaos, weaving among the stalled and burning traffic as coolly as a battle tank. It pulled up in the street between the mob and the apartment, and the rear passenger door opened, and Kemal got out. He beckoned to the men at the apartment door, who turned and yelled up the stairs. They were evacuating Zoe, and I had only seconds to stop them.

'Cops!' I yelled. 'Cops!' The mob around me ducked as if they'd been shot at, and looked around in every direction. At any second, I knew, they might panic and scatter like birds, and I had no way of stopping that – all I could do was wade in and hope they'd follow. I dashed out into the road, swung the pole and slammed it into the tinted windscreen of the Merc. It bounced clean off – I hadn't even chipped the glass. Kemal saw me, and his gaze narrowed in fury, and from the corner of my eye I saw the crowd around me watch, and tense, and I felt their collective mood seething and swirling like volatile chemicals mixing in a tank. 'They're undercover,' I yelled. 'They got cameras!'

Kemal lumbered round the car towards me, and I braced myself and hefted the scaffolding pole. It wasn't the cocky, macho Dean I was facing now: Kemal was one hundred and twenty kilos of cold flint, with fists like sledgehammers, and he was relentless.

He was halfway round the car when there was a single *crack* and everyone ducked. I glanced towards the flat's doorway, and saw Blue Shoes with a revolver in his hand. He had fired a shot – in the air, or at me, who knows? – to drive the crowd back, and that was the catalyst. The crowd didn't disperse, they boiled over. A hail of projectiles came flying down on the two guys at the apartment door, and a few were hurled at Kemal himself. He was still behind the Merc when a brick slammed into the side of his face, splitting the skin, and he barely had time to turn before two hoodies were onto him, hacking away with the crowbars they'd been using on the jeweller's shop.

Kemal grabbed one attacker's arm, twisted and snapped it like a twig. The injured guy screamed and fell to his knees, but two more rioters took his place, one grasping a broken bottle, the other a chain, and Kemal flinched as the first guy's crowbar bit into his scalp, and in that instant the broken bottle was stabbed into his neck. In another instant the crowd was all over him like jackals crowding on a lion, ripping, tearing, yowling – was it them screaming, or Kemal? – and as he slowly sank to his knees they rained down kicks and punches and broken bricks. Vomit rose in my throat – the mob attacking Kemal seemed something less than human, as if I'd conjured up serpents from the hottest depths of hell. But it was too late to stop them, even if I'd wanted to.

The doorway to the flat was now empty and dark, and the smoke pouring out of it was lit from within by fire – Blue Shoes and Popeye had vanished. Up the street furious rioters were racing, pursuing someone, yelling threats and curses – was that where the two men had gone? The Merc's engine roared and it jolted into gear, ready to reverse, but the crowd behind the car was still thrashing and stamping on Kemal's slumped body, and the door Kemal had left open was still gaping wide. Someone in the rear seat reached out to pull the door shut, only to be grabbed by the arm by a rioter who tried to drag the passenger out into the street.

Leaping onto the Merc's bonnet I scuttled across and jumped down on the driver's side. Whoever was in the back could wait – I didn't want this car going anywhere. I rammed the end of the scaffolding pole against the driver's window, near the frame where it was weakest. The glass crazed into a mosaic, and the next swing of my pole punched a hole clean through it and connected with the driver's head. He recoiled, but he couldn't escape – he was strapped in – and when I followed through with a fist into the side of his face he sagged and fell forwards over the wheel like a crash-test dummy.

A sudden deafening bang, and my face was sprayed with fragments, scorching my eyes and sending me reeling backwards. I ducked, my ears ringing, and tried to blink away the pain, vaguely aware that the passenger in the back had shot at me. I stumbled round the front of the car, staying low to keep the engine between me and the shooter while I tried to clear my eyes. His shot must have hit the headrest – it had stopped the bullet but blasted burning crumbs of leather and padding into my face. I heard another shot, and high-pitched screeches of pain, and the yells of the crowd redoubled, and rocks and bottles started slamming into the Merc's body-work. Forcing my eyes open I found I could see OK, though my head was ringing and my eyelids were on fire. I peered round the bonnet.

The shooter had emerged from the back seat. It was the Turk, and he held a massive chrome-plated pistol in his right hand. The guy who had tried to drag him out of the back of the car lay balled up in a foetal position on the wet tarmac, whimpering in agony – he'd been shot in the belly.

For the first time ever I saw the Turk's cat-like calm had deserted him – he had lost control and he'd lost his crew, and now he clearly feared he faced the same fate as Kemal. In his free hand he clutched a slim briefcase, the same one I'd seen earlier that day, and as rocks bounced off the roof of the Merc and past his head he held it up as a shield, looking around for the best direction to run in. Part of me wanted him to run, so I could focus on going in after Zoe, but another part of me wanted to grab that briefcase – if he was so keen to keep it, it had to be worth taking from him.

He decided to head towards the blazing skip

truck, now just an empty metal shell consumed by flame. Raising his gun, he fired two more shots into the mob, almost at random, and now the crowd yelled in panic and anger, ducked and scattered in all directions. The Turk wasn't looking in my direction, but in the two seconds it took me to reach him he could turn that gun on me.

I stood up and hurled the stump of scaffolding pole at him, using all my strength. It caught him at an angle, right between the shoulder blades, glancing off the back of his head. He staggered and fell, and the briefcase went flying – not far, but far enough for one foolhardy kid in a greasy tracksuit top with a smoke-stained bandanna round his face to dash over, grab it and run off whooping. The Turk scrambled to his feet, waving his gun, but more bottles exploded on the tarmac around him, and a massive lump of concrete missed his head by a couple of centimetres. He stood up and ran. I let him go and doubled back.

The kid in the bandanna hadn't gone far – he'd taken shelter in a shop doorway and was fumbling with the straps of the briefcase to see what was inside. Just as I reached him he'd pulled out a folder full of papers and a slim laptop computer. The folder he threw away, its pages fluttering wildly to join the rest of the garbage scattered across the street, and he was just about to check out the laptop when I yanked it out of his grasp. He spat and swore at me, unleashing a flurry of punches that sort of connected with my face and head, so badly thrown it was like being attacked by a flock of moths. I smacked him in the face with the laptop – not hard enough to damage it, but hard enough to knock him backwards through the broken window. As he went down he cracked his head on the corner of a stripped display shelf and knocked himself out cold.

The crowd had closed in on the stranded Merc, and they were piling into it the same way they had gone for the four-by-four – dancing on the roof, wrenching off the wing mirrors, ripping away the windscreen wipers like crazed baboons in a safari park, while the shot rioter's friends gathered around him and hauled him to his feet. They dragged him away, semi-conscious from pain and loss of blood, with his trainers trailing behind him along the dirty wet tarmac, leaving the driver still slumped over his wheel.

Nobody was watching me, and the kid I had mugged for the laptop was still out for the count on a bed of broken glass. I stuffed the laptop into the nearest litterbin, burying it under a heap of greasy fast food wrappers, and just at that moment four figures came tumbling out of the smoke-filled door-way, coughing and choking. One of them was Zoe, in that T-shirt dress and unlaced trainers, dragged along by Roly-Poly who kept her right arm clamped in his big hairy left hand.

They turned left, heading away from me, Swarthy taking the lead, Blondie to the rear. I raced after them. Blondie wasn't much good as a rearguard, being more concerned about where he was heading than what he was leaving: by the time he heard my foot-steps behind him and started to turn I was already on top of him. His right hand plunged into his jacket, leaving him wide open to a haymaker to the jaw, delivered square on with all my momentum behind it. The impact nearly broke my fist, but it sent him spinning on the spot and falling in a stunned heap just as Dean had done.

Swarthy – ten metres up ahead – glanced over his shoulder and bawled something to Roly-Poly, but Roly kept going, shouting something back in what I presumed was Turkish. They hurried on up the street, away from the heart of the riot, straight towards an off-street car park.

I stooped over the comatose Blondie and pulled his right arm out of his jacket; his fingers were still curled round the handle of a gleaming black pistol, not as ostentatious as the Turk's but presumably just as lethal. I grabbed it. There was no time to go back for the scaffolding pole, and against two armed men it wouldn't be much use anyway. I checked for a safety catch but couldn't see one, and I scrambled up and after Zoe.

I caught up with them just as they approached a sleek BMW saloon a few years old. Roly-Poly was fumbling in his pockets – it looked like he was searching for his keys – but Zoe was wriggling in his grasp so hard he was finding it impossible to get them out. He released her with his left and tried to grab her with his right, but she dived under his grasp. He fumbled after her and snatched the neck of her T-shirt dress, pulling her up short.

'Let her go!' I yelled. I held Blondie's pistol out in front of me, two-handed, hoping it looked as if I knew what I was doing. The three of them looked round in amazement, just for an instant, and Swarthy reached inside his jacket for his own gun. I pointed mine at him and squeezed the trigger.

The bloody thing bucked in my hand – I'd known it was going to happen but was still completely unprepared for it – and the shot went wild, pinging off the rough stone wall a metre above Swarthy – but instantly his head jolted forward. He raised a hand instinctively to his head, where the ricochet had struck, before his knees folded and he fell on his face. All the while Roly-Poly had been cursing and wrestling with Zoe. He tried to drag her back towards him, but her dress stretched and started to rip, and it gave her enough room to turn round and hurl herself at him, screeching like a rabid tigress and driving her fingernails into his face, aiming for his eyes.

Now it was Roly-Poly's turn to yell, and he pulled his head to one side and grabbed at Zoe's hands, pulling them free, and he still had both his hands full of furious, writhing, spitting girl when I caught up with him. I tossed the gun away – I didn't trust myself with it when Zoe was so close.

He was a big man and I knew a blow to the belly would likely bounce off, so I went for the face, bending his nose sideways with a right and following through with a hard left that splattered it over his face. He yelled in pain and fury, dropped Zoe and came for me, swinging wildly and trying to grab me, while I ducked and dodged and came back, landing more blows to his face, splitting his lips against his teeth, knocking his jaw sideways – but the bastard wouldn't go down. It was like one of those arcade games with an end-of-level boss that just soaks up the damage and keeps coming, and I was wishing I'd kept hold of the pistol or even the scaffolding pole when my right foot went into a pothole and I stumbled backwards.

It was only for a second but it was all the time the big man needed, and his fat right hand grabbed my shirt and held me steady while he cocked his massive left for a backhander, shrugging off my blows to his face as if I'd been swatting him with a duster.

There was a crack, and his fingers loosened – then a second crack and a third, and Roly-Poly looked puzzled and scared, and the blood flowing from his mouth and nose became a gush, and he toppled side-ways like a tree, his short bitten fingernails gouging scars in my skin even as I wrenched myself from his grip.

Zoe was standing behind him, panting, tears of anger making tracks down her soot-stained face, her ripped dress hanging off her bare shoulder, Swarthy's gun smoking in her shaking hand. Roly-Poly was lying slumped and dying, three holes in his back bubbling blood as air escaped from his punctured lungs. Zoe tossed the gun to the ground beside him and hurled herself at me so hard she nearly knocked me off my feet. I buried my face in her neck and breathed in her scent, hardly daring to believe I was holding her again. When she grabbed my hair and hauled my face to hers and kissed me I knew it was true – and that we had to hurry. I pulled away, grabbing her hand to tug her after me.

'We can take their car,' she said. 'I can drive—'

'There's something we need to pick up,' I said.

We were just in time. The skip truck had nearly burned out, and through the thinning pall of smoke I saw blue lights flashing off helmets and riot shields. The cops were massing for an assault on the mob, and the mob knew they were coming. With the shops just about stripped bare and nothing left to destroy, they were starting to disperse, running off in hooting knots of six and seven, a few of them still lugging battered cardboard boxes. One guy was pushing a supermarket trolley loaded with cigarettes and booze down the street, but like a typical supermarket trolley one of its wheels had gone wonky. It veered off at an angle towards the kerb, caught on a brick and went toppling over, spilling his booty all over the road in a soggy heap. The looter abandoned it and ran.

And that bloody kid with the bandanna was up again, rooting through the litter bin where I'd dumped the laptop. He must have seen its edge protruding from under the garbage, and now he tugged

it free and wiped the grease off its lid with the sleeve
of his grotty tracksuit top.

'Oi!' I shouted, and he ran for it. But he wasn't
much of a sprinter and I was on him in six paces. I
grabbed his greasy hair and hauled him backwards,
yowling. He swung at me with the laptop, and I
seized it with my free hand, ripped it out of his grasp
and sent him on his way with a kick.

'You thieving prick,' he spat. Then he ran for it.

And so did we.

EIGHT

The nearest Underground station had closed early, metal grilles dragged across its entrance and locked with heavy chains, either to protect the staff or to prevent more rioters turning up by tube to join the party. I bashed the cage pointlessly in frustration, and we ran on.

Night was falling properly now and the rain had stopped as abruptly as it had started, leaving the roads shining under the sodium street lights and huge filthy puddles along the gutters where the drains had been overwhelmed. News of the rioting must have spread because the streets had emptied of traffic – no buses, no lorries, and only a few cars. One of those came past us at a crawl, crammed with middle-class kids pressing their smartphones up against the windows in the hope of catching footage of an actual riot – like tourists in an urban safari park.

Zoe kept her hand in my mine and followed me wordlessly, never asking where we were going or what had happened to me. I was glad, because I had no idea where we were headed – I just wanted to put as much distance as I could between us and that havoc I'd unleashed.

But that wasn't so easy. There was a weird electricity in the air, a diffused version of the tension I'd sensed leading up to the riot. Knots of youths were gathering on every corner, wondering when it would all kick off in their area, unaware of how riots worked. It's not like a football match: nobody blows a whistle – one yob will try something on, another will take it further, a few of the more timid types will ape them, until everyone's at it and no one knows how it really started. Everyone just suddenly understands that policing only works as long as the people being policed go along with it. The line separating law and order from anarchy is in our heads; it's less substantial than the plastic tape coppers use to cordon off crime scenes.

We passed one kid with his ear glued to a mobile phone, shouting to his mates that Camden and Walthamstow and Ealing were burning, that the cops were overwhelmed and couldn't keep up. I tried not to think about how much of that was my fault, how many businesses were being destroyed, how many innocent people were being hurt, just so I could save one person – Zoe. And when I thought about it like that, I knew I'd do it all over again if I had to.

Zoe glanced behind her, and abruptly changed direction, dashing out into the road with her hand still clamped in mine. She tugged me backwards so hard I nearly dropped the Turk's laptop before I turned to see what she was up to.

A lone black taxi was heading our way, its yellow light gleaming in the dusk, the rattle of its diesel engine reassuringly normal – except it was hammering along at about thirty, rather than the leisurely trundle of a driver scouting for business. Zoe had realized that as well, and she'd dashed into the road right in front of it – waving to the driver from the kerb would never have worked. The cab slowed a little, and I saw the driver think about swerving round her, but then he seemed to change his mind, and hit his brakes. There were only two of us, after all, and we looked like an ordinary couple, and besides, Zoe's dress was ripped and wet and clinging to her body, and that would have been enough to distract any London cabbie – the straight male ones, anyway. All the same this driver didn't quite halt; he slowed to a crawl and rolled down his passenger window to hear where Zoe wanted to go before he'd commit himself and unlock his doors.

'Can you take us to Richmond?'

'Which bit, love?' He was sixty-something, with a sunburned face wrinkled by too many cigarettes, and thick white hair slicked back. I could guess why he was on the streets when all other public transport had been suspended – he'd been in the cabbing business forty years, he'd seen everything, the odd riot didn't bother him. And he needed the money.

'Richmond Hill,' said Zoe, and she tugged at the passenger-door handle. The cabbie hesitated half a second, then he stopped the cab properly and jabbed a switch on his dash to release the rear door locks. His eyes kept checking his mirrors as we clambered aboard, watching for any sudden burst of activity on the street behind us, and the instant I'd slammed the cab door shut he floored the accelerator, throwing me backwards into Zoe's lap. She yelped and squirmed out of my way, giggling, as if we were running off for a dirty weekend rather than fleeing from gangsters and anarchy and slaughter.

'If you'd said Hammersmith, or Croydon,' the driver's voice came over the speaker system, 'I would have told you to sling your hook. Half the bloody city's gone up – it's worse than last time. I mean, all the people they threw in jail back then, the ones who nicked stuff and set fires everywhere, and called in all their mates on mobile phones – they're at it again! A lot of good prison did them. They should cut these people's hands off like they do in Saudi Arabia . . .'

Zoe lifted my right arm and snuggled under it, up close to me, while the driver babbled on like one of those talk-station DJs, or rather like one of the clueless guests that ring up talk-station DJs to spout half-baked opinions based on gossip they'd heard in the pub. But after all the fear and madness his patter seemed normal and reassuring, and the taxi, kicking up massive waves of spray as it sped through the empty streets, felt like a lifeboat ferrying two shipwrecked survivors to shore.

I glanced at the purple digits on the dashboard in front, jumping up by thirty pence every twenty seconds, and a worrying thought occurred to me.

'Have you got any cash?' I said to Zoe.

'Think so,' she said, and she raised her backside from the seat and fumbled underneath for a moment before producing a crumpled wad of twenties. She saw me staring at it in confusion.

'Was that in your knickers?' I said.

'I lifted it from Nico's wallet just now,' she said. 'The guy you took down with the ricochet.'

'You robbed him?' I said. 'Who taught you that trick?'

'You did,' she said.

The cab dropped us off twenty-five minutes later on the north side of Richmond Bridge, at the foot of a hill lined with huge houses. I'd heard of Richmond Hill; tax-exiled rock stars owned properties here, for the few times a year they visited the UK. The reek of money reminded me of the Guvnor's neighbourhood, but these weren't big tarty palaces with fake plaster columns – they were elegant white-painted Georgian mansions, hiding coyly behind elms and cherry trees. It was respectable, fashionable money round here, the sort that bought class and calm.

This neighbourhood seemed a world away from burning high streets and mobs with arms full of loot, and I wondered what two scruffy, exhausted fugitives like us were doing here. Zoe led the way, taking a left turn, then a right, into a narrow cobbled backstreet running parallel to the Georgian avenue. Here the houses were much smaller. A mews terrace, I realized – the stables where the big houses had kept their horses years ago, and which had long since been converted into homes for servants. Not that many servants lived there now; these were what estate agents called pieds-à-terre, cottages owned by people with business in the City and proper homes in the country. Through the tiny windows I glimpsed cosy sitting rooms with artfully placed antiques and works of art above snug little marble fireplaces. More than one cottage had a steel lattice on the inside of every window: a sight that always made me wonder why so many rich people are prepared to let their homes look like prisons. Is it worth being that wealthy, having all those exquisite possessions, if you live in constant fear of getting robbed?

At the furthest end of the terrace was a glossy black door wreathed in ivy. Like all the other cottages its three sash windows faced onto the street, one directly above the front door. In this one all the curtains were half drawn, which suggested the owners were away and thought this arrangement would fool prowlers into thinking they weren't. Zoe was fumbling under the ivy on the doorframe, looking for something. When she found it she tugged the leaves away to expose it – a small metal box screwed to the wood, with twelve silver buttons in a grid, like an entry panel.

Zoe punched in six numbers. Nothing happened.

She cursed under her breath. She punched them in again; still nothing. Then I heard her gasp 'Oh!' at her own stupidity, and she hit the button at the bottom left, marked with a star. The panel popped loose and swung open, and Zoe pulled it back fully to reveal a single silver key hanging on a hook. It was like no other key I'd seen – a long tongue of metal with a pattern of drilled dimples – but it slipped into the front lock like any other key, and Zoe pushed the door open and stepped inside.

A burglar alarm buzzed, and in the cupboard-sized porch it was deafeningly loud. Zoe marched into the living room – there was no hallway – found the alarm panel and once more punched in six numbers. The buzzing stopped.

'That's a relief,' she said. 'I thought she might have changed the combination. Do want a drink of something? There's bound to be some booze.'

'Whose house is this?' I asked, as I followed her into the living room. I was scared to sit down; like the other houses in the street, this one was crammed with antiques – here they were mostly hand-painted porcelain figurines, the sort so delicate they'd explode if you so much as brushed against them. There was a tiny little chintzy sofa and a single, compact armchair, both of them immaculate – if a little dusty – and I stood among them awkwardly, aware I was still soaking and filthy and bloodstained in places.

'My aunt,' she said. 'My mother's sister. She spends most of her time in Italy. I haven't been here in years.'

'Will she mind us being here?'

'I don't really give a toss,' said Zoe. She was checking out the tiny kitchen next door – smaller than the kitchen in my dad's house – and I saw over her shoulder that the fridge was empty and switched off.

'If you had this place, why . . . ?' I said. Then I realized I didn't want to know the answer to the question I had in mind, and dropped it.

Zoe turned to look at me. 'If I had this place, why did I call Patrick?' she said.

'Yeah,' I said.

'Because my aunt is a toxic bitch,' said Zoe. 'And I trusted Patrick.'

'I knew he was a prick,' I said. 'I should have said something.'

'I knew what you thought,' said Zoe. 'You're not very good at hiding your feelings. Actually I thought he was a prick as well . . . I just didn't know how big.'

'Are we talking about the same thing?' I said.

Zoe started checking out the cupboards, found a

few packets of flavoured instant noodles and examined the packaging to see how out of date they were.

'I knew he wanted to get into my knickers,' she said. 'I just thought it was for the usual reasons. Guys like him think they can have any girl they see ... I didn't know he was only chasing me because the Turk had told him to. That's what's really insulting.'

'I'm sure that wasn't the only reason,' I said. 'Who wouldn't want to get into your knickers?'

'You don't,' said Zoe. She tossed the packet onto the counter and turned to me. 'Ever since I shopped you to the Guvnor's people, and nearly got you killed. In fact, I don't know why I'm having a go at Patrick. I'm no better than he is.'

'You apologized,' I said. 'I got over that a long time ago.'

'Does that mean you do?'

'What?'

'Want to get into my knickers.'

'I can't be that bad at hiding my feelings, then.'

'*Carpe diem*,' said Zoe, walking over to me.

'I don't know what that means,' I said.

She coiled her arms around my neck. 'It means come and get it,' she said.

* * *

After what Zoe had been through, I thought she'd want to take things gently, and I kept meaning to stop and ask if what I was doing was OK, but she made it pretty clear she didn't want me to ask questions or slow down or stop for anything – not even when a porcelain shepherdess took a dive off the mantelpiece and shattered into a hundred razor-sharp fragments that ended up embedded in my arse. Maybe Zoe needed to wipe away the fear and degradation she'd been through – she wasn't going to be anyone's victim, and refused to behave like one – but at that moment I needed her as much as she needed me. We threw off the guilt and the torment and the terror with our clothes; we were safe together, for a little while at least, in this twee little doll's house nobody knew about. London could have burned to the ground around us and neither of us would have noticed till the roof fell in.

The antique carpet was coarser than it looked and its weave was biting into the skin of my back, mostly because Zoe was lying on top of me with her hair tickling my face. It was suffocatingly hot and stuffy in that tiny sitting room and my backside was bleeding and I was ravenous and knackered and I hadn't felt so happy in months.

'I saw you,' said Zoe. 'As soon as they dragged me out into the street. That's when I knew everything was going to be all right.'

'It nearly wasn't,' I said. 'That fat guy nearly had me.'

'You would have taken him,' said Zoe. 'Eventually.'

'Then why did you shoot him?' I said.

She grimaced at the memory, then shrugged. 'I was in a hurry,' she said.

When I laughed I realized how much my ribs ached, how much everything ached.

'How did you find me?' said Zoe.

'I asked Patrick,' I said.

'And he told you?'

'He didn't want to,' I said. 'But he got the impression I'd rip his balls off if he didn't.'

'I wish you had.'

'He would never have given me a lift down here if I had.'

'He drove you all the way from York?'

'It was fun,' I said. 'We listened to his CDs. Talked about you.'

'Piss off.'

'No, we didn't. We barely said a word the whole way down. I ended up wishing I'd taken the train.

But he dropped me off up the street from where they had you, and pointed to the door. I got out, and he drove off.'

'And left you to it?'

'I don't think he would have been much use, to be honest.'

'What would you have done, if that riot hadn't started?'

'I have no idea.'

'How did it start anyway? Did you see?'

'The police tried to arrest some black guys in a boy racer, and the crowd turned ugly, and somebody had a go at the cop car with a scaffolding pole, and after that it all went crazy.'

Zoe frowned. 'Who did?'

'Everybody did.'

'No, I mean, who took a scaffolding pole to the cop car?'

How the hell had she zeroed in on that? I wondered. I hadn't been boasting – it wasn't something I felt proud of. 'Some guy,' I said.

She sat up, her hands resting on my chest, her green eyes puzzled and her full lips parted in surprise. The sight of her was so distracting I didn't hear her question.

'Sorry?' I said.

'Was it you? Who started the riot?'

I hesitated. 'It was all I could think of,' I said.

She stared at me, as if she was too shocked to speak; then lay down across me again, her breasts pressing into my chest, and she kissed me, tenderly at first, then more urgently, and I ran my hands through her hair and rolled her over, knocking into a side table and sending another porcelain shepherdess tumbling to her doom.

An hour later we'd shared a hot bath and something to eat. The instant noodles were two years past their sell-by date and tasted like ready-salted sawdust, but we were both so hungry we didn't mind. Now wearing only a bath towel Zoe lay across the double bed – a big brass monstrosity draped in lacy white sheets that took up almost the whole main bedroom – examining the Turk's laptop.

It was one of those sleek ultra-slim numbers in brushed aluminium with no moving parts, not even a DVD drive. As soon as she opened the lid it sprang to life – well, to the log-in screen anyhow: a bland blue field with a generic silhouette for a picture and a single empty log-in box, with the caption in a curly foreign script that I took to be Turkish.

'Did you grab the power adapter?' said Zoe.

'Bollocks,' I said. 'No.'

'Never mind,' she said. 'Finding a new one shouldn't be a problem. Provided there are still some shops left tomorrow.'

'We don't even know if there's anything on it we can use.'

'I'll find out,' said Zoe. 'It's not as if I have anything else to do.'

'Does this place have Internet?' I said.

'No, but one of the neighbours will,' said Zoe. 'I'll just piggyback on their wireless.'

'So you can hack it? The laptop?'

'Anything a human being can program, another human being can hack,' said Zoe. 'In theory. Given enough time.'

'I'm not sure if we have much time,' I said. 'The Turk got away in one piece. He'll find what's left of his people soon, and they'll regroup, and he's going to want that laptop back.'

'Let's hope he does,' said Zoe. 'Because that would mean there's something on it we can bargain with.'

Later that night we unlocked the bedroom windows and hauled them open and lay naked in the draught. The rain had cooled the night air, and after months of stifling heat getting goose bumps was a novelty; besides, it gave us an excuse to cuddle up more closely. We talked and dozed and shagged and talked and dozed again; she told me a little about the bored, resentful cops who had been babysitting her in the safe house. She'd mentioned her dad to them, not so much to impress them as to make conversation, but they seemed to know the story already, and they weren't impressed. Maybe they knew the truth behind the official version: that DCI Prendergast had been on the take from the Guvnor, and when he was no further use the Guvnor had murdered him. When the call came to shut down the safe house and send Zoe back to York the cops guarding her couldn't oblige quickly enough, and ignored all her protests; less than twenty minutes later she'd found herself on the street, alone, in some Midlands city of rotting concrete. She couldn't reach me, and Patrick was only an hour or two away by car . . .

She didn't go into detail about what the Turk's men had done while they'd held her prisoner, and I didn't ask, because it didn't matter any more. But when I told her about my time at the Guvnor's place in Maida Vale and about Richard killing the nanny and going after McGovern's kids, and how I'd stolen his phone, she turned her head towards me.

'What time was that?' It was dark in the little room but I could sense her frowning.

'About three in the morning. No, four . . . the Guvnor let me go about half four.'

'Someone rang the Turk,' she said. 'He was at the flat, I heard them talk.'

'Richard, I know.'

'No . . . this was later. About seven in the morning – no, exactly seven – Nico had this stupid digital watch that used to beep the hours, and I heard it go off. The Turk had arrived really early, to talk to his guys, and someone called him, and the two of them spoke in English. The Turk didn't say much, but I think it was about how you'd killed that guy, because he looked really pissed off.'

'You mean it was someone else on the Guvnor's crew?'

'It must have been. Who else knew that Richard was dead? But I heard a bit of what this other guy said – he made it sound like Richard had been his best friend; it was weird.'

'Shit . . .' I stared upwards into the darkness. The wind swept the sounds of the city over us: the rumble of a passenger jet coming in to land, two dogs in the next street having a barking competition, and as ever, the wail of sirens – tonight there seemed to be more of those than ever, their wails overlapping and distorting each other like a dozen drunken singers mangling the same tune.

That was the question I hadn't wanted to ask the Guvnor, but I'd asked Junior: *If the Turk turned Richard, how do you know he hasn't turned someone else?*

From what Zoe was saying, it sounded like the Turk had. Which was fine, in one way, because the sooner the Guvnor was defeated the sooner this war would be over, and the Turk wouldn't need to use Zoe or me as pawns any more . . . Except after today the Turk wasn't going to be interested in playing chess. Thanks to me three of his people had been crippled, two killed, and he himself had only just escaped being stoned to death in the street like a whore in the Bible. I was headed for that shredder of his, and knowing the Turk he'd find a way to have Zoe lower me in while he watched. And if the police ever found out I had started that riot in Clapham, they'd happily let him.

I knew now where Amobi and the other cops stood in this battle – on the sidelines, watching. Why would they care if the Turk had a mole in the Guvnor's mob? They had no use for that information. The only person who might find it useful was the Guvnor himself. Right now, maybe just for a day or two, the Turk was weakened and on the defensive; this might be all McGovern needed to finish him off.

I had to get back to the Guvnor, and tell him. Somehow.

The next morning, after a breakfast of baked beans warmed in the microwave, Zoe retrieved a second laptop from a wall safe concealed behind a painting. She explained to me her aunt used the same number combination for every lock, with a roll of her eyes that suggested she considered anyone who did that a total cretin. I nodded agreement, omitting to mention I too used the same password for almost everything online . . . but then unlike her aunt I owned nothing worth stealing and I had no secrets worth knowing.

While I looked on Zoe fired up the second laptop, decrypted the next-door neighbour's wireless security, logged on to the Net using a proxy, and downloaded a suite of utilities from some Finnish hacker site. Then she set about creating a VPN, or something, into the Turk's laptop. At first she explained what she was doing, but as the work got harder her explanations tailed off. I'd stopped listening by then anyway: computer hacking isn't exactly a spectator sport, and I had a job of my own to do that wasn't nearly so straightforward. I had to find the Guvnor again, this time without Amobi's help.

That afternoon I kissed Zoe goodbye like a dutiful husband heading to the office. Neither of us mentioned that this might be the last time we ever saw each other; to say so seemed to invite disaster somehow, and if I'd thought about it too hard I might never have left. It took me fifteen minutes to walk to Richmond station; there were cop cars patrolling the streets, looking for would-be rioters, and I didn't want to draw attention to myself by running. I caught a tube train that would take me all the way across London, albeit very slowly, and sat hunched in the end carriage with my hood up, trying to look inconspicuous. Every tube train and platform and forecourt was dotted with surveillance cameras, but before very long I gave up worrying about them or even looking for them – what was the point, when they were everywhere? The time to avoid being caught on CCTV would have been during that riot, but in the heat of the moment it had never occurred to me.

During the last outbreak of rioting, before the London Olympics, the cops had eventually come piling in with shields and batons to clear the streets – but they made relatively few arrests at that point. All that came later, when they'd gathered every scrap of

CCTV footage they could find and analysed it frame by frame, identifying everyone they could who'd been present, regardless of what those people had actually been doing. About four weeks after the riots came a wave of dawn raids: snatch squads had kicked in doors across the city, rounding up hundreds of suspects at the same time. When the accused came up in court the magistrates refused to hear any denials or excuses or explanations. It was like everyone who'd witnessed the unrest was infected with a plague virus and had to be quarantined before an epidemic of rioting brought down our civilization. One guy had been sentenced to a year in prison for taking a plastic bottle of water from the wreckage of a shop long after the real looters had been and gone.

Eventually the cops would come for me, I knew, but they'd have to find me first, and I wouldn't be their top priority; they'd start with the teenagers who lived at home with Mum and Dad: police always go for the easiest targets first – it boosts their productivity figures. I was less worried about them than I was about the Turk; his people were better motivated, and he didn't have to worry about paying them to work anti-social hours. All their hours were anti-social.

The tube journey took less time than I expected because so many stations along the route were closed, and the train rattled echoing past empty, fully lit platforms. Each time, the guard announced beforehand in a bored drone that due to the 'current situation' the next station was not operational and passengers for such-and-such a place should change somewhere else. I didn't know if there were actual riots in progress on the streets above me, or whether this rush was just a precaution; but all the same the guilt weighed down on me like the million tons of earth hanging over my head. If the judges were right and riot was a transmissible disease, I was Typhoid Mary.

The nearest station to The Horsemonger pub was open, though. I ran up the escalator – I hate standing and waiting, it makes me feel like a cow on a slaughterhouse conveyor belt – half expecting to emerge into a scene from the Blitz. But life here, just as in Richmond, seemed to be carrying on as normal; there were buses rumbling and squealing along the street, and cabs, and traffic, and a flower-seller cheerfully hawking his wares to passers-by. All the smashed windows and burning vehicles, all that was happening in some other London a million miles away. I set off down the street towards the

Guvnor's pub, and it seemed no distance compared to last time, now that I knew where I was going.

But when I found the place, and stood looking at it from across the street, my first thought was I'd been wrong about the riots not coming here.

The Horsemonger was an empty blackened shell with fresh plywood nailed over its broken windows. The pavement around it had been swept clean of debris, but it was still streaked with charcoal, and the once-gleaming crimson tiles that ran along the facade were all cracked and blackened and dulled. I knew the Guvnor's stock was low, but I hadn't expected this; I'd thought even rampaging local yobs would still have feared his reputation enough to give any business of his a wide berth.

My second thought was: no, I hadn't been wrong. There had been no rampage here. The Horsemonger was the only business I could see that had suffered. This wasn't riot damage – it was another act of war by the Turk: hitting McGovern in his heartland, advertising his weakness to the world. It had certainly left me stranded; I knew I'd been taking a long shot coming here, but I had no other way of contacting the Guvnor.

'You want a drink, you'll have to go to the corner shop, like all the other kiddies,' quavered a voice beside me. It was an old man sitting on a bench behind me, wearing a quilted anorak and a flat cap pulled down over his eyes – far too hot an outfit for this weather. When I glimpsed the grey hair sprouting from the old man's ears and the woolly cardigan peeping out around his collar, I finally recognized him: Slasher Eric, the amateur plastic surgeon. Out here on the street, sitting alone with his fists in his pockets, he looked shrunken and harmless, like a shark out of water. I felt a twinge of pity for him, till it occurred to me to wonder what he was clutching in that pocket. It was probably best to keep my distance, so I sat down at the far end of his bench.

'Looking for someone?' he said, without turning his head. He was staring at the pub as if he thought it might spontaneously refurbish itself and re-open.

'Same someone as last time,' I said.

'There were cops watching this place round the clock till two days ago,' said Eric. 'They disappeared after it went up. Makes sense, I suppose – why would anyone come here now?'

Interesting. It was probably Amobi's people who'd been keeping the pub under surveillance. They must have witnessed the arson attack, and done nothing to prevent it. It fitted with what Amobi had said.

'I have some information the Guvnor needs,' I said. Old Eric looked at me, an ancient toothless Rottweiler patrolling a derelict bombsite, growling at anyone who stopped to look.

'What information?' he said.

I sighed. I felt sorry for the mean old bastard, but not sorry enough to waste my time giving him the message and hoping he remembered it long enough to pass it on. I guessed he wanted to feel important, especially now he had to spend his days on a bench in the street instead of his regular stool at the bar; but I wasn't a social worker who'd come round to cheer him up. Sooner or later, I suspected, he'd pick a fight with someone and open their face with his razor, just to get nicked. Then he could spend his last days enjoying the routine and food and company that prison offered.

'You have a number for him?' I said.

'I have a number for somebody who does,' said Eric. He didn't seem to mind me going over his head; the fight had gone out of him, and he just wanted to be useful.

'Could you call them?' I didn't say please: it would have sounded patronizing.

Eric pulled a bony fist from the right-hand pocket of his coat – it held nothing but a crumpled tissue –

and rooted around inside his cardigan a while. Eventually he fished out a mobile phone just like the one my dad used to have, the sort that could go a week on one charge. Fumbling inside his clothing some more he produced a pair of glasses, then spent so long putting them on his face I started to wonder if he'd forgotten how. He muttered numbers under his breath as he stabbed out eleven digits and raised the handset to his ancient hairy ear.

Twenty minutes later I was in a black taxi, heading north-east to some corner of Essex I'd never visited before. The meter wasn't running. It might have been the same driver who had picked us up in Trafalgar Square after the shootout, but I didn't get a good look at his face, then or now. I was surprised how easy this had been; McGovern had trusted me enough to let me go, yes, but a lot had happened since then – thirty-six hours earlier I'd been psyching myself up to kill him.

The taxi pulled up to the kerb in what appeared to be an industrial estate, and the driver waited word-lessly, not even turning his head. I took the hint and climbed out, and as soon as I'd shut the door the taxi wheeled round in a tight circle and sped away.

I stood there squinting in the sun for a few

minutes until another car drew up – a people carrier with darkened windows – and the rear passenger door slid open. Before I could even clock who was inside another black hood was pulled over my head.

Half an hour later, when the hood was pulled off, I wondered where I was. Obviously somewhere still on the outskirts of London, but this sprawling building looked more like a university campus or an office complex built in the 1970s than someone's home. It was all square angles of pale concrete and floor-to-ceiling windows, like an expensive architectural experiment, but one that had been abandoned a decade ago. There were clumps of grass bursting out of the roof, and the extensive grounds were shaggy and overgrown: ornamental shrubs were bunched up so close they were strangling each other, and five-metre rose trees that had once been bushes were exploding with blooms and trailing long thorny suckers like living razor wire. It reminded me of the unkempt garden in front of Zoe's student house, except this one was a few hundred times bigger, and Zoe's didn't have several pairs of thickset blokes in leather jackets strolling round the perimeter, smoking.

Two heavies were waiting for me as I climbed out of the people carrier. Both wore leather car coats; one had long greasy hair and an earring, and the other no hair at all – just tears tattooed on his face. The bloke in the van with me, the one who'd pulled the hood off my head, I'd seen before: one of the Guvnor's junior thugs abruptly promoted after Martin and Gary got shot. He took my arm as if he meant to lead me into the building.

'No,' said Longhair. 'Get back in van.'

There was a brief staring match, and the younger bloke lost. He climbed back into the people carrier, slid the door shut, and it reversed away down the drive. The heavy who'd spoken looked at me and flicked his head upwards.

'Raise your hands,' he said.

His bald-headed companion frisked me, quickly but efficiently, then stood back and nodded.

'Move,' said Longhair. Interesting, I thought. The Russians are supplying the Guvnor's muscle now? I was pretty sure they were Russian – this heavy sounded like McGovern's friend Dimitri. I remembered my father telling me how the Russians didn't have a word for 'the' and didn't seem to need one. Dad had found this fascinating, God knows why – I'd barely been listening. The men patrolling the grounds, they were Russian too, from the look of them – not that they were wearing furry hats or swigging bottles of vodka, but their clothes and hair-cuts seemed twenty years out of date, as if they got their fashion inspiration from twentieth-century mafia movies. Longhair and Baldy smelled like chain-smokers who liked lots of tar in their tobacco.

Before me and my escort had reached the front steps the barrel-like figure of Steve McGovern emerged from the gloomy interior. He too looked gloomy, and tense. I could imagine his problem: he had been second in the pecking order until the Russian reinforcements arrived, and suddenly a whole lot of foreigners he barely knew were senior to him. When he looked at me the loud-mouthed cockiness I'd encountered when we first met had gone; but so had the humility and directness he'd shown last time.

'Why'd you come back?' he said.

'I've got some information your dad might find useful,' I said.

'Tell me,' said Steve, 'and I'll decide if it's useful or not.'

'Thanks,' I said, 'but I've come all this way, I might as well tell him myself.'

Steve shook his head, glanced around at the Russian heavies patrolling the garden, then at Longhair and Baldy, who were standing behind me slightly bored, waiting for this conversation to end.

'Finn,' said Steve, 'you only got away last time because I put in a good word for you. That's all changed now. The stakes are way higher. Tell me what you know and you might just get out of here in one piece.'

It was a tempting offer, but somehow I knew the Guvnor would give me more credit than Steve, and I was going to need all the help I could get. The info I had was slim at best – McGovern might already have found the second mole, for all I knew – but he owed me, more than his son did. If I had only one punch left to throw I had to make it count.

'If he's busy, I can wait,' I said.

Steve shook his head in irritation – *stupid prick*, his look said – and he stood aside. Longhair and Baldy stepped forward, forcing me onwards into the house, riding a wave of stale tobacco smell. Steve trailed after us.

The building's interior had polished concrete floors, doors of polished wood, and empty white shelves; the look was chic and minimal, or bleak and brutal, depending on your point of view. My escort steered me towards a flight of mahogany steps mounted on a single central pillar, leading up to a platform with a long glass partition obscured by vertical window blinds. Maybe that look had been trendy back in the 1970s, but now the decor seemed shabby and sad. I tried the polished steel handle of the central glass door; it was open.

Steve followed me in and nodded at our escort to get lost. Longhair hesitated, as if he and Baldy had been planning to leave anyway, but didn't want to look like they answered to him. Then he decided he didn't care how it looked, and headed back downstairs.

Inside I found McGovern in jeans and an open-necked shirt, muttering into a mobile phone. The room was laid out like an office, with slender furniture of chrome and white formica, cold abstract paintings on the walls, a white rug on the polished concrete floor and a leather sofa that might have been white once but was now way, way off-white.

'Well, get a message to him and tell him to call me,' McGovern was saying. 'I don't care if he's got the NSA, the FBI and the Salvation fucking Army listening to his calls. He can use his initiative.'

There was a huge map of the UK stuck to the wall behind him. This was a war room, I realized. But where were all the generals?

'Right. Goodbye,' said the Guvnor. He hung up and turned, and his icy grey stare drilled into me.

I could smell the adrenalin pumping through his system, but somehow he remained calm and focused, like a boxer working out how to take on three opponents at once. At that moment he looked capable of it. For an instant I wished I'd blurted out my message to Steve and done a runner.

'Still trying to reach Dennis?' said Steve.

His father's cold glare flickered from me to him. 'Wanker's playing hard to get. Wouldn't be the first time he'd sat on the fence.'

'We can manage without him,' said Steve. 'Karakurt won't know what hit him.'

'Not the point,' said his father.

'Karakurt?' I said.

'The Turk's real name,' said Steve.

'You sure about that this time?' I said, and immediately I wanted to kick myself. I'd just wanted to make conversation, but it had come out as snide.

McGovern looked at me, considering whether to reply or have someone throw me down those hard-wood stairs on my face. 'My friend Dimitri used to be KGB,' he said at last. 'He has contacts all over the old Soviet Union, right down to Turkmenistan and all them other Stans. Yeah, the intel's good. So what's this you've got for me?'

Jesus, I thought. If he's got the bloody KGB working for him, he won't need me.

'After I left you that time,' I said, 'the Turk – Karakurt – grabbed my girlfriend. Held her hostage.'

'What for?' said Steve. He'd moved round from behind me, trying to insert himself into the conversation, closer to the man in charge.

'He wanted me to do a job for him,' I said.

'What sort of job?' said Steve.

'What do you sodding think?' said McGovern, with more than a hint of contempt. 'He wanted Finn to whack me.' Steve's eyes widened, and he reached around to the small of his back. 'And don't start waving that bloody shooter about, they've already frisked him.'

Sheepishly Steve returned his pistol to its hiding place.

'I got her out, anyway,' I said.

'How'd you manage that?' said McGovern with a flicker of genuine curiosity.

'There was a riot. Somebody set fire to their building. When they all ran for it, I grabbed her.'

McGovern grinned hugely, and I got the impression he hadn't laughed in a long time. 'You jammy little sod,' he said. 'Why aren't you working for me?'

'My girlfriend overheard someone calling the Turk,' I went on quickly, before he had time to volunteer me. 'To tell him Richard was dead, that I'd killed him.'

'Christ!' said Steve.

'It must have been someone on your crew,' I said. 'No one else would have known, would they?'

'Who?' said Steve.

'I have no way of knowing,' I said. 'I thought maybe you could find out.'

Steve snorted. 'How, exactly?'

'I don't know,' I said, trying not to flounder. 'Check your people's phones? She said the call came in at seven . . .'

McGovern seemed lost in thought, like he was running through the potential candidates in his head. Steve just seemed disgusted and angry. 'That's it?' he said. 'All this fuss, all this bollocks, *this* is the inside gen you have? Jesus . . . there were twenty-four people in that house, you expect us to check all their phones? How do you know they weren't using a burner, like Richard?'

It was a good question. Why the hell had I dived back into this snakepit with so little to protect me? 'Zoe – my girlfriend – said it sounded like a friend of his . . . like the Turk had been really close to

Richard, though it didn't make any sense – I don't know if that . . .' I tailed off. I had nothing left to say, and the more I talked the more of an idiot I sounded.

McGovern was rubbing his forehead, as if a thousand black thoughts were swirling in his head. Steve was doing exactly the same, mirroring his dad – I didn't know if he was doing it consciously or not, but in his case it looked less like deep thought and more like panic.

'Shit,' said McGovern calmly. He glanced at his son. 'You called someone around then, around seven.'

'Me? No I never.'

'Yeah, yeah,' said McGovern. 'I came in when you was on the phone.'

'Oh, yeah,' said Steve. 'That was Richard's mum, I told you. We owed her that much.'

'Right,' said McGovern. 'You said.'

There was a short silence. McGovern's cold gaze rested on Steve, who chewed his lip nervously.

'She won't have said anything, though,' Steve blurted. 'She knows the drill.'

'Right,' said his father again. 'So if I called her, this minute, she'd back you up, would she?'

'What?' Steve looked offended. 'Course she would. She's getting on a bit, but—'

'Fine. Lend us your phone,' said McGovern.

Steve stared at him, and so did I. Was the Guvnor really implying what I thought he was? Shaking his head in disgusted disbelief, Steve reached into his pocket. Except he didn't go for his phone – his hand slipped round to the small of his back. His father strode forward, grabbed Steve's right hand with his left behind Steve's back, and Steve's throat with his right. Steve wheezed and started to choke, while I just stood there, uselessly, trying to figure out what the hell was happening and who I should help.

The two men were standing face to face, inches from each other. Steve's left hand flailed; it tugged at McGovern's wrist, then clawed at and scratched at his face, but McGovern shook him off like a midge. Steve's right hand, pinned behind his back, was gripping his gun, I realized. His face was turning deeper scarlet by the second, but McGovern's face was deathly calm and pale, like he was holding a puppy down in a bucket of water.

I remembered the first time I saw McGovern kill someone. 'Don't mess about, don't make speeches,' he'd said. 'Just do it.' And he was doing it now, while I looked on, as useless as a shop-window manikin.

Steve started to sag; his knees were going. With all

the strength he had left he wrestled his right wrist free and brought his gun up in his father's face and fired a shot, but at the very last second McGovern tilted his head, so the bullet just nicked his ear and shattered the glass wall behind. The pane fell to shards in a discordant clatter that was all too familiar now, and under that racket I heard a tiny *crunch*, of Steve's windpipe collapsing, and his eyes bulged from his purple face. His arm dropped and the gun dropped and his whole body deflated.

His father released his grip and Steve fell in a heap, while shouts and running feet from the hallway downstairs told us the Russians were coming back. McGovern stared down at the crumpled heap that had been his son and I couldn't tell what he was thinking. Last time he'd killed someone in front of me, he'd held a gun to my head until I'd convinced him I wouldn't tell anyone what I'd witnessed. This time he seemed so appalled – at what he'd learned, or what he'd done – it was like my presence didn't matter one way or the other. Pulling a handkerchief out of his pocket he held it to his bleeding ear, then checked the bloodstains to see how badly he'd been hurt. His shoulder was soaked in red, but the bleeding was already stopping; he was probably in more pain from the powder burns to his face than from the wound.

It was Longhair and Baldy who burst back into the room, holding machine pistols. Taking in the scene Longhair cursed under his breath and barked an order in Russian to Baldy, who turned and hurried out again, presumably to fetch someone.

McGovern stooped, picked up Steve's pistol and checked the action. I tensed, wondering if I would be quick enough to dodge when he turned the gun on me, but instead he stood up and tucked it into his waistband at the small of his back.

'He didn't speak to me for years,' said McGovern abruptly, without looking at me. 'After I left his mum. After she died he comes back. Said all that was in the past, we were family.' He rubbed his hand down his face, held it over his mouth. 'I tried to help him. He wasn't the brightest kid in the world, but . . .' He turned to me with a crooked, wry grin, tinged with something that looked like shame. 'It's like whatsisname, innit? Oedipus. Wanted to screw his mum, kill his dad. I knew it, I knew he still hated me, deep down. Just didn't want to see it.'

Longhair was watching both of us calmly, his gun hanging loosely in his hand, pointed at the floor. I didn't know how much he understood. Come to that, I didn't know how much *I* understood. Longhair looked relaxed, but I noticed his finger was stroking the trigger, and I suddenly wondered which of us he saw as the threat. McGovern was oblivious. He stared down at Steve, blinking rapidly. 'He was a great kid,' he said, his voice suddenly hoarse. 'A real rascal.' He blinked. 'It was me who screwed up. Some dad, eh?'

Did he expect me to argue? He was standing over the strangled corpse of his firstborn son. But I felt compelled to say something. 'Kelly's a good kid,' I said. 'And Bonnie. It's not too late.'

'You think?' said McGovern, and his cold grey eyes settled on Longhair, still standing there with his pistol swinging free. Was the Guvnor asking me for reassurance, or . . . ? There were more footsteps on the staircase outside, slow and steady ones, and when I saw Longhair stiffen and straighten up I knew who he had sent Baldy to find.

Through the glass door I saw Dimitri's white-haired head appear, one step at a time. Today he wore a lemon-yellow shirt with glinting crystal cufflinks. As before, it was unbuttoned to the chest, where his gold medallion glinted from a nest of bristly grey hair. I didn't see any diamond in his teeth this time, because he wasn't smiling; his lips were pursed tight. He pushed the door open and stood in the doorway, taking in the scene.

'I found our grass,' said McGovern. 'We need

to change the plans. He'll have told Karakurt everything.'

Dimitri sighed and nodded, sucking his teeth.
'Then house too is compromised,' he said. 'We move.'

That seemed obvious to me, but McGovern was
silent a moment as if he was thinking something
through. 'The warehouse,' he said.

Dimitri looked at me.

'I should go,' I said.

'Too late for that,' said McGovern. His next words
were directed at Dimitri. 'We need to sort out this
piece of shit as well.' He nodded at me. 'He's been
with the Turk from the start.'

My stomach dived and twisted. What the *fuck*?

'That's not true,' I said. 'I came here to help.' I
tried to keep my voice as calm and steady as I could
– the shriller I got and the more defensive I sounded,
the less they'd believe me. Steve's voice had climbed
an octave before his dad had grabbed his throat. But
when Dimitri looked at me and shrugged, I knew it
would make no difference what I said or how I
pitched it.

'Not in here,' grunted Dimitri. 'Outside.'

Was he worried about his white rug? Did he want
to save his men the effort of lugging my corpse out of
the house? No, I realized. If they were abandoning

265

this place, they wouldn't want to leave bloodstains and DNA behind. The delay might offer me a few precious seconds – what if I grabbed Dimitri as a shield? I'd heard machine pistols sprayed bullets in all directions . . . but how would I get out of this house, or clear of this place, dragging an un-cooperative old man?

In the time it took me to think about this and not come to any conclusion, Longhair had stepped forward and grabbed my arm, hauling me towards the door. Yes – I'd let them take me outside, then I'd run. There was no way any of these chain-smokers would catch up with me, and they wouldn't dare to start blasting away in the open – the noise of their guns would carry for miles, and nobody would mistake the racket for a car backfiring.

As Longhair marched me down the stairs the house was already bustling with activity. Some of the guys I'd seen patrolling earlier were packing weapons into black duffel bags, while others ran upstairs past me carrying what looked like a body bag: I wondered idly how many of those they kept in stock. The interior was no longer gloomy – the high ceilings were lined with halogens that flooded the room in a wash of cold, stark light, because night was falling.

Outside three Mercedes saloons had pulled up in a line before the front door, headlights burning. Bags were thrown in the boot, and though the evening was warm, Baldy brought Dimitri a camel-hair coat and helped him shrug it on, as tenderly as a young mum dressing her toddler for nursery. I flexed the muscles in my legs, checking for a gap in their lines, waiting for the moment when Longhair's attention would be distracted. When I noticed the short guy standing off to my right carrying what looked like a hunting rifle, my heart sank. One shot from that wouldn't draw anyone's attention, even out here in the suburbs – and one shot was all it would take.

That decided it; I'd run straight at that guy, and take him down before he had a chance to open fire. I wouldn't grab the rifle, but keep running – by the time someone else picked it up, I'd be two hundred metres away in the dark. And it was getting darker all the time.

McGovern emerged, shrugging on a lightweight blazer over his bloodstained shirt, and he didn't even throw me a glance. Coolly he tugged out his shirt-sleeves and tripped down the steps to the first Merc in line, heading for the rear passenger seat, but the Russian waiting to open the door – a guy of around twenty, with black teeth and pitted cheeks – shook his head.

'You sit front,' he said. 'Boss in back.'

McGovern shrugged, and Black Teeth opened the front passenger door for him. Now McGovern turned to me, with a sardonic grin. Too late I remembered Amobi's warning about how the Guvnor could turn on anyone, even people who'd thought they were his friends. 'Ta-ta, Crusher,' he said. 'Thanks for trying, eh?' What the hell was that supposed to mean?

From the corner of my eye I watched the short guy with the hunting rifle. He was facing the line of cars, his weapon poised and ready for action, but when the cars moved off he'd be watching them, not me. I tensed my muscles, ready to let rip. Black Teeth shut McGovern's door and stood back. There was a brief pause, as if everyone there was waiting for a signal from Dimitri, but he said nothing – he just fished in his breast pocket to check he had brought his glasses. I needed a distraction, and I was running out of time.

But something was happening, in the Guvnor's car. There'd been a swift, shadowy movement from the rear seat, and now McGovern was pulled back hard against his headrest, clutching at his throat. Through the glass I saw him shudder, and writhe, and kick – he pulled his foot clear of the footwell and braced it against the dashboard, trying to push his seat back, but it was useless. At first I couldn't comprehend what I was seeing, but eventually I understood: the Guvnor was being garrotted, and all the people he'd counted on as friends and allies were standing around watching, waiting for the end. His agony seemed to go on for ever, and in the gathering dusk I even thought I could hear the last of McGovern's breath hissing through his nostrils as he fought for life. The whole car shook and bounced on its springs as the Guvnor threshed and writhed and fought for life, and then abruptly, all movement stopped.

A few moments of stillness later the shadowy figure in the back seat slid out of sight again, and the Russian crew relaxed and turned to light each other new cigarettes. With a hum and a rustle of gravel under its wheels the front Merc moved off, carrying the Guvnor's wilted body away to God knows where.

That had been the moment to run, I realized, just then, while everyone was calmly watching the execution of the man who had once been the most feared gangster in Europe. But I had missed it – I had frozen in shock and disbelief, and now it was too late. I waited for Longhair to push me towards the second Merc, but first Dimitri turned to me.

'You work for Karakurt, yes?' he said.

I looked at him. I didn't know which answer would save me, so I gave him no answer.

He nodded, as if my silence had confirmed something. 'Tell your boss we have deal,' said Dimitri. And turning he walked slowly back into the house, Baldy shadowing his steps, watching the old man's feet in case he tripped.

NINE

'Jesus,' said Zoe. 'They killed him?'

'He knew what was going to happen as soon as they told him to sit in the front of the car.'

We were lying together in the big brass bed. We'd kicked off the fancy lace counterpane and the white embroidered cushions, and they lay discarded on the floor, taking up the little space that was left between the bed and the walls. Longhair had dropped me at the nearest tube station and driven off without looking back, and I was so shocked and sickened and blindsided by everything that had happened I had barely registered the journey back to Richmond. When Zoe opened the door she'd tried to ask a question, but I'd piled in like a landslide, slammed the door behind me and grabbed her. We didn't even make it up the stairs the first time. She sensed my desperation and my need – she'd have to have been carved from marble not to – and asked nothing more, until an hour or so later, when we lay tangled together, half covered by a damp and rumpled sheet. Then I told her everything that had happened since I'd left that afternoon.

'Sounds like he knew before that,' said Zoe. 'That he'd lost, that it was only a matter of time. When he told the Russians you were working for the Turk, it was so they wouldn't kill you too.'

'But why did he even care?' I said.

'Because he liked you? Because you were the only one there who hadn't betrayed him?'

'I can't believe Steve sold him out,' I said.

'Not every child loves their dad as much as you did, Finn.' She spoke gently, trying not to sound superior, but I knew she was talking from experience. 'You said McGovern left Steve's mum, for that younger woman, Cherry? Steve probably felt like his dad had walked out on him too. He probably hated the Guvnor's new kids.'

'Yeah . . . Karakurt must have found that out, and used it.'

'Just think, all these years, the cops and SOCA have been trying to nail the Guvnor,' said Zoe. 'And the Turk took him down in, what? A fortnight?'

'Blitzkrieg,' I said. 'You hit your opponent so hard and so fast they have no time to work out what's happening or how to hit back. And you buy off their friends with a promise of peace, and a big cut of the proceeds.'

'And always have someone on the inside.'

'Funny,' I said. 'The Turk probably learned all that off McGovern. That's what he used to do, back in the 1990s, to anyone who got in his way. It's how he got to be the Guvnor.'

'He got old,' said Zoe.

'He got married,' I said. 'He had kids. That's what makes you weak. Loving someone.'

There was a short silence, and I wondered if I'd said the wrong thing.

'Do I make you weak?' said Zoe.

'Every time I look at you,' I said, and I rolled over on top of her. She giggled, and slid her arms round my neck. She didn't make me weak everywhere.

The night was silent, except for the sound of Zoe's soft breathing. The riots had been snuffed out in thirty-six hours; the cops must have been stung last time by all those critics who'd wondered – from the comfort of their armchairs – why the Met had stood by and watched London burn instead of piling in and cracking heads. This time round they hadn't made the same mistake. In the early hours of that morning I heard no more sirens – well, just one or two, a reassuringly normal number.

Except I wasn't reassured. The Turk had won his war, and the authorities had helped him by getting the police and the NCA to back off. Of course, if anyone accused them of taking sides, Government ministers would deny it and call it an outrageous slur, and there'd be no written evidence to prove they were lying. And as long as the Turk helped them catch terrorists, and kept a low profile, the establishment would happily let him run the UK's crime network. Why not? Every other British industry had been taken over by foreign corporations.

But to the Turk, Zoe and I weren't just a loose end. I'd brought about the death of Kemal, who'd been the nearest thing the Turk had to a friend. I knew a gang leader once who'd had a favourite pit bull terrier, and I recalled how he'd wept when his dog was mauled in a fight, and what he'd done to the owner of the other dog . . . that guy was now in a care home somewhere, being fed pap with a spoon.

The laptop. I'd forgotten all about it. I must have gasped when I remembered it, because Zoe stirred, as if she hadn't been asleep at all, but just dozing.

'Hmm?' she said.

'I meant to ask,' I said. 'How's the hacking going?'

'Oh, shit,' she groaned. 'I didn't tell you.'

'You wiped the hard drive?'

'*I* didn't wipe it. It was an automated security routine.'

I was sitting naked at the tiny kitchen table, staring at the Turk's sleek laptop, stabbing the power button like an idiot. Nothing happened; the machine was dead. I checked the power flex – the indicator light was on, so power was going in ... but nothing was coming out.

'The Turk must have used a dongle,' said Zoe.

'A what?'

'Like a memory stick – it slots into a port, and when you log in it asks for a code from the user. If you enter the wrong code, or the dongle's missing, a program in the memory starts to format the hard drive. And this one's SSD – solid state – so it happened really fast.' She was leaning against the sink with her arms folded, angry at failing, but defiant too because she'd tried every trick she knew. She was wearing her aunt's gold kimono, which looked good on her; I was uncomfortably aware of my bare arse sticking to the vinyl of my chair.

'But you can recover data from a formatted drive, you told me, you've done it before—'

'Usually, yes, but it zeroed all the sectors—' Her shoulders drooped, and she gave up explaining. 'I'm sorry, Finn, I got nothing. Just a few fragments from the cache before the power died.'

'What sort of fragments?'

Back in the bedroom she flipped open the laptop she'd taken from her aunt's safe, logged in and double-clicked a file on the desktop. A bright square of blue appeared, daubed with blocks of white text. I squinted, trying to make sense of it, but as usual the letters swam and shuffled as I looked at them, like hyperactive kids running amok in a playground.

'You know I'm dyslexic,' I said. 'I can't make head or tail of this.'

'Nobody can, Finn,' sighed Zoe. 'It's a memory dump in hexadecimal. It could be part of a photograph, or an MP3, or a program – anything. I've got dozens of these but there's nothing I can do with them.'

'What if it was just text?' I said.

'It could be, yeah, but there's no way of knowing.'

'All right, so if it is a photo or a program we're screwed. But why not try to open it anyway?

With a word-processing program, or something.'

'It would just come out as garbage. The header's probably missing.'

'Probably? So you haven't tried?'

She glared at me, and I wasn't sure which irritated her more, my stupidity or my stubbornness. Clambering across the bed she pulled the laptop away from me and propped herself up against the brass frame, tapping away at the keyboard. Her eyes flickered as she concentrated, slid one finger along the touchpad, and double-clicked. For just a moment she looked hopeful; then she signed in exasperation and tossed the machine back towards me.

'Garbage,' she said. 'Told you.'

I pulled the laptop round so I could look at the screen. Now the characters were black on white, but they were still in garbled blocks: the whole thing looked like a picture a toddler might make if you offered them a stick of glue and a pot of spider's legs. Zoe was right; this was hopeless. 'It might as well be in Arabic,' I said.

Zoe stared at me. 'Which part of Turkey is he from, do you know?' she said. 'Karakurt?'

'McGovern thought he was Kurdish,' I said. 'The bit next door to Russia. But that might have been bullshit.'

Zoe dived forward and snatched the laptop back. Tapped on the keys again, slid and clicked. This time her eyes widened and her mouth fell open.

'Shit,' she said. 'I was using the wrong character set. Fifty-one twenty-nine . . . ?'

'What?' I said.

She showed me the screen. Now the text was in orderly paragraphs, and I could almost make out some words – except the letters weren't any shape I recognized. The Ns were backwards and the Os had bars across them so they looked like 8s. I checked, twice: it definitely wasn't just me.

'I'm an idiot,' said Zoe. 'I didn't try Cyrillic.'

'You can read this?' I said.

'No, you pillock. But I can read this.' She pointed to the middle of one line, where I saw a row of figures: *51°29.915' 0°20.188'*.

'What the hell does that mean?' I said.

'I think they're map coordinates,' said Zoe.

Night was falling again by the time I left the house; I needed darkness for what I had in mind. Zoe was still on the laptop. She'd spent most of her day at it – she thought that fragment we'd decoded might offer a clue to decoding the rest, but we must have been lucky the first time, because none of the others seemed to be text documents.

While she worried away at the task like a dog working marrow from a bone I caught up on some urgent sleeping. Around midday I got up and ransacked the cupboards to see what I could use or we could eat, and managed to knock us up a meal of rice and tomatoes and artichokes that was almost edible. Neither of us wanted to leave just to go shopping for groceries, in case our presence was noticed by the neighbours. In a London street like this it was quite possible that none of the inhabitants knew each other well enough even to exchange hellos if they happened to pass on the pavement, but it seemed wiser not to take the risk.

After we ate I persuaded Zoe to take a nap with me, which didn't involve much sleeping. We had no idea what lay ahead, and we knew the Turk and his people were probably looking for us, and that the cops might well be looking for me; but for a few hours in that little house we were safe and secluded and we were together, and that was all we wanted or needed.

I dressed soon after it got dark. She saw me to the door; we kissed goodbye quickly, she wished me good luck in a whisper, and she shut the door softly behind me. I walked briskly down the street, my head high as if I belonged there, but with my hood pulled up all the same to hid my face; at the end I turned west towards the river and the towpath and started to run.

The towpath wasn't the straightest route – the river curved and kinked back on itself in places – but it was the least conspicuous, and I fitted in with the other runners pounding along in the dark – almost all of them men, it had to be said. Few women felt comfortable along the river because woods and bushes grew so thickly, and so many stretches were unlit that at times it felt as creepy and menacing as London must have been two hundred years ago, when every shadowy alley teemed with tarts and muggers and the Thames at the Tower of London yielded a nightly harvest of corpses.

A few sprinters overtook me, and I let them – I wasn't there to compete and I knew I'd overtake them again anyway a few minutes later, when their pace flagged. It was about two miles to the junction with the canal, and from there another mile north along the towpath before I'd reach my destination. I cleared my mind and just ran, hard and steady. No point in worrying what I'd do when I got there, until I got there.

Near its junction with the Thames the canal was a

mass of chic new waterside apartments overlooking picturesque lines of narrowboats moored semi-permanently. The barges glowed from within; they looked as cosy and warm and welcoming as the house where I'd left Zoe, and I had to block those thoughts from my head and keep running north. Very soon the lights and the life faded away behind me, and the sleek granite paving of the waterfront gave way to the crumbling potholed tarmac of the old towpath. There were no designer apartments any more, and few narrowboats; one white shape in the water turned out to be an old motor launch that had sunk, and now lay rotting and abandoned, three-quarters submerged in four metres of murky water. There were occasional patches of pinkish-yellow sodium light from the road that ran parallel to the canal, but soon even they died out, and the only light was the glow of London itself to the east, reflected off high thin clouds. Plenty of stars, but no moon yet; another lucky stroke of timing.

When I came to an arched, narrow iron bridge I knew I was nearing my destination. Zoe and I had entered the coordinates into an online map and even reconnoitred the place online by clicking through to a street-level view, though half the images were obscured by passing trucks. There had been no pictures covering the side I was coming from, but that was an advantage; it was pitch-dark back here, and there would be no traffic to betray my approach.

The only building at those coordinates was an old industrial unit, standing by itself in the middle of a tarmac yard surrounded by chain-link fencing topped by barbed wire. The unit's rear perimeter backed onto the canal, about ten metres from the water itself. Between the canal and the fence was a sloping bank overgrown with butterfly bushes, sycamore saplings and brambles. Not so long ago these banks had been regularly trimmed, but then whoever ran the canals decided to let it grow unchecked – as a resource for wildlife, they said, but everyone knew it was to save money. As I ducked down and fought my way on hands and knees into the undergrowth, the only wildlife I encountered was slugs between my fingers, and a stink of foxes so strong it made my eyes water.

I didn't know what the Turk was keeping in that place. Maybe more sex slaves? I knew one of his operations involved trafficking girls in from Europe – that beating the other week from Kemal and his pals had been payback for telling the police about their last warehouse – but somehow that didn't seem likely. The other place had been a mansion miles from anywhere with plenty of rooms; this was a crumbling industrial unit, surrounded by other industrial units. Too many witnesses would have noticed women being dragged in and out in chains, and whatever foreigners might think, the English are not so obsessed with privacy they'd ignore something like that. Then again, maybe his crew drove the cargo in and out in vans? I'd seen that before too. Whatever was in there, the Turk had gone to a lot of trouble to hide it by installing a self-destruct routine on the laptop, and risking the wrath of a mob to carry the machine with him out of a riot. If this place meant that much to him, I had to know what it was.

It took me ten minutes to crawl the thirty metres up the bank, maybe more – I took a long detour round a vicious bramble bush. As I got closer I saw an old white van with a long wheelbase parked up with its nose against the fencing. Sloppy of them, I thought. Zoe and I had spotted one CCTV security camera on the street side of the building, and we presumed there were more. But with this van in the way no camera would spot an intruder cutting the fence, which is what I proceeded to do, lying face down on the muddy bank, with wire cutters I'd lifted from Zoe's aunt's house. They were lightweight ones, designed for stuff like changing plugs, and they'd be ruined after this, but that didn't bother me very much. When I'd cut a gap in the fence about half a metre long I threw them away anyhow.

Pushing the severed fencing aside like a stiff curtain I crawled through from the mud and thorns of the canal bank onto the greasy gravel of the car park, under the van's chassis. Its length gave me another four metres of cover; that left roughly another sixteen metres to cross before I reached the side of the unit itself. Moving as slowly as possible I crawled as close I could to the edge of the shadow cast by the van's underside; with sodium lights to right and left – in neighbouring yards, not in this one – the pool of shadow was not quite as wide as my body, but it would have to do.

I lay on my back and looked up towards the corner of the building ahead, where a CCTV camera slowly swivelled from left to right, and paused. As I watched, it slowly swivelled back again, and paused again, pointed straight towards me. I froze. Whoever was monitoring it, if they saw anything, would see a shadow in a shadow, but the slightest movement would give me away. At first I didn't even dare to blink, but thinking about blinking made it impossible not to. I blinked – and the camera started to move on again, to the left. I reached up, grabbed the bumper of the van, hauled myself out and dashed across the scarred and pitted car park, trying to keep low until I could flatten myself against the corner of the unit directly underneath the camera. Maybe the operator could tilt it down far enough to see me, but I doubted he would without good reason.

The red-brick corner of the building bit into my back. There was nothing to my right except the rear of the unit, a vast expanse of more red brick without so much as a window or an emergency exit. To my left, though, was what looked like a fire escape running up the side of the building. At its foot was an annexe jutting out, which meant the base of the stairs would only be seen by the camera above my head. I kept looking upwards until the camera swivelled to the right, then dashed for the stairs. Another bloody metal staircase – it was like climbing a ladder made of bells, and no matter how softly I trod, each step still resounded under my tread. But I made it to the top.

There I encountered a solid, smooth, wooden door that had once been painted yellow, or green or white – it was impossible to tell under the sodium lights. But the lock was brand-new, and when I put my shoulder to the door there was no give – because it opened outwards, towards me, which made it impossible to kick in. Even a police battering ram would have bounced off. I had no time to curse, and I couldn't retreat – I had to find a way in. Fumbling in my pocket I found the only other tool I'd managed to find in Zoe's aunt's cottage: a cheap and nasty screwdriver of such soft metal the head had already twisted out of shape.

I forced it into the door jamb by the lock, and pushed; the wood splintered on the surface, but the door itself didn't budge. I dug the blade in again, wrenching and twisting, but I could feel the shaft of the screwdriver bending – it was going to snap clean off before I made an impression on this lock. There was no point having a go at the hinged side; that would take a crowbar and I didn't have one.

I heard the buzz of the CCTV camera swivelling towards me, flattened myself against the door and froze. The lens was tilted down to cover the car park, and there was a chance the operator wouldn't be looking for anyone up at this level, but I was still stuck there, with no way in and one way out – and I wasn't going to run, because then I'd be running for the rest of my life.

That annexe at the foot of the stairs had a flimsy corrugated roof, and I'd fallen through one just like it a few weeks back . . . could I do that again? It wasn't exactly a stealthy way of gaining entry, and last time I'd nearly broken my neck. Maybe I could force a window? But the window nearest to me was a metre from the top of the stairs, and two metres above ground level. They glowed faintly, as if the interior was lit by a couple of strip lights kept on permanently for security. The panes were opaque wired glass, nearly impossible to break, and I couldn't see any sections that opened, assuming I could have reached them. So how was the place ventilated? Were there louvres in the roof I could get through, or an air-conditioning unit I could unscrew? What a bloody stupid idea – as if this dump would have air con.

Then I heard something. A scuffle, a footstep. Someone was moving about inside the building – by the sound of it, not far from this door. I checked the windows and caught a flicker on the glass, a shadow that was moving towards the exit where I stood. Were they on to me? If they put a few bullets through this door, the way they had done at the Turk's flat in Clapham, I'd have no way of dodging them – unless I went back down the stairs. But for some reason I didn't do that; I just stepped back to clear the door. Maybe it was the way the footsteps sounded as they approached – not urgent, not stealthy, just someone walking.

I heard one bolt inside pulled back, and held my breath. Then another. I wanted to brace myself to dive through the door as soon as it opened, but there was only enough room on the platform for the door to swing out, and I had to lean back against the railings to make room, praying it wouldn't fly open so hard it knocked me over. I perched there, completely off-balance and vulnerable, as the lock clicked and the door started to open. The edge of it brushed against my jeans as it swung back.

The man inside was casually dressed and dark-skinned, with a short, neatly trimmed beard. He wasn't looking outwards to start with, but fiddling with something in his hand. In a second he'd registered my presence, but he was still too late. I lunged forward through the doorway, slamming my body into his before he could pull the door shut again. He grunted and swore in some language I didn't understand, and he ducked and writhed and wriggled free of my grasp and tried to dash back along the raised walkway, but I grabbed the hood of his sweatshirt and hauled him backwards.

He twisted, cursing, and something clicked and flashed in the dark, and I pulled back instinctively – that was a flick knife, with a sleek, razor-sharp blade. Now he crouched, levelling it in his hand, and by the way he held it I was pretty sure he'd done this before, and not just in training. The blade barely wavered in his hand and he kept his eyes locked on me in a way that suggested he was ready for any feint or dodge.

What was he waiting for? Why didn't he call out for help? *Because he's the only one here.* It took me a couple of heartbeats to realize that, and now I could see why he was holding back – he was weighing up the risk. He wanted to go and raise the alarm, but that meant turning his back on me. He had to finish me off first, and though I was bigger and heavier, I was probably slower, and I wasn't trained in knife fighting.

I swallowed, nervously, and saw a smile flicker on his face, and knew he'd made his decision. I saw him step forward with his right foot, but move his weight to the left, and I took a gamble too, and let him make his feint, and came in close. His arm twisted and the knife changed direction but I just managed to grab his wrist with my left, and hold it, its lethal tip resting on the skin below my ribs. Straining every muscle in my left arm I grabbed him under the chin with my right and I pushed him backwards. His right arm flailed and snatched at the rail but he was too late. For a few fractions of a second my eyes were inches from his – his pupils were a shining golden brown, the colour of chestnuts – and I could smell his sour breath, and then gravity took over. His legs flipped up and he fell twisting in the darkness below, his yell of terror cut off as he hit the concrete floor, head first, with a muffled crunch. His knife skittered off into the shadows.

I stood there feeling my racing pulse calm down, wondering what else I could have done. Taken him prisoner? Knocked him out? Pointless to worry about that now. I was standing on something, I realized. Lifting my foot I looked down and saw a crushed packet of cigarettes – menthol, low tar. That's why he'd come to open the door in the first place; he'd been sneaking off for a smoke. But why the hell had he bothered? I could imagine the Turk was a scary employer, but I didn't think he'd enforce government regulations about smoking in the workplace.

At the end of the walkway was a cosy office with long windows facing out across the working floor; presumably it had once been used by a manager or foreman. Now it was a security station, where six flat-screen monitors relayed pictures from the CCTV cameras. The images were still moving, the cameras panning back and forth, even though there was no one at the controls. The control panel featured a little silver joystick and an array of backlit buttons, one of which was illuminated right now: the caption on it read AUTO. On the desk beside the control panel was a plastic tub holding a few crumbs of couscous, a cup of juice and a half-read paperback lying face down. Its cover showed a solitary figure hitchhiking on an empty road leading nowhere. By the looks of things the bloke lying in a heap below the walkway had been on guard duty, but had slacked off from sheer boredom.

At the far end of the little office another door led to a steel staircase down to the working floor. I descended as quietly as I could, though I was sure by now there was nobody else here. The unit appeared to be an old transport depot where vehicles had once been maintained; that bitter tang of engine oil takes a long time to die away. There were two troughs in the floor – inspection pits – between hydraulic vehicle lifts, but all the machinery I could see was caked with grease and dust and rust.

In the furthest bay what looked like a small petrol tanker was parked. Was that why matey had been reluctant to smoke inside? Unlike this building, the tanker was relatively new, with gleaming paintwork. Close up, however, I could see that the headlights were splattered with dried-out bugs; this truck had come on a long journey, quite recently – from the continent. It was left-hand drive, with EU number-plates. When I pulled open the driver's door I saw the keys were still dangling in the ignition. There was no branding or logo on the tanker itself, just a series of coloured labels, the sort all lorries carrying chemicals were required to show in case they spilled their load in a collision. I didn't know what the letters signified, but even an illiterate like me could understand that icon at the end: a hand with a crater burned into it. Corrosive substance.

Against the far wall stood three oil drums, also plastered with chemical labels – though these were different to the ones on the tanker. Beside them was a long workbench, neatly laid out. At one end shallow trays held reels of coloured wire and solder; at the other stood several crates of spring water in glass bottles, swaddled in polythene wrappers; beyond that, a neat stack of boxes that turned out to be cheap pay-as-you-go mobile phones – burners like the Guvnor and his crew used, all brand-new.

Beneath the workbench was a wheeled plastic crate. Pulling it out I peered inside and found three cheap backpacks, like you'd pick up in a big super-market – lots of chunky zips and webbing straps and pouches, but not waterproof, so no good for serious hiking. This was the sort of budget kit that people took to rock festivals, then left behind. One was bright orange; I lifted it out and looked at it more closely. It smelled new, but it looked slightly scuffed, as if someone had kicked it about the place to age it artificially. And there was something else about it, something familiar, that I couldn't quite place, something that gnawed at the edge of my mind like a rat.

From the street outside came a clink and a jingle. I froze, and listened . . . but now I heard only silence. Was I getting paranoid? It was probably just a jogger passing by with a pocketful of keys. But the longer I listened the twitchier I felt. Shit . . . the Turk wouldn't have left a place like this supervised by one man – not all the time. There must have been another guy, who'd slipped out to buy supplies, and was now coming back. But why so quietly? Did he know I was here? If he did, what was he waiting for? For all he knew I could be on the phone to the cops right now. Had he cut his losses and run? That's what I would have done.

There was one way I could find out.

I hurried back across the floor and climbed the stairs back to the supervisor's office, as quietly as I could when taking two at a time. At the bank of monitors I switched off the AUTO setting, grabbed the joystick and pushed it to the right, checking the screens to see which monitor I was controlling. The top left-hand camera panned across the entire length of the road out in front of the factory. There was no one out there. The streets were silent and empty - no traffic, no pedestrians, no joggers, no bikes . . .

Nothing at all? The hair prickled on my neck. *That's not right.*

The monitor on the rear of the building was labelled number 6. I punched the button marked 6 and pushed the joystick to the left. The camera responded. Nothing out back either: the white van still nestled its nose against the wire. Beyond the fence the butterfly bushes swayed . . . was that the night breeze? Light glinted from the direction of the canal and then vanished. But that hadn't been a reflection of a ripple on the water – the shape had been distinctive, very much like . . . light glinting off a pair of goggles. I paused the camera, and waited.

There.

A black shape shifted against the fence, a shadow darker than the other shadows. I checked the street out front again and this time concentrated on those patches of black I'd ignored before.

Another.

That made two men at least, dressed in black, wearing goggles. *There* – a third, crouching in a deep doorway directly opposite. Holding something pointed upwards, a stubby pole . . . no, a submachine-gun, fitted with a noise suppressor.

This wasn't the Turk's crew. This was an Armed Response Team, in full combat gear, and they were closing in.

Now I understood exactly what this place was.

I had ninety seconds, maximum, to decide what to do, and it had to be the right decision. I'd seen enough reconstructions and played enough combat sims to have a good idea of what would happen next: the cops would kill the power to the building, then fire flashbangs and tear gas through the windows. Except these windows didn't break . . .

Footsteps on the roof, soft as a cat, but distinct, heading for the ventilator panels I could see on either side of the apex.

I scrambled down the stairs again, but when I got to the bottom I still had no idea what I should do. Come out through the front door with my hands in the air? They'd either shoot me or arrest me . . . most likely they'd shoot me *and* arrest me. Afterwards they'd make sure the ambulance took its time getting through the cordon so I'd bleed to death and spare the NHS the expense of treating me. The same thing would happen if I lay down on the floor and waited for them to storm the place – they'd shoot me twice in the head, just in case I had a detonator in my hand.

Because this place was a bomb factory, and the cops were on to it. Anyone inside would be considered a terrorist and a live threat, and when terrorists get shot nobody objects, except the usual human-rights cranks that everyone ignores. Any awkward questions would be washed away in a flood of speculation and misinformation – that I was a loner, a psycho, another alienated underachiever who'd become a religious fanatic—

Without a sound the lights went out. There was only one thing I could do now and one place I could go, but I couldn't see a thing – my eyes hadn't adjusted to the darkness and there was no time to let them. Those inspection pits were somewhere dead ahead of me, so I shuffled to my right, then forward as fast as I dared, knowing that at any second stun grenades would blow me off my feet and blind me. I stretched out, flailing with my hands – my target was right there, I had been looking at it two seconds ago . . .

I tripped on something hard and unyielding and went sprawling, half expecting to find empty air and go tumbling into the gaping darkness of a pit, but my hands hit concrete, and groped at the greasy dust. A bent nail that dug into my right palm – I was shuffling along the floor now on my knees and my right hand, with my left up in front, swinging left to right and left to right – had I missed it, gone past it? How? High above me I heard a faint screech of bent metal as a door or flap was forced open, and at that moment my left hand brushed something smooth. I scuttled forward, and now my right hand felt it too – the bumper on the front of the tanker. Scrambling to my feet I fumbled my way down the side of the cab, fingers scrambling along the door – that was the wing mirror strut – this was the window – then the handle had to be – yes—

In one movement I pushed the latch down with my thumb, pulled the door open, and heaved myself up into the cab, and as I did I heard a hiss, a clatter and a rattle, and I slammed the cab door shut, and the bang shook the teeth in my head and made my ears ring. A stun grenade. The flash didn't dazzle me – it just lit up the inside of the building, and showed me the roller shutter door, dead ahead. The grenade must have fallen into one of the inspection pits, but I screwed my eyes shut, expecting a second, and there was – another deafening detonation, almost too loud to hear, and a light so bright I could count every vein in my eyelids. I found the gear shift and gripped it, twisted the key in the ignition, and floored the brake pedal. The engine roared into life, and beyond it I heard shouts, but I ignored them. Lights, lights – I tugged and twisted the levers protruding from the steering column – *there*!

The instrument panel blazed into life, and the lettering on the automatic gearbox. Keeping the brake pedal pressed I pulled the gear lever back to D, found the parking brake and released it, lifted my foot off the brake and slammed the accelerator to the floor.

The truck leaped forward, its engine roaring, and the motion threw me back against my seat. I gripped the steering wheel with both hands and pointed the tanker straight at the roller door, bracing myself for the impact, half expecting the truck to stop dead on impact and hurl me through the windscreen. The nose of the cab was a flat wall of glass and steel and it hit the roller door like a giant hammer, ripping it clean off its hinges and knocking it outwards and upwards like a tin cat-flap that rattled and scraped along the roof of the cab. Black-clad figures ahead of me dived to right and left and I hunched down in my seat, waiting for a shower of bullets to shatter the cab windows, but none came. Of course – they didn't dare open fire in case the entire tanker went up.

The engine was still screaming, but I was heading for the fence, not the gate, so I eased back on the speed and hauled at the wheel, turning it to the right. I was amazed I'd made it this far – all I knew about driving I'd learned in one drunken night four years ago, in a stolen hatchback that my mates and I had trashed on wasteland. That had been an automatic, like this, and they were a piece of piss to drive as long as you didn't care what you crashed into.

The gates were dead ahead now, and I accelerated again, just as an unmarked police car roared forward from the right to block my exit. I pulled the wheel to the left, aiming the tanker for the shrinking gap, but I misjudged it and sideswiped the gatepost, skewing it sideways and ripping off my wing mirror. The tanker slewed to the right and slammed into the front corner of the cop car, spinning it aside with a thunderous crunch, the tinkle of shattering headlights, and a scream of metal scraping on metal that set my teeth on edge. The right window exploded and crazed, but not from the impact – one of the armed response guys had opened fire – and even as I ducked down in my seat again and hauled the wheel anti-clockwise I could hear yells and screams over the roar of my engine. Someone was getting an earful.

I was out of the yard and clear, but I'd pulled the

wheel round too hard – now I was driving half on the pavement, heading straight for the concrete post of a street light. When I wrenched the wheel clockwise the truck swerved wildly, bounced down off the left kerb and headed for the right. I eased off on the accelerator but the vehicle barely slowed – it was far heavier and slower to respond than that car we'd nicked. I could hear its chemical load sloshing wildly about in the tank behind me, and feel the truck tilt and sway with its momentum as I wrestled with the wheel. I was almost getting the hang of it. The road ahead of me was clear – all twenty metres of it. The cops hadn't sealed it off because they didn't need to – it was a dead end, a turning circle for trucks, empty apart from one abandoned van sitting rusting on flat tyres. Beyond that van was the kerb, beyond that kerb was a metre of tarmac pavement, and beyond the pavement was a metal crash barrier that I hoped to God was less solid than it looked.

There was no way to tell how close the Armed Response Team was behind me – my right-hand window was a vertical mass of glass crumbs, and I'd knocked the mirror on my side clean off. But it made no difference either way. Uttering a silent prayer to a god I didn't believe in – he'd never believed in me – I floored the accelerator again and hung on for dear life. The engine roared and the tanker surged forward and I felt myself being thrown back in my seat a second time. I glimpsed the speedo, and the needle was heading towards forty when I hit the kerb, and the cab bounced so hard I flew vertically upwards out of my seat and nearly let go of the wheel. A split second later the cab slammed into the crash barrier, which warped and burst asunder like wet cardboard, and now I was bouncing down an unlit slope, veering and swaying wildly, the wheel thrashing in my hands. I had to hold it straight or the whole thing would topple over and take me with it. Under the tortured howl of the engine I could hear a slashing hiss of plants being ploughed up and pushed aside.

There was another teeth-rattling jolt upwards as the tanker's front wheels hit the towpath, and for an instant my windscreen was filled with the dark, gentle outline of trees against the orange night sky; then the cab plunged downwards and hit the canal, throwing me forwards over the wheel, my forehead bouncing so hard off the windscreen I saw stars. I blinked and shook my head to clear it, and when I opened my eyes again the grey slimy water of the canal had nearly reached the top of the windscreen and was gushing into the cab around and under the doors. An instant later the crazed window to my right exploded inwards under the pressure. As the cab filled with stinking lukewarm water the lights of the dash faded into grey gloom, leaving me in darkness. I started to breathe, long and hard, long and hard, keeping it up as long as I could, feeling the water soak my jeans as it climbed up my legs to my crotch and then my belly, until my head started to spin and throb and I knew I was hyperventilating. I tugged off my hooded top, levered my right trainer off with my left, but I couldn't get my left trainer off. I ducked under the water to pull it free and when I straightened up I was still underwater, but now my head was brushing the roof of the cab. It was time to go.

I blew out as much of the air in my lungs as I dared; the bubbles glinted silver in the dark, and they were all I could see. I'd filled my blood with oxygen so I wouldn't need any in my lungs. With my chest full of air I'd be pulled upwards, and as soon as my head appeared above water someone would put a bullet through it. I could taste the canal swilling about in my mouth, and I tried not think of what was in it – the rat piss and essence of corpses – while I fumbled at the door beside me for the window winder, found it and cranked it, fast, until it would go no further. Then I grabbed the frame of the open window, pulled myself out through it, and forced myself down, and further down, till I touched the mud and slime and broken glass of the canal floor. I drove my hands forward and swept them back, kicked my legs, and propelled myself downriver, into the dark.

It was the searchlight that nearly killed me.

I stayed under as long as I could, swimming downstream along with the feeble current, but eventually my chest started to burn and my muscles to weaken for want of oxygen. With no air in my lungs I had to force myself up towards the surface, and I tried pushing off the bottom, but my foot just sank into sticky sludge. I kicked with my legs and flailed my arms to break free and rise, and I was half a metre from the surface when the water above me lit up like a football stadium, and through the roaring of the blood in my ears I could hear the high whine of a chopper overhead – a police helicopter fitted with a high-intensity searchlight, sweeping the canal. Somehow I forced myself down again, every last cell of my flesh screaming for air, and struck out for the bank, hoping if I surfaced up against it I'd be less visible. I felt the interlocking metal plates of the canal's sidewall before I saw them. I knew there'd be no overgrowth here to conceal me, just a hard clean metal edge, but I couldn't stay under any longer. I pushed myself up, scrabbling at the coarse metal with my fingers, desperate to pull myself clear of the water and breathe.

I felt the night on my face, opened my mouth wide and dragged in air, coughing and spitting and hawking, gulping down more oxygen before I shook the water out of my eyes and looked upwards. Now the clatter of the helicopter's rotor blades and the whine of its engine was deafening; it couldn't have been more than fifteen metres overhead. But directly above me was the high metal arch of that last bridge I'd crossed on the way here, and for a few precious seconds I was sheltered in its shadow. I watched the hard beam of light from above flick and swivel, pausing for a few seconds on a punctured football floating in a patch of litter ten metres away, and in those few seconds I took three more breaths, blew the air out of my lungs and dived again. The searchlight was bad enough, but that chopper would have heat-seeking cameras too, which would pick out my shape as soon as I surfaced. I had to keep diving and swimming downstream – it was the only way to stay concealed.

Just as my lungs started to burn again I saw an orange flush on the water above me and recognized the scattered glare of a street lamp. It threw into silhouette a patch of floating garbage – water bottles, crisp packets and rotting leaves – piled up in the twigs of a severed branch that had snagged on the bank. I pushed upwards and surfaced underneath it, trying to tread water without splashing or scattering the litter. The clattering of the chopper overhead was deafening, and the searchlight dazzling, but now it was focused on the white hull of the half-sunk boat I'd passed earlier. A member of the Armed Response Unit was crouching on the far bank peering in through the slimy glass of the cockpit, but after a second he shook his head and looked up – straight across at me.

Surely he could see me, or hear my laboured breathing? I clamped my lips shut and tried to breathe through my nose, but my sinuses were full of filthy water and I had to splutter it out, wheezing and retching with my hand over my mouth. The copper didn't react: the chopper's racket must have drowned me out – and the dazzle of the searchlight was throwing mad dancing shadows over everything outside its beam. The cop paused a moment, listening to a voice in his earpiece, then set off back upstream at a run. I took another three deep breaths and dived again, and behind me the glow of the light in the grey water faded and slid away.

I knew I'd never make it all the way to the Thames like this, not even if I'd been a bloody dolphin. Between here and the river were two locks where the canal level dropped, each one a dead end, impassable under water. The first was another five hundred metres downstream. Maybe the cops would be waiting for me there, but it didn't matter any more: I was done with swimming, and felt almost too weak to float.

By the time I saw the massive wooden gates looming out of the water ahead of me I couldn't even bring myself to dive, though the thrum of the chopper's blades was still so close that the pilot could be over me in seconds with one twitch of the joystick. I focused on that thought, let the fear and anger drive me onwards up to the wooden gates where more rubbish had piled up, swept downstream by the thunderstorms. There were no cops in sight; they must have thought it impossible I could get this far, and I didn't blame them. The water level was high enough to let me reach the wooden walkway overhead, attached to the canal gates themselves with iron brackets.

As I gripped the walkway's edge my biceps trembled and throbbed but I managed to haul myself up out of the water, hook one ankle on the walkway's lip, and with the last dregs of my strength heave myself up and clear, to lie gasping and dripping on the wooden ledge.

I desperately wanted to rest, but I couldn't – not here, out in the open. I had to move, somehow, somewhere, anywhere else. Ten minutes downstream lay the shiny development of designer flats, with all those people and that nightlife to hide in – except among them I'd be as conspicuous as a freshly drowned corpse. On the far side of the canal a steep bank rose to a two-metre grey steel fence topped with spikes. On the near side sprawled a muddy jungle of woods and shrubs – the edge of a park I knew vaguely. I'd picnicked there once, years ago, when my mum and dad were still together. No choice, then.

I scrambled to my feet, staggering with such exhaustion I nearly tumbled back into the canal. Clutching the handrail I hurled myself forward, turned right along the towpath, and a few seconds later cut left into the bushes, heading uphill. I wanted to run, but could barely manage a jog, and without my trainers I could feel every twig and pebble underfoot. All the same I kept running, in a half-crouch, expecting every second the looming thunder of the police helicopter to surge in volume and the searchlight to dazzle and drown me.

The park was dark and empty – no dog walkers, no teenage potheads, not even a lurking flasher. Around me the trees were starting to thin out and I could see street lights flickering through sycamore leaves. The sirens and the chopper's beat were pulsing in volume, growing distant, and no one in this suburban back street was curious enough to come out and look. They wouldn't have seen much anyway; just a tall teenager in dripping jeans, a soaking grey T-shirt and mud-caked feet jogging out of the woods, down the street, then ducking sideways into a narrow passage between two terraced houses.

The passage led to an alley that ran along two sets of rear gardens, back to back. One garden was separated from the alley by nothing more than broken fragments of fence, and in it swung a rotating clothesline draped in washing: three T-shirts, assorted socks, and a few pairs of sweatpants. I hesitated for almost a nanosecond before I swung my leg over the shards of fencing and snatched the joggers from the line, sending the pegs flying. I took a navy T-shirt too – of the choice available it would be the least conspicuous in the dark. I quickly checked to see if these kind people had left any trainers outside on the back doorstep – Dad used to do that with mine when they stank too badly to keep in the house

– but I saw nothing; I guess that would have been too much to ask. I hurried further down the alley and paused in the shelter of a wheelie-bin to tug off my soggy jeans.

Forty-five minutes later I stood at Zoe's door in Richmond, my feet bruised and throbbing from running without shoes, and with barely enough energy left to lift the knocker. I didn't realize how hard I was leaning on the door until it opened and I fell inwards, straight through Zoe's arms and into a heap on the doormat. She asked if I was hurt, and kissed me, and recoiled, and told me I stank like a backed-up toilet. While she ran me a bath I told her what I had found in the Turk's lockup, and she told me what she'd found in his laptop's memory. She went online while I clambered into the bath to soak, but I was so shattered I passed out almost immediately. It would have been ironic if I'd drowned in bubbles after what I'd just been through, but Zoe pulled me out, rinsed my hair, towelled me down and put me to bed. We talked for another twenty minutes, made love for twenty minutes, and slept in each other's arms for twenty minutes.

Then the cops smashed the front door in.

TEN

It wasn't how I'd expected it to happen, but to be honest I hadn't expected the cops at all – or not for another twenty-four hours, anyway. I thought at first it was an Armed Response Unit, but the men who came thundering up the stairs and squeezed into our tiny bedroom – in such numbers they nearly started falling over each other – were packing nothing more lethal than batons and pepper spray. Every one of them was in full Met police uniform, with bulky stab vests, and navy baseball caps pulled down low over their eyes, and every one of them was even bigger than me – it was like a rugby scrum round our bed.

Zoe screamed at them to get out, dragging the sheet around herself and off me, but I was still so dopey with sleep I didn't even notice I was naked. When I'd blearily tugged on my stolen sweatpants and T-shirt, ringed in a knot of uniforms so tight I could feel their breath on my skin, they handcuffed me, and with two cops ahead and two cops behind I was marched down the narrow stairs. We left Zoe behind, hissing and spitting and demanding to see a warrant, as if this house was hers and she was entitled to be there, but I could hear the confusion in her voice: she couldn't figure out why she wasn't being arrested too, on a charge of conspiracy – the catch-all the cops use when they haven't quite figured out who's been conspiring with whom to do what, and need time to ghostwrite a confession or fabricate some evidence.

The tiny downstairs lounge too was heaving with uniformed coppers, wearing latex gloves and with plastic covers over their boots as they raked through cupboards and combed the bookshelves. As the arresting officers led me out into the street I saw the Turk's sleek laptop and the chunky one belonging to Zoe's aunt sealed into thick polythene evidence bags and stowed in the boot of a cop car.

It didn't make sense, any of it. I'd just returned from a bomb factory. I thought the plods would have sealed off the street and sent guys in hazmat suits in to lift the floorboards and probe every crevice with chemical sniffers in the search for explosives. With a cop on either side holding me by the arms I was led to a standard-issue police van, the sort they use to round up drunks on a Friday night. The paintwork was scratched and dented, and one of the side windows freshly cracked; clearly it had been in the wars this week.

Net curtains twitched along the length of the street but nobody so much as poked their head out of a window to ask what was happening as I was bundled aboard and shoved towards a bench seat. The van doors slammed shut behind us and the engine fired up. One cop sat opposite me while the other sat to my left, so when the van lurched off I went sliding into him. He shoved me away again, none too gently. In the dimness of the van it wasn't easy to make out their faces, but the one opposite me was middle-aged, with a neatly clipped greying beard that made him seem almost human. I caught his eye and asked him what I was being charged with.

'Riot,' he grunted.

I nearly laughed in his face.

But they were serious. I thought they'd take me to the local nick, but we drove for more than an hour through the suburbs to a station so massive it looked like a prison, way south of the city. In the huge custody hall hordes of sulky teenagers and surly twenty-something yobs were being led to desks, questioned, charged, searched and locked up. The supervising coppers snarled at us to keep quiet, but rumours went buzzing round the room: there were all-night courts in session upstairs, processing suspects like battery hens, each hearing taking only a few minutes. The same thing had happened after the last outbreak of rioting; back then, out of two thousand accused, not one had got bail, no matter what the charge or the circumstances. Every suspect was remanded in custody, and some ended up serving months of imprisonment before they even came to trial.

And it was my turn next.

'Name?'

'Finn Maguire,' grunted the bearded copper at my shoulder to the custody sergeant, who typed my details up on a computer using two fingers. No wonder this was taking so long.

'Address?'

'Don't have one,' I said. The duty sergeant glared at me, but saw I was serious, and glanced back to the copper.

'What's the charge?' he said.

'Riot and GBH,' said the cop. That sounded even more ominous than I'd feared. Every other charge I'd overheard had been 'burglary' or 'violent disorder'. Grievous Bodily Harm? What was that about?

Oh shit. Dean's kneecap. *They have video.*

This wasn't the time to argue, and there was no point in trying.

'I want to speak to DS Amobi from the NCA,' I said.

'The court will appoint a duty solicitor to represent you,' said the sergeant, in a voice like a speaking clock. 'Turn out your pockets and give me your shoelaces.'

'There's nothing in my pockets and I'm not wearing shoes,' I said. 'Amobi's a detective sergeant in the National Crime Agency. I need to talk to him about—'

'Son, I don't give a shit who you'd like to talk to. It's four o'clock in the morning and all the bloody detectives are in bed asleep, which is where I should be. Now turn out your pockets and give me your shoelaces.'

'Just think, if you were a detective,' I said, 'you'd earn enough to buy your own sodding shoelaces.'

That was probably a mistake. The cops were too busy and tired to bounce me down the stairs, and the corridors were too crowded for them to practise their favourite baton strikes and restraint techniques. But they managed to find me a cell with a young bearded nutter babbling loudly to his guardian angel, a wino who had crapped his pants, and a tattooed Chinese guy who stood with his back to one corner and his arms folded, staring at the rest of us as if wondering who to strangle first. The duty sergeant suggested with a smirk that I should make myself comfortable – I was going to be here a while.

There was only one bench in the cell, and it was moulded out of the same stuff as the wall – hard washable plastic, easy to hose down and disinfect – but the drunk was stretched out the full length of that. The whole cell stank of shit, but it was particularly strong near him, so he had the bed to himself. The mental patient had lain down on the floor opposite and curled up facing the wall, muttering 'Talk to Jesus, talk to Jesus,' and the mute Chinese guy had taken possession of one corner. That left me the other. I hunkered down till my backside hit the floor, rested my head on my legs, and shut my eyes.

'Maguire.'

How long had I been asleep? My knees had locked up. The cell door was open and the duty sergeant was back and he wasn't smirking any more. Behind him stood Amobi, and he wasn't smirking either.

After that stinking packed cell the interview room felt like a penthouse and its stale recycled air smelled like a meadow breeze. I stretched my legs out and breathed it in. Amobi looked twitchy and impatient, like he had better places to be. He seemed less drawn and tense than the last time I'd seen him, but then the last time I'd seen him he was being beaten to the ground by two plods.

'Any chance of a cup of tea?' I usually didn't have to ask the cops for tea, and it was always so pale and weak I didn't bother drinking it, but right now I actually wanted some. Maybe I was getting too used to police stations.

'I don't think so, Finn, and if any officer here offers you a cup, I would advise you not to drink it,' said Amobi. I frowned. 'Too many of them have seen the evidence against you,' he explained.

'You mean me taking part in a riot?'

'I mean you starting a riot.'

'I didn't mean to . . . OK, I did. But I had to create a diversion so I could rescue Zoe.'

'I would not rely on that for your defence. Homes and shops and cars were burned and looted all over London. You cost this city millions of pounds. Three men died, many were injured – one man was crippled.'

'Yeah, and most of them were working for the Turk. I asked you for help, Amobi, and you said no, because the Turk was an informant and you couldn't touch him.'

Amobi's glance slid sideways to the young uniformed officer standing at ease in the corner.

'I don't recall any such conversation,' he said carefully.

'Yes, you do, I said. 'It was right before you got worked over by two racist cops.'

'I don't recall any such incident,' said Amobi. Now he held my look. I knew it wasn't the first time he'd lied to protect his colleagues, no matter how little they deserved it, and I felt anger, but also pity; I'd trusted him once. He must have seen it in my eyes, because he pushed his chair back as if he was about to leave. 'Finn, I came here as a favour to Zoe,' he said. 'She called me and told me you were in custody and you needed my help. But I came to tell you I can't help you any more.'

'You misunderstood,' I said. 'It's you who needs my help.'

He paused, but I could see he wasn't convinced.

'I figured out how they're recruited,' I said. 'Those

suicide bombers you've been chasing. They're not really suicide bombers.'

Amobi said nothing.

'They're smuggled in,' I said. 'From somewhere in the back of beyond, Kurdistan or Uzbekistan. Like all trafficked people, they're promised jobs, but they end up owing the traffickers a fortune and having to work like slaves to pay it back. Only some of them, the ones with no family, no friends to miss them, I think they're given special deals. They're told that if they make one delivery they'll be let off some of their debt. And they're given a backpack and sent off to Liverpool or Bristol or Oxford Street, and when they get there, someone phones the mobile in their backpack that's wired to a detonator, and . . . *boom*.'

'That's an interesting theory,' said Amobi in a non-committal tone, as if he'd heard it before. But he didn't get up.

'It's Karakurt who's recruiting them,' I said. 'That's his trade, people trafficking. He has an infinite supply of volunteers, from all over Eastern Europe.'

Amobi stared at me. 'You can go,' he said suddenly. It took me a second to grasp he was talking to the uniformed cop in the corner.

It took the cop a second to grasp it too. 'Sorry, sir?' he said. 'Do you want me to fetch someone else?'

Amobi turned to him to explain, as patiently as if he was talking to his favourite idiot nephew. 'This isn't a formal interview, it's a conversation,' he said. 'I don't need another officer in attendance.' The officer hesitated, as if he wasn't sure where to be if not in here, while Amobi waited. Then he slunk out.

'Am I getting warm?' I said.

'Where did you hear that name?' said Amobi.

'Karakurt?' I said. 'It's what the Russian mafia calls him. He's teamed up with them now. The Guvnor's not around any more.'

'So where is he?'

'Retired,' I said. 'Or so I heard.' I wasn't getting into what I'd witnessed, and fortunately Amobi didn't insist.

'Did these Russians tell you the Turk was behind the bombings? I wouldn't rely on them, Finn. They have their own agenda. Besides, we just shut down the terrorists' bomb factory.'

'Yeah, the one near the canal. It was Karakurt who tipped you off about that place, wasn't it? That's why you only found one body in there. The poor bastard who was ordered to guard the place when his mates were sent to set up two new bomb factories.'

Now Amobi was staring and some of the colour had drained from his shining black face. I'd once

319

promised myself never to play poker with him, because his expression gave so little away, but right now he looked like a man who'd staked his life on one last hand and been dealt a pair of threes.

'That was you?' was all he said.

'Was what me?' I said. 'The guy who broke in just before the SWAT team turned up and drove the tanker into the canal and disappeared? No. I know nothing about it.'

'Did you say there were other factories?' Amobi seemed keen to change the subject.

'Karakurt's not finished,' I said. 'You guys will be clapping each other on the back and lining up for medals, and in a few weeks it'll all start again, and you'll need him more than ever.'

'How do you know about them?' asked Amobi. 'These factories?'

I told him about the laptop I had grabbed during the riot, how Zoe had downloaded the memory, and how she'd decoded it. Amobi was starting to sweat, I noticed, and twitch in his seat. I could see he wanted to dash out and call his office, to tell them how Karakurt had taken them for a ride, but I wasn't done with him just yet.

'One of the other files Zoe found mentions two

locations up North. I don't know for sure they're bomb factories, but maybe you should go and look. Another turned out to be a recording of a woman who sounds very high up in the security services promising the Turk limited immunity in return for his cooperation.'

'Finn, it's dangerous to be in possession of this sort of information,' said Amobi.

'I'm in a police station,' I said. 'Surely it's the safest place I could be.'

He missed the sarcasm, but then he had a lot on his mind. 'I was thinking of Zoe,' he said.

'They should have arrested her when they arrested me,' I said. 'You're never going to find her now.' I was praying that was true. 'There is one way to make the knowledge less dangerous,' I went on. 'Spread it about. Tell the world everything.'

Amobi had always kept a beautifully folded handkerchief peeping out of his breast pocket; for the first time ever I saw him pull it out and dab his lips like he'd been eating something messy; it was a nervous gesture. I'd finally rattled him.

'I really wouldn't advise that,' said Amobi.

'You wouldn't advise Zoe and me to tell every media outlet and blogger and conspiracy theorist in the world how British security services protected a major criminal who was running a bombing campaign in the UK?'

'That sort of irresponsible behaviour could jeopardize national security,' said Amobi.

'If everyone knew, there'd be no reason for the Turk to come after us,' I said.

'Apart from revenge,' said Amobi.

'Maybe, but with all you lot chasing him, he wouldn't have time for that,' I said.

'Chasing him isn't catching him,' said Amobi.

'Too late, anyway,' I said.

Amobi nearly swallowed his handkerchief. 'What do you mean?'

'I'll tell you now where to find Karakurt's other bases. But the other stuff, the recordings? Zoe uploaded them last night, to twenty different sites on the Net and in the Cloud. She hasn't shared the links yet, but if I get done for riot and GBH, or conspiracy . . .'

Amobi looked disgusted at my cynicism. 'You think we're going to let you walk out of here? It doesn't work that way, Finn. This country has an independent judiciary.'

'You say that as if you believe it,' I said.

'I'm not empowered to make that sort of deal.'

'Then maybe I should talk to someone who is,' I said.

'Nobody is,' said Amobi.

'That's too bad,' I said.

We sat there in silence for a little while.

'Let me make some calls,' said Amobi.

ELEVEN

Spring had come with Zoe. In the week since she'd arrived the stream at the foot of the valley had grown from a thin icy trickle to a gushing white torrent, fed by the melting mountain snows. The craggy peaks to the north were still capped with white, but we could smell the thaw in the air and feel warmth in the sunshine, and see green shoots bursting from the branches of the almond outside the front door. The evenings were still bitterly cold, of course, but I'd chopped up a fallen walnut tree the previous October and between that and the overgrowth I'd cleared from the terraces we had enough firewood to keep us warm for twenty winters.

There'd been no reason to stay in London after I'd been released without charge, and plenty of reasons not to. Karakurt wasn't one of the reasons I left. He'd gone on the run shortly afterwards, a wanted terrorist whose face and many names were plastered all over the media and the Internet. As various whistle-blowers and journalists had learned the hard way, criticize the British royal family, the government or the police all you like, but screw with the British security services and you'll be hunted down like smallpox. The Brits had called in favours from fellow spooks the world over, and soon Karakurt was number one on every Most Wanted list across Europe and the USA. Even the Russians had been looking for him – presumably because he hadn't been able to deliver on the deal he'd made with the Moscow mafia.

I'd headed for Spain, mostly because I had nowhere else to live. My parents' place I'd long since rented out, and the house I'd been living in – the one that had belonged to my old boxing coach Delroy – had been reclaimed by his Jamaican relatives. That was when I'd decided it was time to visit this castle I'd inherited when my dad died, the one that had once belonged to the actor Charles Egerton, and which I hadn't seen since I was eight years old.

It was a lot smaller than I remembered, of course, but it was still beautiful. Five minutes' hike from the border with France, in the foothills of the Spanish

Pyrenees, it was more farmhouse than castle – a ramshackle, wandering farmhouse with its roof collapsed in places, but with some castle-like ruins nearby: stone colonnades surrounding a marble bath left behind when the Moors had retreated to Africa. In the years since Charles had died the bath had been used as a sheep dip by my grizzled ancient neighbour Estaban. When I'd moved in he'd come round to ask nicely if he could carry on grazing his flocks on what had been Charles's pastures and were now mine, in return for produce from his farm. I said sure, since I hadn't been planning to use the pastures myself. I think that's what we agreed, anyway: I didn't speak much Spanish when I arrived, and I very soon learned that few people in those parts spoke Spanish either – this was Basque country, where everyone spoke Euskara, and all the road signs were in two languages. Trying to read Euskara made reading English suddenly seem straightforward, but between conversations with the locals and videos on YouTube I learned enough at least not to embarrass myself when I drove into town for supplies.

Yes, drove. I'd taught myself, in a four-wheel-drive that Charles had left behind, which Estaban had also 'borrowed'. It was still in good nick when he returned it, if you didn't mind the faint whiff of livestock, and I didn't, because for the first few months I smelled pretty ripe myself. There was no running water in the house, so I washed in the icy stream, and that was after spending all day cutting back the jungle that had grown up around the house, repairing the broken windows and fixing the roof with Charles's rusty tools. I didn't know much about traditional Basque roofing, so I just copied the bits that were intact, and I'd managed to make it watertight in time for winter. One gable wall of the adjoining barn was unfinished but its fallen stones were lined up on the top floor, waiting for warmer weather, when there'd be less chance of frost damaging the fresh mortar.

'If that bloody dog brings me one more dead rat I'm going to shoot him,' said Zoe sleepily.

'It's a present,' I said. 'It's 'cause he likes you.'

'It's you he likes,' she said. 'And he's jealous. He brings me the rats to gross me out and piss me off.'

'You'd be a lot more grossed out and pissed off if he brought you a live one,' I said.

It was late afternoon, and we were in bed together, in the dim whitewashed room that had once been a byre, having a siesta. The weather wasn't really warm enough, and we didn't do much sleeping, but

327

calling it a siesta made it sound less lazy and self-indulgent.

Zoe was probably right about the dog. He had turned up in the depths of that first winter, so underfed I could count his ribs. I hadn't encouraged him to hang around, but I had sort of tolerated him, and maybe that was more affection than he had ever been shown, because he stayed. I couldn't blame whoever it was had thrown him off their farm; he was the ugliest dog I'd ever seen, with the head of a greyhound, the body of a boxer, and the brains of a sparrow. He was good at catching rats – and there were a lot of rats to catch – but he never warmed to Zoe. When she wasn't around he slept in the kitchen next to my bedroom; when she came to stay and shared my bed he made himself scarce, like now.

'You should use that stuff Estaban gave you,' she said. As a Christmas present Estaban had brought me a rusting can of white powder and explained in toothless Euskara that it was for killing rats. I thanked him profusely and hid it in one of the outhouses along with all the other rusting cans – mostly banned garden products Charles Egerton had left behind.

'That stuff's ancient, and it's lethal,' I said. 'If I put down poison, Zakur will eat it, and it'll kill him, and he smells bad enough as it is.'

'Zakur,' said Zoe. 'You've even given him a name. You're stuck with him now.'

'It's not a name,' I said. 'Zakur is the Basque word for dog.'

She raised her head and looked at me in sleepy indignation. 'I can't get over the fact that you've been here six months and you can speak Basque.'

'I can't really,' I said. 'But don't tell the dog that.'

Zoe had come here every spare week she had from her course, and like most students she seemed to have a lot of spare weeks, but I wasn't complaining. The work she had missed while stranded in the safe house she'd caught up with before the end of that first September, and she had resumed her studies; she said it was going well, but I got the impression she was bored because the course wasn't challenging enough. Maybe writing essays seemed a little dull after hacking a laptop and blackmailing MI5 with the contents. Patrick Robinson had dropped out and disappeared to the USA, and she'd officially taken over the room he'd rented in that shared house, but when term began she still had the feeling she was being watched.

As indeed she was: Amobi cheerfully admitted it when she'd contacted him. NCA and 'certain other agencies' were keeping an eye on her, supposedly to intercept the Turk if he came looking for revenge. Zoe suspected their real motivation was to ensure that no harm came to her, accidentally or otherwise. She still hadn't sent out the links to those compromising documents she'd hidden on the Internet, but she had set up an automated routine that would do it for her, unless she logged in every few days. It was by way of a failsafe – if anything did happen to her, or me, the world would find out about Karakurt's deal with the British security services. Whenever Zoe stayed with me in Spain she logged on using the wireless Internet connection the local IT geek Txaparro had supplied to the farmhouse. It was slow, but it worked, and Zoe seemed happy, and we were never bored.

The weird thing was that even without Zoe releasing that information, all sorts of rumours and conspiracy theories about Karakurt had bubbled up: that he'd been working for Al Qaeda or the Taliban, that he'd been a double agent who had gone rogue, that he was really working for the Chinese, or the UN, helping to usher in the New World Order. I'd wondered where all this stuff was coming from; Zoe suggested it was coming from British security services themselves, stirring up smoke and mud to create confusion. That way the actual truth, if it ever did come out, would sound like one more loony conspiracy theory.

If that was really the plan then it was already working, as far as I was concerned, because I didn't know what to believe. I took a few precautions, and laid in some supplies around the house, but as the months passed they began to seem absurd and paranoid, a bad habit from a previous existence I'd already begun to forget.

Especially after the Turk was caught.

By February government militia had cornered him in a villa in Cyprus that had caught fire during the shootout and burned to the ground; what was left of Karakurt was identified by DNA extracted from his teeth. His only other remains were the millions in various currencies frozen in offshore accounts; millions that were now being squabbled over by the Brits, the Turks, the Russians and even Kurdish separatists. Some of that money was mine, as it happened – stolen from my lawyer's client account the night she disappeared – but I wasn't bothered; I had my farmhouse, I had my fields, and I had Zoe . . . and of course there was the insurance payout I'd collected after the theft.

And now spring was coming and there was a pot

of lamb stew simmering on the stove and Zoe was here in my arms. Which reminded me . . .

'We're nearly out of condoms,' I said.

'Don't worry about it, I'm sorted. And I'm not seeing anyone else, so we don't need them.'

'What about me? I might be seeing someone else,' I said.

'Like who?' she snorted. 'Estaban? Bit old for you, isn't he? Oh God' – she looked round – 'tell me it's not the dog.'

'It gets lonely up here,' I said. 'And the sheep run too fast.'

She smiled at me. 'You're disgusting,' she said. 'Sometimes I think you—'

'Wait,' I said. In the distance Zakur was barking.

'What is it?'

I sat up. 'What's up with Zakur?'

'Jesus. You really do care more about that dog than me.'

'Hsh . . .'

Last autumn I'd heard Zakur barking like that, frantic and furious, and it turned out he'd found a hedgehog and was trying to harass it into uncurling. When I'd caught up with him his muzzle was all bloody from biting the spikes, but he was too stupid to stop. I hoped this was another hedgehog, but somehow I knew it wasn't; I could hear snarling and snapping between the barks, and what sounded like a man's voice cursing.

Then there was a single shot, and the barking stopped, abruptly. It wasn't the blast of a shotgun like the locals used for chasing off wild boars and foxes – it was a pistol shot. Zoe realized that too, and her eyes widened in fear as she turned to me.

'Go,' I said. 'Hide.' She scrambled out of bed and tugged on her clothes.

We'd talked a few times about what we might do if everything we'd heard was wrong, if the Turk was still out there and looking for us, if somehow he had tracked us down to this place. But lately we'd let our guard down, allowed ourselves to hope the nightmare really was over. Maybe it was, maybe this was a false alarm, but I was going to assume the worst. No point in calling my neighbours or the Guardia Civil; it would take the cops at least an hour to get here, and I didn't want to get old Estaban mixed up in this. Whoever it was I would have to face them down myself.

I headed for the old dovecot that poked out of the roof of the barn. From up there I could see in every direction, right down the valley and up the hill trail. I pressed my face up to the slats still dotted with ancient birdshit and feathers, and peered out. Damn it. I should have known.

It was the Turk.

I could see three men approaching from different directions – one coming down the mountain trail, another limping up the path, but it was the Turk who was coming up from the stream. There'd be another guy coming down from the treeline above the house to the west, I assumed, through the vineyard. I could take all four, one by one, if I was lucky.

I took another look at the guy limping up the lane with a heavy pistol held in both hands. That was my old friend Dean, his greasy hair grown long again, his face still crooked from the battering I'd given it almost a year ago. I hadn't seen him since he'd been carried unconscious out of the riot, and if he was still limping now I must have injured him more severely than I'd meant to. That was a comfort.

I checked the terraces to the west where the vines were just starting their spring growth, sending delicate tendrils up the struts and wires I'd spent the last few weeks building. There he was, the Turk's newest recruit – a short, unshaven guy, Spanish by the look of him. He was an ugly son of a bitch, with a squint, and one thick eyebrow across the width of his forehead. I wondered where Karakurt had found him

– and how, with every cop in Europe on his trail. Was there some employment agency for thugs, where your criminal record served as your CV? How much was this new guy getting paid, or was this an internship?

Squinty was following the path I'd beaten into the earth as I'd slogged up and down from the vineyard. It led round the old walnut store, hugging tight to its ancient wall, under the unfinished gable. I scrambled down the dovecot ladder as softly as I could, hoping the creaking wouldn't give me away, and crept towards the gable where the old stones were waiting to be re-laid. Here the roof was held up by rusting steel struts, leaving the attic open to the weather. I peeked over the edge and down. There was Squinty, following the path as I'd thought he would, holding his pistol pointing upwards like cops did in the movies, pausing at the corner to check the courtyard was clear.

I didn't waste time thinking whether what I planned to do was right or not – I just did it. The topmost stone of the unfinished wall was not mortared into place, and it took barely any effort to roll it over, and it made no noise at all until it hit Squinty four metres below so squarely on the head it drove his skull down into his chest cavity. I didn't wait to check my handiwork, but scuttled over to the west corner of the barn, where I'd left the ladder. Squinty had been covering that side, so with any luck the others wouldn't see me coming down.

My luck ran out at the foot of the ladder.

'Stand still,' said Karakurt. His voice was behind me, about two metres away, too far for me to turn and jump him no matter how fast I moved. Raising my hands I joined them on the back of my head without waiting for him to tell me, because I knew from experience that whatever he told me to do I'd feel compelled to do something else. I turned to face him.

Interesting. He was paler than I remembered, and he'd put on weight. A life in hiding didn't seem to suit him. Those weren't his usual designer clothes, either – his jeans were saggy, and his thin leather jacket looked like it had come from a market stall. But his self-satisfied grin was still there, the smile of a man who knew he was finally going to have the last word, and the hand pointing the silver pistol at my head was rock-steady. Was that the same silver pistol I'd seen in the riot? Amazing he still had it. Maybe it had sentimental value; maybe Kemal had given it to him.

'Who was the guy in Cyprus?' I said. 'The one who died in the fire?'

'I don't know,' said Karakurt. 'I never met him.'

'I thought he'd be family. Considering the sacrifice he made for you.'

'Families are a liability,' said Karakurt. 'When I need relatives, to say that a dead man is really me, I hire them. Where is the girl?'

'You just missed her,' I said.

Karakurt smiled and flicked his gun, *That way*. This time I obeyed, and led the way round to the front of the walnut store. We had to step over the crumpled remains of Squinty, who now sported a boulder for a head, and I took care to avoid stepping in the blood that had puddled around him. If I had to run I didn't want to leave red footprints. Dean and the other new recruit were waiting in the potholed courtyard in front of the main farmhouse.

'*Dónde está Javier?*' said the other new guy. He was tall, bearded and balding, with a long scar on his right cheek where someone had once widened his mouth with a blade. He wore a padded leather jacket – a serious biker jacket, not just for posing – and there was blood on his jeans: my dog's blood, I guessed. At the sight of it cold rage boiled up inside me; but I forced it down.

'*Javier está muerto*,' said Karakurt.

Biker glared at me, clearly shocked and

disbelieving. What had Karakurt told him to expect? Some clueless gringo kid living alone miles from anywhere? And if they turned up at my farmhouse waving guns I'd invite them all in for sherry and tapas?

'I'm sorry,' I said. 'Was that your boyfriend?'

I expected Karakurt to translate, but from the look on the biker's face he spoke enough English not to need it, and he moved fast for a big man. I saw the kick coming and I managed to shift my weight, but the toe of his heavy boot still caught me in the balls hard enough to send pain erupting up the length of my body, flipping my stomach over and filling me with nausea.

I dropped to my knees on the cobblestones and bent forward, trying to absorb the agony and let it wash over me. I wanted to look weak and vulnerable at that point, but I'd kind of been hoping to act the part, and right now I didn't need to act. I felt my stomach roil and convulse and I went with it, spewing up bile, spitting and retching, all the while keeping an eye on Biker's big heavy boots a metre from my face. If he pulled one back for a kick to my face I was going to take him before he blinded me; it was a gamble, but I figured at this point the Turk would sooner lose this guy than kill me. For now I kept my fingers laced behind my head; I knew that made me look helpless and cowed.

'Where is your girlfriend?' Karakurt repeated. He strolled round to stand in front of me, Biker behind him, and stooped so his eye could meet mine, and I could look into that cold empty abyss he had in place of a soul.

'She ran,' I said. The Turk shook his head, stood up and stepped aside. Biker pulled back his fist; I just had time to notice he'd slipped on a brass knuckle-duster before he slammed it into my face, splitting it across the cheekbone, and spraying my blood onto the cobblestones. He had opened the old scar Kemal had left. He had little of Kemal's power or technique, but he had enough; a few more punches like that and my head would start to look like a burst watermelon. From the corner of my eye I saw Dean chuckle.

'She did not run,' said the Turk patiently. 'We would have seen her. She is still here, hiding some-where, and we will find her sooner or later, and the sooner we find her, the sooner this will be over, for both of you.'

I knew that was a lie: Karakurt would draw our deaths out for as long as he could, whatever I told him. After six months on the run he might be out of practice, which meant the torture might last a day or two rather than a week, but I wasn't going to volunteer for either option.

'She ran,' I said. The Turk rolled his eyes and gestured at Biker, who lifted his fist. The same knuckledusters, the same cheek, the same pain and the same stars bursting behind my eyes. But this time I felt something crack in my face, and my mouth filled with hot salty blood.

'Please,' I said, blood spluttering from my lips and spilling down my chin. 'I told her to run and hide, I don't know where she went—' I looked up again at Biker and flinched away, and my look rested just a little too long on the crooked door of the woodshed directly opposite the farm. I shook my head to try and conceal what I'd done and lowered my eyes, spitting blood and snot on the cobblestones, feeling my cheekbone grate under the bruised and torn flesh of my face. Biker cocked his fist again.

'Wait,' said the Turk.

'She went into the woods,' I babbled, 'hid out in the old smokehouse. She'll have gone for help—' There was so much blood in my mouth I was almost gargling, but the Turk wasn't listening. He had followed my careless glance over to the woodshed ten metres away from where we stood, its rickety door held shut by a rusting loop of wire running from the handle to a hook cemented into the doorpost.

'Quiet,' said the Turk. He gestured to Biker with a tilt of his chin. '*Buscar allí,*' he said.

I groaned and coughed and spat. 'She'll have called the police by now—'

'I said be quiet,' said the Turk.

I watched helplessly as Biker strolled over to the woodshed. His pistol poised in his right hand, he untangled the wire from the hook with his left. The door, hanging crooked on its ancient hinges, swung back halfway with a lazy creak. I dropped my hands from the back of my head to wipe the blood from my mouth and rested my palms on the cobblestones. Dean had turned his back on me to watch Biker; the Turk's body faced me, his gun hanging loose in his hand, but he'd turned his head away.

Biker peered cautiously round the doorpost and squinted into the dark; it was pitch black in there, and all he could make out were shelves lined with tins of ancient chemicals. Taking his pistol in both hands, he stepped into the doorway, raised his biker boot and kicked the door fully open.

With a massive flat bang a fireball exploded from the open doorway in a burning cloud, and lethal splinters of oak shrapnel flew outwards from the dis-integrating door. The blast blew the roof off the shed and Biker off his feet, and when his back hit the cobblestones his clothes and hair were singed and smouldering and his face was a blackened mask oozing blood.

Dean and Karakurt had both recoiled instinctively, but it was the Turk I went for, diving forward to slam my body into his and sending us both tumbling in a heap. He was flabby and out of condition, while I was half his weight again, rock-hard from my work in the fields. His pistol went flying and I landed two good punches to his face, knocking him into a daze, before I hauled him to his feet.

And then my left knee burst apart in a shattering explosion of pain, and I fell, dragging the Turk down with me. When my right leg hit the cobblestones the pain redoubled, coursing up my leg and my spine to my mouth, but I was already screaming in agony. I felt the Turk wrench himself free of my grasp and instinctively my hands dropped to clutch at my knee instead, but all I found was a mess of broken bone and torn ligaments. I could hear Dean cursing and the Turk panting; I didn't know which of them had shot me in the leg. I fought desperately to focus, to put the agony someplace else, to try to think clearly – this wasn't over, I couldn't give in to the pain—

I opened my eyes and spat blood. The cloud of

dust and smoke from the explosion was clearing, and the ringing in my ears was slowly fading. I didn't look down at my knee – that wouldn't help – so I turned my head to the sky, and saw a tendril of smoke wisping from the muzzle of Dean's pistol, pointed straight downward at my face. He staggered a little, and his hand was shaking, but at this range that wouldn't matter.

'You fucking prick,' he was saying, over and over. There was blood running down his cheek from a splinter embedded in his face a finger's width from his left eye. 'You fucking prick.'

'Not yet, not yet,' shouted the Turk, also half deafened by the blast – but his tone was one of annoyance rather than anger. When I turned to look at him he was laughing – at my ingenuity or my malice, or the fact that neither of those had been sufficient to kill him. He had survived yet again, only now he had one less employee to pay off.

'Sodium chlorate!' whooped Karakurt. 'Fertilizer bomb! Did your father teach you that? The Irishman?'

I didn't answer; my leg was going numb. Either I was better at this mind-over-matter shit than I thought or I was losing too much blood.

Karakurt chuckled as he bent to retrieve the big

silver pistol I'd knocked from his grasp. 'Any more surprises, Crusher? The dog, the rock, the booby trap, what else have you got? The girl, she is hiding here somewhere with a shotgun, isn't she? And the first one to find her will get his head blown off. But that will still leave one of us, and whichever one it is, believe me, both of you will pay.' He looked about. 'But we are not going to do this your way.' He pointed his pistol at my uninjured right knee. 'Your girlfriend is going to come to us. And she had better not be carrying any shotgun.'

'I told you,' I said. 'She ran.'

'Too bad for you,' said the Turk. 'Do you like it here? Living the life of a farmer? It's hard, isn't it? Have you thought about how much harder it will be when you are a farmer in a wheelchair?'

He cocked the pistol and I saw his knuckle whiten as he tensed his finger on the trigger.

'Don't,' called Zoe.

I angled my head towards the house and groaned, and not from the pain in my leg. Zoe was walking out of the door towards us, empty-handed but for an old towel. I'd thought she'd agreed to the plan – that she'd hide, and while I distracted the Turk she'd run into the woods; or if she couldn't do that, she'd bunker down in the cubbyhole where I'd stashed

Charles Egerton's old shotgun and wait for them to come looking. Instead she was here, kneeling beside me, tearing the towel into long thin strips, blanking Dean and Karakurt like a paramedic would ignore rubberneckers at a road accident.

'Why?' I whispered through clenched teeth. I knew what she was planning to do and I wasn't looking forward to it.

'You came for me,' was all she said. And lifting my leg she bound the bloody mess with the towel, cinching it as tight as she could, and the pain nearly made me pass out.

'Inside,' said the Turk.

Now the dressing helped. When Zoe grabbed my arm and heaved, and Dean reluctantly lent her a hand, the crude bandages helped me push the agony to the back of my mind and focus on how we were going to get out of this. Soaked in cooling blood, the left leg of my jeans flapped against my calf, and I could feel the material stick to the skin and peel off with every step. I couldn't take any weight on that leg, but supporting myself on Dean and Zoe I managed to hop along, the Turk to the rear shepherding us back into the house at gunpoint. It did occur to me to grab Dean, but I couldn't shield both myself and Zoe with him, and anyway the Turk would happily shoot either of us right through Dean.

The kitchen was warm and full of the smell of stew, but it wasn't cosy and homely any more with Dean and Karakurt strutting around it. While the Turk lifted the lid of the pot and sniffed, Dean pulled the chair facing mine out and sat down. I saw a twinge of pain on his face as he bent his right leg, the one I'd stamped on a year ago.

'Good meat,' Karakurt said to Zoe, who was standing by the hearth with her arms folded. 'But you should not use green peppers in stew, it makes it bitter.' Zoe and I exchanged a glance. The stew was mine, not hers – Zoe couldn't boil an egg. But we weren't going to share any more of our lives with the Turk than we had to.

'It's not for you,' was all Zoe said.

The Turk frowned, as if disappointed. 'It's funny,' he said. 'I grew up in a place just like this. But smaller, not so much land. My uncle worked us eighteen hours a day, all the year round, and still we never had enough food. But he understood the ancient laws of hospitality.' While he spoke he laid out two bowls from the rack, picked up the ladle and filled each one with stew. 'When guests come, even uninvited, you feed them. He would make the women lay out all our meat and olives and cheese, and he and our guests would feast. And for weeks afterwards the rest of us would have to eat leaves from the trees.'

He placed a bowl in front of Dean, took a seat at the head of the table, and picking up a fork speared chunks of green pepper and set them aside on a saucer. I knew what he was up to, and it had nothing to do with the laws of hospitality. He'd explained to me last summer, in the shadow of that massive shredder: *It is not enough to kill a man. You must first enter his house, eat his food, defile his wife, and slaughter his children, while he watches.*

'And now,' said Karakurt, 'the wheel has come full circle. I find you hiding here. It was not hard, by the way – the details of the will are on file, accessible to anyone, for a modest fee. And I like this place. I like what you have done with it. I think it will suit my purposes very well. I will tell the locals you sold me the farm and returned to England. They are used to that. Gringos come, looking for a new life in Spain, then discover to their amazement that no one speaks English, and they cannot buy baked beans, and then they slink off home with their tails between their legs.'

Karakurt was a surprisingly fastidious eater who never spoke with his mouth full, but soon his spoon was scraping the bottom of the bowl. Dean was less enthusiastic; I saw him pushing aside the mushrooms and onions to pick out the lamb, as if he was only eating to oblige his boss and piss me off.

'Talking of hospitality . . .' said Karakurt. He pushed his chair back, stood, then went to the doorway to the old byre, pushing aside the curtain we had hung there as a door. He checked out our rumpled bed and nodded approvingly, then turned to Zoe. 'In,' he said.

She didn't look at me, and she said nothing, and she didn't move.

'Or we can do it in here,' said Karakurt. 'On this table. This is your home, so it's your choice.'

I tried to push my own chair back, only to feel a surge of pain from my smashed knee that made my head swim.

Karakurt looked at me and grinned. 'Relax, Crusher,' he said. 'You don't have to watch. But when I am done with her it will be Dean's turn. *Then* you will watch.'

Zoe's face remained impassive, but I saw her clench her fists as she walked round behind Dean, who sat there slurping gravy, and entered the bedroom.

Karakurt dropped the curtain behind her and

leered at me at he slipped off his leather jacket. 'How does she like it, your girlfriend? Actually, forget I asked, I don't care how she likes it. I like it rough. I like it when they put up a fight. And I bet this one will defend her virtue like a wildcat – the little virtue she has left. Hey, you think I can take her? Come on, I trained in your gym. You want to lay a bet?'

'I bet she walks out of there and you don't,' I said.

The Turk snorted. 'Sit back, relax,' he said. 'I am going to make this last.'

'I'd get a move on if I were you,' I said. 'You'll be dead very soon.'

'Please,' snorted Karakurt as he unbuckled his leather belt and pulled it free. 'You are the one bleeding to death. And now you are trying to delay the inevitable, to irritate me with silly threats.' He wound the belt round his fist with the buckle outwards. 'If he tries to move again,' he said to Dean, 'shoot him in the other leg.' He pushed the curtain aside and followed Zoe into our bedroom.

Dean grinned at me, wiped gravy off his chin and shoved the bowl aside.

'Whoever fixed your teeth that time,' I said, 'they were rubbish. You dribble like an old man taking a piss.'

I needed to talk, and to get him to talk, to cover the

noise of what was happening next door. The heavy curtain muffled nothing; I could already hear blows and whimpers.

'How's your knee?' said Dean. 'Hurts, doesn't it? I've been looking forward to that all year. Come on, have a go – I'd love to give you a matching set.' He pulled the pistol from his belt and laid it on the table, resting his hand on it, daring me to make a move.

I folded my right leg back under my chair, kept my left relaxed. The pain from my shattered knee was now a constant burning throb, which made it easier to push aside. But I was losing blood, and I didn't know how much time I had before I'd be too weak to act.

'And when I've done the other knee,' Dean was saying, 'I'll do your ankles and your elbows. Then we'll start on your teeth.' Reaching inside his jacket he pulled out a pair of pliers and brandished them at me. 'Kemal gave me a few tips. You think my teeth are bad? Just wait till I'm finished with yours.'

'Oh yeah, Kemal,' I said. 'I heard they had to pick him up with a street sweeper.'

Dean grimaced as if he'd eaten too quickly. His chair creaked as he leaned back; it didn't quite drown out an animal groaning from next door, but Dean seemed not to notice.

'How much is the Turk paying you?' I said. 'Can't be as much as you'd make turning him in.' I dropped my hands into my lap and felt for the frame of the table.

'It's not about the money,' said Dean. 'Working with him I get to do shit like this to big annoying twats like you.' A thought occurred to him, very slowly, like treacle dripping. 'You know what? I think I'll do your girlfriend's teeth before I do yours. You can sit there and listen. I've only tried it once before – I'll probably break a few, but practice makes . . . perfect.' He was sweating, I noticed, and pallid, and the hand holding the pliers trembled. ''Cos if she doesn't have any teeth, she won't be able to bite me when I stick my—'

He dropped the pliers with a clatter on the table and clutched his stomach. Then he stared at me, and started to gag, and suddenly he knew what I'd done, and his right hand reached for his gun, but he was too late. Taking all my weight on my right leg I stood up, gripping the edge of the table and heaving it up with the last dregs of my strength, flipping it over to land on top of him. It knocked Dean out of his chair, bouncing the back of his head hard off the rough stone wall, and I hurled myself across the upset table to grab him. My lame injured leg sent jagged shards of pain ripping up my spine, but I let my hate and my fury overwhelm it and one hand closed around Dean's throat while the other pinned his wrist to the ground.

He was full of fury too, and he thrashed and writhed under my grip, but the rat poison burning into his stomach was sapping his strength. His fingers clutched at my face and tried to gouge my eyes, and his dying desperation drove his fingernails into my face, scoring my skin, but I screwed my eyes up and kept my grip hard round his throat, and held it there, and finally his fingers flexed and relaxed and fell, and his whole body sagged. When I opened my eyes again Dean was staring upwards and white foam was bubbling from his mouth, running through his crooked teeth and down his chin onto my hand.

I snatched my hand away and wiped it on his shirt; strychnine can be absorbed through skin contact. It works faster if it's eaten, but it's too bitter to be used as poison in food, unless you mask the taste with something more bitter still – like green peppers thrown in at the last second.

It is not enough to kill a man, the Turk had told me. *You must first enter his house, eat his food, defile his wife . . .* We were lucky he'd tried to do it in that order.

I sat back, panting, and listened; there was no sound from the bedroom. Hauling myself upright using the leg of the upturned table as a prop, I limped to the bedroom doorway and dragged the curtain aside.

The Turk was dead. His eyes were staring, his back was arched, and both his arms were thrown back in an absurd pose, as if he was diving out of a window. I knew strychnine could do that, but I'd never seen it; I'd never wished that agonizing death on anything, even a rat, until today. Zoe had helped things along, I could see; I recognized the handle of the knife protruding from the Turk's belly, pointing upwards into his heart – it was the razor-sharp kitchen knife I'd used to prepare the stew.

'You all right?' I said. It didn't sound like a stupid question till I heard myself ask it.

Zoe, still in my oversized red T-shirt, sat on the edge of the bed, her face pale, her eyes closed. 'I wasn't sure if you'd done the poison,' she said. 'I hid the knife in here before I came out to you.'

'That was smart,' I said, limping round to hold her.

'No, it wasn't,' she said, and rising to meet me, she swayed a little. 'I'm sorry,' she whispered. I noticed she was clutching her side, just under her ribs. When she lifted her hand away there was a spreading stain, a darker crimson soaking the red cotton. 'He fought back,' she said.

'Oh Christ,' I said. 'Lie back, lie still, I'll get help.'

'No, no, not in here. Not with him. Take me outside.'

Somehow we carried each other out of the bedroom, through the kitchen, back into the afternoon sunshine, although I could feel her growing weaker with every step. Outside the front door she finally sagged and I let her sit down for a moment on the stone bench under the almond tree.

'I'll take you into town,' I said. 'Get you help. Can you make it to the car?'

'Finn, you can't drive,' she said. Her voice was growing softer. 'How will you change gear?'

I'd been so worried about her I'd forgotten my smashed knee, and when I looked at it now I saw the struggle with Dean had opened it up further; the strips of towel were soaked in red, and the left leg of my jeans was glistening with fresh blood.

'Christ, look at the state of us,' I said, and I fumbled for the mobile phone in my pocket, and found a contact.

'Txaparro? Finn. We're hurt ... *Gaude – zauritu?* Help ... *lagundu. Bai ... bai ...*' He'd already hung up.

'He's coming,' I said.

'I still can't believe you can speak Basque,' she giggled.

'Don't go to sleep,' I said. 'Stay with me.'

'I just want to rest for a bit,' she said. 'It's so beautiful here.' She laid her head on my shoulder.

'Wait till you see it in the summer.'

'I'd love to. But I don't think I can.'

'No, Zoe, stay with me—'

'I love being here with you, Finn. I never want to leave.'

'Then don't. Stay with me, OK? Please. I love you.'

She smiled. 'Must be bad. You never told me that before.'

'I'm sorry. I hoped I didn't have to, I hoped you knew.'

'I knew. But it's nice to hear you say it.'

'Stay awake, Zoe. Stay with me.'

'Love you too,' she whispered.

I took Zoe back to England six weeks later. She'd loved the farmhouse and so did I, but I couldn't stay there without her, even when the place had been hosed down and the bodies carted away. That had taken a while: first two Guardia Civil turned up, then a hundred; they'd taped off the farm while their forensics people had scoured it for evidence, trying to piece together what had happened. After them came an army of suits in unmarked cars from unnamed security agencies eager to confirm that this time Karakurt actually was dead. Txaparro, the local IT geek, had told me all about it when he visited me in the hospital in Barcelona where they'd been rebuilding my knee.

It was Txaparro who'd come roaring up the track in his battered old Subaru twenty minutes after I'd called him. He'd carried Zoe to the back seat, then helped me limp over to get in with her and rest her head on my lap as he drove us to the nearest emergency unit. I remembered clutching her hand and talking to her as the car jumped and jolted down the track; I didn't remember much about the later part of that journey, because I had lost so much blood I was semi-conscious by the time we arrived. Everything that had happened afterwards seemed like fragments of a dream: being heaved onto a gurney, lights gleaming in my eyes, frantic doctors and nurses cutting my clothes off, barking orders and readings to each other in lightning-fast Spanish. I didn't recall asking about Zoe, but I must have done, because I remembered someone telling me, 'We are doing all we can do. Relax now, let us help you.'

When I came round twelve hours later they told me they might be able to save my knee, but they were sorry, because they hadn't been able to save Zoe.

The spring we had seen reborn in Spain was stillborn here in England. Gaudy daffodils under bare birch trees shivered in the bitter east wind, and glowering grey clouds rolled overhead. Reaching down I grasped a handful of heavy crumbling clay from the heap and tossed it into the grave; it burst with a rattle across the lid of the glossy wooden coffin. I hadn't wanted to bury Zoe on the farm in Spain; when I'd gone back there it seemed to me the whole place smelled of death. But weeks later in here in England, as I stood in that freezing breeze and felt rain spit on my face, I realized it was me – that I smelled of death, and that I'd never be able to escape it.

I'd arranged for Zoe to be interred in the same plot as her mother and father. I knew how little love there'd been between them towards the end, but what did that matter now they were all dead? I wasn't going to perpetuate their family quarrels. They must all have loved each other once, if only briefly, and that was as much as any of us could hope for.

Besides, having the funeral here in London gave Zoe's friends and what was left of her family a chance to say goodbye. There were a few fellow pupils from her girls' school, but most of the mourners were students and tutors who'd come down from York. From the stories Zoe had told me of her time at uni I knew how much she'd liked it. I'd never admitted it, but I'd envied her the fun she'd had there, and I'd never understood why she'd chosen to spend so much time with me instead. None of them had ever put her in danger the way I had – except Patrick maybe, but he'd had the decency to run. When Zoe's other friends queued up to shake my hand and tell me how sorry they were I nodded and mumbled my thanks and I hated myself for a hypocrite. They pitied me, and I didn't deserve any of it.

Zoe was dead because I'd loved her. I would never make that mistake again.

A few of her relatives had turned up too, but more out of duty than affection. That heavyset man with the nervy, stick-thin wife – he must be an uncle, on her father's side, I guessed. I'd seen those heavy jowls before, and those stubbly cheeks red with broken veins. He didn't come over, but merely gave me a nod from the far side of the grave before he turned and stumped away after his wispy wife, who didn't seem able to get out of there quick enough. Two distant cousins of hers had come down from the Midlands. In their mid-twenties, they had some of Zoe's beauty – the bright green eyes, the flawless skin – but none of her fire; where she'd looked sulky and sultry, they looked sullen. As soon as the service ended they were wandering through the graveyard texting on their smartphones. I wondered if they were going to catch a West End show while they were in town.

Of Zoe's aunt, the one who owned the mews cottage on Richmond Hill, there was no sign, but I had heard from her, or from her solicitors anyway. They'd written to tell me I was being sued for the damage caused to the house when the cops kicked the door down and turned the place over. Also for the rent we hadn't paid. It had taken me half a morning to decode the legal jargon, and half a second to screw the letter up and bin it.

I realized I'd been staring down at the coffin so long most of the mourners had drifted away, and the gravediggers were hovering in the background, fiddling with their shovels, waiting for me to go too. They looked incongruous in their muddy jeans and hi-viz waistcoats, but of course this was just another morning's work to them; it was the rest of us, with our best suits and black ties and shiny shoes, who were in fancy dress. All the same I was curious to know why gravediggers needed to wear hi-viz jackets. Had any of them ever been run over by a hearse? Even council employees didn't move that slowly.

I turned from the grave all the same to let them get on with it, and almost immediately stopped again, and took a deep breath and counted to ten, trying to ride out the jolt of pain from my leg. Standing still for so long it had nearly seized up. The Spanish physio had ordered me to stay in a wheelchair for six weeks and use crutches for two months after that, but I'd given up on the wheelchair after seven days, and dumped the crutches a fortnight later. Screw Karakurt, and Dean; I might never run again, but I was never going to be a cripple on account of them.

Not everyone had left, I noticed, as I limped towards the tarmac path that led down between the rows of graves. Two men in suits and long raincoats were observing from a distance, one of them wiry and pale with rimless specs and thinning ginger hair, the other black, with skin so dark it shone. I didn't know whether Amobi and his colleague had come to pay their respects to Zoe or to ask me more questions about Karakurt, but I wasn't interested either way. I owed the cops nothing – the only favours Amobi and his people had done me had been grudging and half-hearted, to save themselves from some bad PR.

I walked straight past them, heading for the cemetery gates. I'd organized a reception at a riverside pub, because that's what you did after funerals. Zoe's friends from York were headed there, and I was going to join them. Not to swap stories about Zoe, but to find out if my dad had been right, when he'd told me that booze might not be the answer but it did help you forget the question.

'Finn, wait.'

There was no point in trying to outrun Amobi: my knee felt like it was on fire. I'd left my painkillers in my hotel room, and now I cursed the macho pride and stupidity that had led to this – to me standing in the rain, forced to listen to Amobi spouting clichés about sorrow and loss, and to Zoe lying in a dank London graveyard, fading away into the clay.

'I am very sorry for your loss, Finn,' said Amobi.

'Yeah,' I said.

'I am sorry for everything that happened. You must not blame yourself. None of this is your fault.'

'Yeah,' I said, because I couldn't punch him in the face, not in a cemetery.

'I know this is not a good time, but we would like to talk to you, before you go back to Spain.'

'I told Interpol everything I know,' I said. 'Ask them.'

'Not about Karakurt.'

'What, then?' I don't know why I asked that, because right at that moment I didn't give a shit.

Amobi bowed his head briefly; his hair had gone properly grey, I noticed, almost silver, and now it glinted with tiny beads of rain. When he looked up again his eyes were full of pain and shame, and for a moment I forgot how much I hated him, and how I'd once thought of him as a man too decent to ever succeed as a copper. He sighed, as if it was too late to turn back, and he had to get this over with. For a moment I thought he was going to arrest me.

'I wanted to know if you might be interested in working for us,' he said.

I stared at him, then at his red-haired friend standing wordlessly behind him, then back at Amobi.

'You must be out of your fucking mind,' I said.

And I turned and hobbled away.